Darcy stood on her doorstep, flowers in hand.

Emma checked through the peephole again. Yep. He held a fistful of purple irises and orange gerberas. Great. Just when she was totally completely angry and hated him, he brought her flowers.

Emma opened the door. One bare foot crept over to rest on top of the other. "What brings you here?"

He presented her with the bouquet. "Sorry I acted like a jerk."

In his button-down shirt and with his tousled dark hair he looked sexier than he had any right to. And younger than his forty years. How could she possibly feel attracted when she was so angry at him?

Why was she even angry? She wasn't supposed to feel anything anymore.

"Thanks," she said, accepting the flowers. Their fingers brushed. She felt nothing. That was static from the carpet, not a spark of electricity.

And any second now she'd actually believe that.

Dear Reader,

Do you ever wish you could have a do-over of some day, week or month in your life, some moment in time when everything went bad because of some wrong choice or a decision you wish you could take back? I'm fascinated by the idea of *Sliding Doors,* where even a tiny choice, like turning right or turning left, or arriving a minute earlier or later will change the course of a person's life. We all have trillions of such moments over a lifetime.

When my hero and heroine both make wrong choices, a tragedy ensues that destroys their marriage and threatens their future chance at happiness. Afterward, while they appear to be moving on with their lives, they're stuck in a limbo of regrets and thinking "if only" they'd done something different on that fateful day.

In real life we don't get a do-over, but we can learn from our mistakes. I believe that even if you make a wrong decision you can usually fix it by recognizing where you've gone astray and working hard to get back on the right track. You might not get where you would have been had you not made the mistake in the first place, but life is made up of an infinite number of paths. If you're self-aware, and know what you want and where you want to go, you'll usually get there.

Getting there can be a hard lesson and a painful one, as my hero and heroine found out in *Maybe This Time.* The rewards can be joyful and at the same time bittersweet. But as the saying goes, life is all about the journey, not the destination.

I love to hear from readers. Contact me through my website, www.joankilby.com, or c/o Harlequin Enterprises Ltd., 225 Duncan Mill Road, Don Mills, Ontario M3B 3K9, Canada.

Warmest wishes,

Joan Kilby

Maybe This Time

JOAN KILBY

HARLEQUIN® SUPER ROMANCE®

Recycling programs
for this product may
not exist in your area.

ISBN-13: 978-0-373-71839-9

MAYBE THIS TIME

Copyright © 2013 by Joan Kilby

This edition published by arrangement with Harlequin Books S.A.

For questions and comments about the quality of this book,
please contact us at CustomerService@Harlequin.com.

® and TM are trademarks of Harlequin Enterprises Limited or its
corporate affiliates. Trademarks indicated with ® are registered in the
United States Patent and Trademark Office, the Canadian Trade Marks
Office and in other countries.

Printed in U.S.A.

ABOUT THE AUTHOR

Joan Kilby enjoys writing about the fictional seaside town of Summerside, Australia, because it bears an uncanny similarity to the town where she lives with her husband and three children. Although her pubbing days are long over, she has a soft spot for the colorful and quirky pubs found in small Australian towns. When she's not writing Joan likes to read, cook and go to the gym. She's a longtime member of Toastmasters International.

Books by Joan Kilby

HARLEQUIN SUPERROMANCE

*Summerside Stories

Other titles by this author available in ebook format.

CHAPTER ONE

January
Melbourne, Australia

DARCY LEWIS STRAIGHTENED his cream linen jacket. The cruise ship's crowded ballroom was decked out in a Brazilian Fiesta theme and the live band's spicy Latin beat had him tapping his foot. Hot women in sexy dresses clustered around the room, sipping cocktails and eyeing up the men, including him.

How long had it been since he'd done something new and exciting? Way too long. His mates in Summerside were right. Twelve months of celibacy was too damn long for any red-blooded man with fully functioning hormones. They'd known what he needed even if he hadn't.

"Have a fling," Riley Henning had said as he and John Forster—Darcy's old surfing buddies and now both police officers—presented him with a ticket for a weekend singles cruise. The three of them had gathered one night after hours in Darcy's pub for a few drinks in honor of his fortieth birthday. "No strings attached. No emotional commitment. Definitely no moping. Just hot sex and fun."

Darcy cleared his throat, a little choked up at the generosity of his good mates. The past two years had been hard, really hard. "Thanks, guys."

John clapped Darcy on the shoulder. "Riley's right, sex and fun. When was the last time you had either?"

"Been a while." First Holly's death, then the divorce… His cocooned existence had involved eating, sleeping and working—not necessarily in that order. It was time he made an effort to get into the dating scene. And this cruise was just the ticket, so to speak.

He dragged his thoughts to the ballroom and the nearest woman—a brunette wearing a red dress sipping from a drink with an umbrella. "Would you like to dance?"

"Thanks, but I've got a partner for this one. He'll be back any second. My friend would like to." She pushed forward the petite woman wearing a blue dress standing behind her.

"Tracey, I can find my own— Oh." Emma's blue-green eyes widened. A smattering of freckles stood out against a peaches-and-cream complexion framed by flaming red hair. "Hey, Darcy."

Darcy swore silently. What were the odds? What were the frickin' odds? Of all the ballrooms on all the singles cruises in the world… He pasted on a smile. "Hey, Em. What are you doing here?"

"On a cruise. Same as you." She glanced around desperately, as if hoping someone would rescue her. Or a fire would break out, or the ship would hit an iceberg. Anything to put an end to this awkward moment.

Was she looking for a good time, too? A roll in the sack? Well, why shouldn't she? She was absolutely free to sleep with whomever she wanted. It did *not* make him jealous. Or hurt. Much.

He started to ease away. "Sorry to bother you."

The brunette grabbed him by the arm. "Where are you going? Do you two know each other?" She turned to Emma and whispered, "Come on, Em—he's hot. This makes the third man you've passed on."

"This is Darcy," Emma hissed. "My ex-husband."

"Oh!" The woman dropped his arm as if it were infected.

Nice. What exactly had Emma said about him?

"Wonderful running into you." He gave them double thumbs-up as he moved away. "It's a big ship. I'm sure it won't happen again. Now if you'll excuse me, I have to see a man about a dog."

"Huh?" Tracey's nose wrinkled. "What dog?"

"Forget it." Emma waved a hand. "Let him go."

He felt Emma's glare burning a hole in the back of his jacket all the way to the bar. What was she saying about him to Tracey? Was she warning her? *He likes to party but if you're looking for happily ever after, forget it.*

Darcy slid onto a stool, automatically taking note of the efficient, uncluttered layout of the bar. It was set up mainly for cocktails with features he would never use. But those sliding doors on the fridges would be great instead of the swinging ones he had.

Seeing Emma unexpectedly was almost as disconcerting as sitting on this side of the bar. He had an urge to hop the divider and start polishing glasses. He caught the bartender's eye. "Coke with plenty of ice."

"Everything okay, mate?" The bartender, a man about his own age with receding blond hair, tipped a scoop of ice into a glass and squirted in the soft drink.

"Just ran into my ex-wife." He lifted the glass and took a big swig. Whiskey would have been more welcome right now.

"Still got a thing for her, do you?"

Bartenders had an instinct for people and their troubles. He knew he did but he didn't care to be on this side of the conversation. "It's complicated."

He wanted to hate Emma—but couldn't. He wished he could love her the way she wanted to be loved—couldn't manage to do that, either. Would have liked to stay friends—that was too painful after what they'd had together. He wished he could ignore her—one look and every other woman in the ballroom faded into insignificance.

So where did that leave him? In limbo, that's where—unable to forget her, unable to move on. This cruise was supposed to be his first step toward a new life.

Instead he was torturing himself by watching her on the dance floor. Even though their last six months together had been the worst of his life, even though they were divorced now, the thought of her on the prowl for another guy twisted his insides into knots. Through the bobbing heads he glimpsed her doing the mambo with some bozo with two left feet. The guy's hands were all over her. Darcy didn't know which was worse, the liberties the guy was taking or that a terrific dancer like Emma was wasted on him.

Darcy turned around, unable to watch. He hadn't seen her in nearly six months, not since the house had sold for a song. Both of them wanted rid of the memories and had been unwilling to wait for a decent offer. She'd moved to Mornington, to a rental unit. He'd moved into the apartment above the pub once the previous tenant's lease was up.

The first night of this cruise and already her presence had ruined the whole experience for him. How was he going to chat up other women with her on board? Sure he was divorced, but it would still feel like cheating on his wife. He would be constantly looking over his shoulder. Even now he imagined he could smell her perfume—

Hell. She slid onto the next stool.

Blue-green eyes fringed with dark auburn lashes flashed at him. "I can't believe you're here, too."

"I'm fine. Thanks for asking." He gulped his soda, wishing it was Scotch more than ever. They'd both resorted to animosity to cover a whole host of more difficult emotions. It worked but it was draining. "You?"

"Pretty crap, actually, now that I've run into you." She signaled to the bartender. "Can I have a mojito, please? Only instead of rum I'd like vodka, and instead of lime, I want pineapple juice. Oh, and no mint leaves, thanks. Lots of ice. And just a dash of pomegranate."

Fixing his gaze on the row of liquor bottles lined up in front of the mirror, Darcy gave an irritated chuckle. "Now I remember why I divorced you. Only those cute freckles and that pert nose allow you to get away with orders like that."

"My freckles suck. And not every bartender is a purist like you." She dipped fingers with short blunt nails into a bowl of peanuts. "Just for the record, *I* divorced *you*. But never mind that, we need to talk."

It had better not be about Holly, or their relationship or his many faults.

"Don't eat those." He shoved the bowl down the black marble bar. "You don't know whose hands have been there before you. You ought to know about germs."

She wrinkled her nose. "I'm on holiday. Don't mention nursing or hospitals or sick people or bedpans—"

"Okay, okay, I get the idea."

Instead of getting down to what she wanted to talk about, she said, "How's the pub? Business good?"

"Fine. The same." He didn't know why she asked.

She'd always resented the time he spent there. In her opinion he should have been home with her and Holly more. But the sixty-year-old country-style pub he'd bought from his father when he retired was not only his heritage, it was his livelihood. The fact that he enjoyed the atmosphere and considered his local customers part of his extended network of friends was a bonus.

"How's the hospital?" he said, playing along. "Are you still in post-op?"

"No, I'm in geriatrics now. I work with Tracey. She's my friend in the red dress. Oh, and I've applied to do a master's degree in nursing. If I get in, classes start next semester."

"That's great. You always wanted to finish that."

She looked him over. "You've lost weight. Are you cooking for yourself or relying on takeaway?"

He'd lost a few pounds after he'd stopped drinking, but that was none of her business. "I'm living on peacock's tongues and caviar. You said you wanted to talk?"

She reached for the tall drink in front of her. "Why are you here?"

"Why does anyone go on a singles cruise? To meet people. And in this case, for the dancing."

"Well, I won't get in your way if you stay out of mine. That's what I came over here to say. After this one drink together we should act like we don't even know each other."

He cast her a sidelong glance. "We wish, eh?"

She played with her straw. "Are you seeing anyone? I haven't noticed you on the internet dating sites."

"I prefer to meet people face-to-face. You should be careful, hooking up with men online. There are a lot of creeps out there, married men just looking for a fling." What she did was none of *his* business but she'd started it by asking if he was seeing anyone. And damn it, he might not be married to her anymore but he still didn't want to see her hurt.

"I sort those out pretty quickly."

He bet she did. Emma was nobody's fool. She would tell them what she thought of their illicit activities before they could say, *my wife doesn't understand me.* He swirled his drink of melting ice and watery cola. "Quite the coincidence, us coming on the same cruise."

"Not really. There aren't many singles cruises sailing out of Melbourne. Even fewer cruises that feature Latin dancing, something we're both passionate about. We've been divorced for a year, the usual milestone for separated couples to take a significant step into dating. If you add up all those things, it was almost inevitable we would find ourselves on this ship together."

Great. Even single, his life had become predictable. An uneasy thought struck. "Did you hope I'd be here?"

"No, are you crazy? If I'd known you'd be on board, I wouldn't have bought a ticket. Who needs the reminder of—" She quickly glanced away.

Bloody hell. Darcy reached out, his hand hovering over her shoulder. *Don't touch her. It'll make seeing her even harder than it already is.* His fingers curled into his palm as he withdrew his hand.

Emma lifted her head, unaware of his near caress, and shook off her distress. "I told myself I wasn't going to think about her this weekend. Or talk about her."

He grunted, not trusting his voice. Grief was like that. It came out of nowhere, struck like a ninja when you least expected it. He missed Holly, too, and wished he and Emma could have found comfort by talking about her with each other. But the grief was still too raw, and there was too much blame on both sides. Their daughter was one topic that was strictly off-limits.

Emma looked him in the eye, waited a beat then said, "I'm here to meet someone. I want to get married again. I want another baby."

Darcy's sympathy hardened instantly into a simmering resentment. In the months following Holly's death Emma had pressured him to try for another child right away. She'd pushed and pushed him to get her pregnant on the grounds it would bring them closer. Nope. Eventually she'd pushed so hard he'd gone right out the door.

"You can't replace her."

"I *know* that." She blinked and touched her eyes with a cocktail napkin. "I'm thirty-five. The clock is ticking. This time around I want to fall in love with a man who wants the same things I do. A home and family."

When they'd married he'd wanted those things, too. He'd loved Emma passionately and thought he couldn't be happier. Then Holly came along with her red-gold curls and sparkling eyes like her mother's. He'd adored her with an inexpressible joy. And then…then… Suddenly she was gone, his little girl run over in the driveway by a drunk friend leaving their party.

He couldn't understand Emma wanting another child so soon. How could she just forget Holly? Where did she find the courage to risk that kind of anguish again? He'd tried to tell her it wasn't like getting a new puppy when the old dog died, although any dog lover knew that wasn't easy, either. She hadn't listened. She wanted everything to be perfect and she went to great lengths to achieve that. She didn't understand that life wasn't perfect. People weren't perfect. God knows he wasn't.

Having another child to make up for the loss of her first one wasn't fair on her next baby. And what about the guy, rushed into marriage to satisfy Emma's longing for a family? It was a recipe for disaster for everyone concerned.

"I think you're making a mistake—" He held up his hands at her glare. He would have to be a masochist to have this discussion again. "But what do I know? Just don't settle for the first man who is willing to give you a baby. Don't sell yourself short."

"Of course I won't." She paused. "What about you? I would have thought the ladies would be lining up once you were free. I thought you'd have a girlfriend by now."

"I'm not looking for a relationship."

"In other words, you're here for sex."

"Don't make it sound so crass." The opening bars of a salsa had Darcy swiveling to face the dance floor. "Women go on singles cruises looking for a fling, too."

"*Some* are looking for a fling. Some are looking for the white picket fence." Emma turned around and crossed her legs, the side slit in her dress revealing smooth bare thigh. She nodded discreetly at a woman wearing a modest dress, a frozen smile and a red hibiscus tucked behind one ear. "She's searching for Mr. Right."

"How can you tell?" Darcy was truly curious.

"She's trying to look 'fun' and not pulling it off. She's probably a librarian from the suburbs who never gets asked out. She came on the cruise hoping to meet a dentist or an accountant, someone respectable but not too challenging."

Emma wasn't that mean. She was only trying to wind him up. "She's probably perfectly nice. I'll bet she's a great cook. And a good listener."

"I bet she has five cats that she texts daily with twee

messages. I bet she uses those old-fashioned dolls with crocheted skirts to hide toilet rolls."

"My great-aunt Gladys makes those dolls."

"I rest my case." Emma sucked on her straw, slurping the liquid at the bottom of the glass. "The point is, would you want to have sex with her?"

"Aunt Gladys?" he asked innocently. At her exasperated look he conceded, "All right, I know what you mean. No, I probably wouldn't be interested, not if you're right about her wanting to settle down. Anyone out there take your fancy?" he added, prepared to hate whoever she picked on sight.

"Hmm." She scanned the room. "That guy in the dark jacket, the one with the gelled hair."

"Are you kidding me? He looks like a serial killer."

"He's cute. Harmless."

"Your children would look like Ted Bundy."

The band segued into a samba. Darcy's feet tapped restlessly on the rung of his stool. Almost more than wanting to have sex—although that was top of his list—he wanted to dance again after a drought of over a year and a half. The best partner he'd ever had was sitting beside him.

She gathered her clutch purse. "I'll get out of your way. You don't want me to cramp your style."

"Hang on." Would it be wrong to dance with Emma one more time? She tensed, half-off the stool. How would he put this so she didn't get the idea he was interested in anything more? "If we dance together, everyone would see how great we are. You'd have your pick of the men after that."

She gave him a dry glance. "No false modesty."

"No point. We're good and we know it." Latin dance

might be the only thing they did well together anymore but they could outshine anyone.

Still she hesitated. He understood her wariness. With them, an evening of Latin dancing invariably led to sex. That wasn't his intention tonight. No, sir, not going down that road again.

He hopped off his stool and held out his hand. "It's *only* a dance. Promise."

"All right," she said reluctantly. "One dance. For old time's sake."

Darcy led her into a clear space on the floor, spun her around and then pulled her in close. Excitement thrummed through his blood. Emma locked gazes with him, their faces mere inches away. With their bodies pressed together from chest to thigh, they moved as one to the sensual, hypnotic, intensely erotic beat. Emma's body twisted and turned, her breasts and hips swiveling in opposite directions. The rest of the room faded away....

The music ended with a flourish. Emma flung her arm out and bent backward, her head falling back dramatically. She was breathing hard, her breasts rising and falling beneath the thin fabric of her dress. Applause brought Darcy's attention to the room. The dance floor had cleared around them. Someone whistled.

"You've still got it, babe." Darcy pulled her upright. Nodding to the ring of admiring men and women, he added, "You can take your pick. I don't trust Ted Bundy. Just my opinion, of course."

The music segued into a salsa. He stepped away and reluctantly let go of her hand.

Emma's eyes sparkled. Perspiration gleamed on the upper curve of her breast. She captured his hand again. "Let's not stop yet. One more?"

This was the old Emma, the woman he'd fallen in love with. He shouldn't. It would be a mistake—for both of them. But he couldn't resist either the invitation in her eyes or the moment of fun. What was the harm? One more dance then they would move on, Emma to begin searching for her next husband, him to find comfort for the night. With a grin he tucked her into the crook of his arm.

Of course he should have known it wouldn't end with one dance. After the salsa came a lambada, hot and fast and sexy. Then a tango had them moving across the floor, arms outstretched, cheeks pressed together. Darcy gave up any pretence of looking for other partners. No way was he giving Emma up to some geek with two left feet. They belonged together—at least on the dance floor. At least for this one night.

And to think he'd almost refused to join the Latin dance class Emma had dragged him to at the community center the first year they were married. This wasn't something he'd ever thought he'd be interested in, but after three lessons he'd been hooked. After that they'd frequented the Latin clubs in the city, once even entering a contest and placing second.

The music segued into a rumba—the dance of love, and his and Emma's favorite. Their hips moved sinuously, thrusting and retreating in a mock display of the sexual act. Damp tendrils of curling red hair framed Emma's face. Her cheeks were flushed and a fine sheen of perspiration gave her face, chest and arms a glow. Hot. So hot. She pressed her butt against his groin and rotated her hips. It was a move they'd done countless times before. He was getting hard. He hoped she couldn't feel him. This was only a dance, not a prelude to something more.

But the dance was bigger than both of them. He forgot himself, totally focused on Emma in his arms. The room became a blur. There was only the sexy beat of the music and the two of them moving in sync. When Emma spun to face him, blue eyes locked on his, her lips slightly parted, he knew she was aroused, too. Seeing her nipples stand out against the silky fabric of her dress, his blood heated to fever pitch.

The dance ended. Breathing hard, Darcy held on to Emma's hand and hip, waiting for the next. She waited, too, trembling slightly. The bandleader spoke into the mike. They were taking a break. Back in twenty. People began to leave the dance floor, heading for the bar and the tables ringing the ballroom. Others streamed through the open doors onto the deck.

Emma gently disengaged from their dancer's embrace. "I could use a glass of water."

Darcy needed a cold shower. Hell, Niagara Falls might not be enough to put out the fire in his blood. He needed to put distance, physical and emotional, between himself and his ex-wife. This was the perfect opportunity to thank her for the dances and let her go gracefully.

Instead, he said, "Let's go outside."

CHAPTER TWO

EMMA HESITATED. She'd known the dance would be erotic. What she hadn't expected was the emotional upwelling. This was the first time they'd danced together since Holly's death, the first time they'd done anything that didn't involve grief and guilt. She'd been transported back in time to *before,* when she and Darcy had been deeply in love, innocently happy. How she missed, and longed for, those days.

Darcy's black hair was slicked to his temples and his cheekbones slashed with red. His dark brown eyes were burning her up. It didn't take much effort to picture him naked, in bed, broad bare shoulders, muscled chest and sheets twisted around his lean hips.

Her heart was still beating fast, not only because of the athletic dancing. Being in Darcy's arms again, feeling him pressing against her brought back all the best parts of their marriage. In bed and on the dance floor they were hot and passionate. If they could have done nothing but rumba and make love they might still be together.

Tracey was at the bar with a couple of men, motioning her over. Emma should make an excuse to Darcy—bathroom, drink, anything to get away from him before she did something stupid. She was starting over, looking for someone new, someone to build a life with, have a home and a family. Darcy was her past, not her future.

If only his presence wasn't so compelling. If only he wasn't the only man on this cruise she'd like to spend time with. She heard herself say, "Fresh air would be nice."

Outside, couples leaned against the railing, arms entwined, gazing at the moon spilling liquid silver across the inky waves. Ghostly gulls wheeled and soared into the night sky. Her heeled sandals ticked on the metal deck as Darcy led her past the others, seeking a secluded area.

She must be insane to hook up with him when she'd come on this cruise expressly to try and forget the man. But she'd also come to have fun. It had been too long since she'd laughed, or danced. Darcy was excitement on legs, a party in a pair of pants. If she were looking for a fling, if they didn't have history, he would be her go-to guy.

Despite the way their marriage had ended—with anger and recriminations—she trusted and respected him…even if he was now cruising for casual sex. They'd met in the E.R. at the Frankston Hospital when he'd brought in a woman who'd been slipped a date-rape drug at his pub. Even though he hadn't known the woman, he'd stayed till she was treated and personally called his friend Riley so she could report the matter to the police. When he'd asked Emma out she'd said yes right away. Guys as caring as Darcy didn't come along every day.

That seemed a very long time ago. Since then Holly's death and the aftermath had eaten away at their love until there was nothing left.

They rounded a bulkhead onto an empty stretch of deck. Nervous, she tugged her hand free and went to the rail. A warm wind pushed her hair every which way and lifted the skirt of her dress.

Darcy's arms came around her from behind, sliding across her midriff below her breasts. Warm and solid—and yes, still aroused—he felt so good. She leaned away to tell him she couldn't do this. After all the pain they'd gone through to extricate themselves from each other's lives, it was a mistake. Before she could speak he kissed her behind the ear, sending tingles rippling across her skin.

"I've missed you," Darcy murmured against her neck.

Her eyes shut, her chest aching. She'd missed him, too. More than she'd realized. Missed his humor and caring and strength. Plus, with Darcy she didn't have to pretend to be happy. He knew what she'd been through even if they didn't agree on where fault lay. Unlike a stranger, he wouldn't ask awkward questions about her broken marriage or unwittingly probe deeper so she'd be forced to either lie or confess she'd lost a daughter in tragic circumstances. Someday she might heal enough to speak of Holly without bursting into tears. But not yet.

Darcy traced the curve of her waist with his fingers, sliding up to cup her breast. His hand was warm and alive, but he waited, allowing her time to decide if she wanted his touch. The needs of her flesh—and her emotional needs, too, if she was honest—overrode her good sense. She missed the comfort of being held. Missed, too, the mindless pleasure of sex. Those few moments in which she could blank out the gaping hole in her life left by Holly's death.

She covered his hand with hers and pressed his fingers into her breast, pushing his thumb across her nipple. His sigh, deep as a groan, rippled through her, and she turned in his arms. His heart thudded against her chest as she slipped her arms around his neck and leaned up for a kiss.

Now there was nothing demure in her approach, or

tender in his response. The kiss was hot, wet and deep, almost violent in their mutual need. Abstinence might not have made their hearts grow fonder but it fueled desire. Over the past year she'd had opportunities to sleep with men, but hadn't. She'd thought her libido had crashed. Apparently not. All it had taken to resurrect it was Darcy. Scary thought.

"Em." His voice was ragged. "I know I'm not what you need—"

"Shh, you're what I *want*." She dragged him down for another scorching kiss that left them both breathless. "For tonight, that is. This doesn't mean we're getting back together."

"Hell, no," he said vehemently.

She knew where she stood with him. There would be no coy handing over her phone number and wondering, hoping he would call. No worries that he would expect more than she was able to give. One night together and they'd be done. Almost as if it had never happened.

"My place or yours?" Darcy asked.

"Yours, if you've got a cabin to yourself. I'm sharing with Tracey."

"This way." He looped his arm around her waist and with his other hand, reached behind for the door to the passageway leading to cabins. "Is Tracey going to worry when you don't come back to the ballroom?"

"Probably not. She'll assume I met someone. The singles cruise was her idea," Emma added in a burst of nervous chatter. *Was she really going to sleep with Darcy?* "She wanted to go to Vanuatu, but when I saw the Latin dance theme it was case closed as far as I was concerned."

Darcy's hand slid over her butt as she spoke, letting her know he wasn't really interested in Tracey. His subtle squeeze reminded her of their courting days when he'd been so eager to get her to bed he couldn't keep his hands off of her.

They weren't courting now, she reminded herself. There would be no happily ever after. Tonight was simply about two people who knew each other better than anyone else, and who cared enough that they could give comfort and release, but who had too many issues to be together. She blinked against an unexpected pricking of her eyes. This wasn't sad. It wasn't.

He stopped in front of a door and slid his key card in the lock, then let her walk in first. He had a single cabin, cozy, but big enough for two people who wanted to get close. And impersonal enough that she wouldn't associate the bed or the room with anything in their past.

She dropped her purse on the table and slid her arms around his neck for a kiss that instantly reignited her desire. He clasped both hands on her hips, pulling her tight to his, leaving her in no doubt he was ready, willing and able to satisfy her needs and wants.

Without thinking, she turned to let him unzip her dress. The pang hit her unexpectedly. This used to be a ritual, one of many small rites built up over their brief years of marriage.

His hands paused.

Was he remembering, too? "Something wrong?"

He pressed a kiss on the nape of her neck as he slid the zipper the rest of the way down. "Not a thing."

The straps of her gown slipped over her shoulders and the dress puddled around her hips. With a hand on his shoulder for balance she stepped out of it and stood before him, slightly self-conscious in her high heels and brand-new violet lace bra and thong she'd ordered online from Victoria's Secret. If there was an upside to being single with no kids, it was that now she had time for the gym. Months of working out showed in her toned arms and legs, and thinner waist.

Darcy's eyes widened and he whistled under his breath. "You look amazing." He stroked down her arms and took her hands in his, then raised their clasped hands to twirl her around, the better to admire her new figure.

"Thanks. I've been working at it."

"I'm honored to reap the benefits—even if I'm not your Mr. Right." He made a wry grimace, as if to acknowledge that at one time, he *had* been, and yet had turned out to be so wrong.

"Maybe we shouldn't talk too much," she said.

"Good idea." Humming a rumba he locked eyes with her as he unbuttoned his shirt. His hips swiveled to the catchy Latin beat.

His mellow baritone and the smooth circular motion of his hips had her twitching in response. Swaying closer, she helped him with his pants, tugging them down his legs, leaving him in black knit boxers that clung to his muscled butt and hugged the thick bulge of his erection.

She hummed along as they reprised the tango in the confines of the cabin. With even less fabric between them the dance was almost unbearably sexy. Darcy's hands whispered over her bare waist, spun her then brought her bottom in snug to his groin. Seeing them move together in the mirror was an added turn-on. Her nipples peaked against the lace, tender and aching to be sucked and touched. Between her legs she was wet and hot and heavy. Their steps slowed, became languorous and even more sensual. He kissed her neck, his breath hot on her skin. His hands slid around her front, one slipping inside her bra to mold her breast, one covering her mound. He pressed her against him, their hips moving to his increasingly breathless humming.

Emma closed her eyes, her hands roaming over herself, his legs, his arms, anywhere she could reach. She moaned as he slipped his fingers inside her panties and found the slippery folds of sensitive flesh. He eased back enough to drop his boxers and then his cock was nudging her from behind, seeking and finding her entrance while his fingers brought her tantalizingly close to climax. She sagged in his arms as her knees turned to jelly. He moved inside her, thrusting and whispering hot sexy things in her ear. He was close, too. She recognized the ragged state of his breathing and the tension in his muscles.

"C-condom," she managed to moan. She'd almost completely fogged out and forgotten. Lucky...

"You...IUD."

"No." It was all she could say.

He groaned but he pulled out and guided her over to the bed. She sank onto the turned-back sheets while he found a plastic packet in the bedside drawer. Within seconds he was sheathed, sliding on top of her and into her almost in one motion.

She met his thrust with a strong surge of her hips, clenching her muscles so she didn't come immediately. His gaze focused on her as if she were the only thing in the universe. As he was to her. When his eyes started to glaze over she abandoned control. A cry tore from her throat and she was swept away in the climax that she'd been waiting for.

"HOLLY, STOP!" Emma waved a gloved hand holding a trowel dirty from planting pansy seedlings next to the front porch. "Come back now."

Holly's bright red-gold curls bounced in slow motion. Her small sturdy legs sprang toward the red ball rolling along the driveway. She laughed, unaware of the black 4WD reversing toward her....

"No, Holly!" Emma tried to run. Couldn't...move. She looked down. She was buried up to her hips in the garden bed. "Stop!" she screamed again—at Holly, at the faceless driver, at the universe. "Stop!"

A flash of white face in the driver's window, panic and confusion. The 4WD jerked once then zoomed backward, smashing into Holly, throwing her through the air—

"Holly! Oh, God. No, no, no, no..."

Emma awoke sobbing, dripping with sweat. She blinked her eyes open and peered at the dark unfamiliar room. Collapsing on the pillow, she closed her eyes but the dream still permeated her mind. Images flashed. Holly, a broken rag doll on the pavement, blood running from her nose. Darcy, hauling Emma off their daughter's body. The ambulance, siren wailing, then abrupt silence. The paramedic pulling a blanket over Holly's face. *My baby, my baby...*

"Em, what's the matter? Are you okay?" Darcy, his voice groggy with sleep, cupped her shoulder.

She shook his hand off and rolled out of bed, now as repelled by his touch as she had been eager for it earlier. The grieving mother in her longed for comfort. Darcy should have been the one to give it to her. Except that even though he wasn't driving the vehicle, he was to blame for Holly's death.

"No, I'm not okay. I'll never be okay again."

He turned on a lamp and squinted at her. "What's wrong?"

"Holly." She dragged her dress over her naked body

and managed to zip it halfway before she got on her knees to hunt beneath chairs for her shoes. How could she have been so stupid as to sleep with Darcy?

He groaned and flung himself on the pillow. "Not this again."

"Yes, this again." She should leave this subject alone, but she was still gripped by the horror of the nightmare. "You, a bartender of all people, should know better than to serve your friends alcohol and then let them get behind the wheel."

Darcy sat up in bed and crossed his arms over his chest. "I barely knew the guy. He came with someone else. And I get tired of being the booze police. I have to do that at the pub. I shouldn't have to in my own home. People brought their own grog. I couldn't monitor everyone's intake. Whatever happened to personal responsibility?"

That was all very well in theory—except that her child had been killed. Someone had to be accountable.

She caught sight of herself in the mirror, makeup smeared, her hair a fright. Who cared? Darcy had seen her at her worst and this wasn't it. She wanted to get to her own cabin so she could cry. "Where the hell is my other shoe?"

"What about you?" Darcy said. "You were right there in the yard with her. You were supposed to be watching."

"I *was* watching. Could I help it if her ball rolled into the driveway? When did you ever watch her for even five minutes? You played with her but you didn't watch over her. You didn't look after her."

Ah, there was her shoe, under the bed.

"How could you not have noticed that guy was staggering drunk when he left the house?" she continued. "When the police tested him he blew 0.15."

"I didn't see him leave! If he was staggering, how come you didn't stop him from getting in his vehicle?"

She turned away. They'd gone over the day in forensic detail a million times. "If we'd gone on a picnic the way I wanted, it never would have happened."

"It was the footy grand final! I've been watching with these guys every year, since long before you and I got together. But that's just like you, Emma, not wanting me to have a life outside the family."

"That's not true. But you seemed to enjoy your outside life more than spending time with Holly and me. Why weren't we enough for you?" She threw up her hands. "What am I saying? Nothing's ever enough for you. There isn't enough excitement, people, activity in the world to satisfy you."

"You like reading books. I like being around people. Does that make me a criminal?"

Emma sat to strap on her sandal, sick to death of the familiar litany, the going off on tangents. They'd been through this over and over with no resolution. "This was a mistake, thinking we could have one night. Let's forget it ever happened."

"Fine by me." He slumped farther down in the bed.

She grabbed her purse, made sure her key card was inside, then went to the door. There she paused to look at Darcy, hoping for...what? For him to call her back, hold her, find the magic words that would somehow make all the pain go away?

He opened his mouth as though he would speak. Something flashed in his eyes, a hint of vulnerability that went so deep it was scary. She almost went over and hugged *him*. Then his jaw clamped shut and the lines around his eyes hardened.

She shook her head. What was she thinking? Darcy

wasn't vulnerable. He was Mr. Goodtime Charlie. He didn't exactly laugh off tragedy and adversity, but he somehow set it aside and carried on. Nothing gave *him* nightmares or had him weeping in the middle of the day. He wasn't as affected by Holly's death as she was because family life simply wasn't as important to him.

"Goodbye." Before she closed the door, she added, "Next time fate throws us together let's hope we have the sense to walk in the opposite direction."

FRIDAY NIGHT AND THE PUB was hopping. Darcy poured beers as fast as the foaming head would allow. Kirsty, a young and mouthy waitress with spiky black hair and arms of steel, picked up a loaded tray, grumbling good-naturedly, "I should be paid by the glass on Friday nights."

Darcy blotted the overflow from a pint of Cascade Lager and passed it down the bar. "How does five cents per round sound?"

"I was thinking more like five dollars. Do you know how much these things weigh?"

"Look at it as saving on a gym membership," he teased. He paid her well and she knew it; she just liked to joke around.

Darcy's gaze moved over the crowded room. Ten o'clock and it was standing-room only. A roar of laughter came from the far corner by the dartboard, where his father was holding court with his cronies. With his thick head of white hair and black eyebrows, Roy Lewis stood out in a crowd. Seeing him lean on his cane to limp to the table, Darcy frowned. His dad was waiting for a hip replacement and living on painkillers in the meantime. Roy glanced over and made eye contact, giving Darcy an approving nod. Darcy turned his frown to a smile. At least the old man still enjoyed himself.

Darcy liked that his father had owned the pub before him, liked the continuity and the community. This was Darcy's home, where he belonged. Here in the pub he was among friends, some he'd grown up with, others he'd met as recently as last week. He thrived on the energy and buzz of people having a good time. Emma had never understood that.

When the pub had been built sixty years ago Summerside had been in the country instead of the outskirts of suburbia the way it was now. The dark wood-panel walls were covered with photos, cricket and football pennants from local teams and other bric-a-brac. His older regulars kept their own special beer mugs on a high shelf over the bar, a motley array of ceramic, pewter and glass.

Occasionally he thought about upgrading the pub but really, why should he change? His was a classic small-town watering hole. Everyone knew everyone else. It had suited him and his customers for the past ten years.

He bent to open the fridge for a bottle of imported beer and the door swung out, letting out cold air and blocking Kirsty's passage to the till. Of course a few modernizations like sliding doors would be welcome. He would get around to them one of these days.

Riley came in with Paula, his new wife and a detective on the Summerside police department. Darcy automatically reached for a frosted glass and a bottle of James Boag classic. He had it poured before Riley elbowed his way to the bar. As he passed it over, he winked at Paula. "Gin and tonic for the missus?"

"If you call me *missus* one more time, I swear, I

will arrest you." Paula's blue eyes sparkled. "I'll have Cinzano with a twist, just to keep you on your toes."

"Careful." Riley sipped his beer and regarded his wife with relish. "She's in a feisty mood tonight."

"I love a strong-minded woman." Darcy grinned at Riley as he poured a measure of ruby-red vermouth over ice and added a sliver of lemon. "Makes for a challenge."

"Speaking of women…" Riley raised his eyebrows. "How was the cruise?"

"Well…" Darcy deliberately let it dangle, trying to figure out a way *not* to tell Riley what happened.

"If you boys are going to talk dirty, I'm going to see if I can find a table." Paula saluted Darcy with her glass and headed off into the crowd.

Before Darcy could answer, one of his regulars, Tony, a young bricklayer with russet sideburns and an angel tattooed on his right arm, came up to the bar. "Six pots of Carlton Draught, thanks, Darcy." He doffed an imaginary cap to Riley. "How's it going, Sarg?"

Riley replied easily and made a comment about football. Darcy watched the exchange as he poured beers and lined them up on the bar. The bricklayer's deferent but friendly attitude masked a wariness of cops. Tony had had a couple of run-ins with the police in his younger days over minor infractions but he'd kept his nose clean for some years. Darcy was glad. He liked Tony.

"Cheers, mate." Tony paid for his drinks and left with six glasses clutched between his callused fingers.

"He's a good kid," Darcy said.

"Did I say anything?" Riley asked mildly. He leaned forward and beckoned Darcy in close. "So, I want to know how you fared on the cruise. Did you get laid?"

Darcy affected a pained expression. "So crude."

"Well, did you? John and I want you to get our money's worth from that ticket."

"I suppose you think that entitles you to a blow-by-blow." Darcy took an order from another customer and moved down the bar to pour a Scotch from the liquor bottles lined up in front of the mirror. No way was he going to mention he'd hooked up with Emma. It was not only indiscreet, he felt foolish.

"Blow-by-blow?" Riley said with a twinkle in his eye when Darcy returned. "Are you saying you engaged in rough play?"

Darcy picked up a cloth and began to wipe the beer-splattered bar, recalling the sexy love-dance between him and Emma. "Vigorous and athletic, but no, not rough."

"You did get laid!" Riley grinned widely. "Was she hot? Are you going to see her again?"

"She was hot," Darcy admitted, getting a visual flash of Emma in that blue dress—and out of it. He was getting hard just thinking about her.

Would she tell her friends? He didn't want to be a source of gossip. They'd already weathered that storm and he was glad it had died down. Their friends and acquaintances had pretty much split down the middle when they divorced. Everyone *said* they didn't want to take sides but inevitably, they had—some more than others. For instance, Riley, seeing the hell his friend was going through during the marriage breakdown, had been critical of Emma. In turn, Emma's sister Alana had been hard on Darcy for "treating Emma so badly."

"Come on, tell an old married man the juicy stuff. Blond or brunette? Tall or short?"

"Redhead, slender but curvy."

"Like Emma." Riley shook his head. "Jeez, mate,

you're supposed to be getting over the woman, not banging her body double."

Darcy rubbed his cloth in circles, the wood getting shinier and shinier. "So what do you think of Geelong's chances to make the final this year?"

"Huh? You don't watch football anymore—" Riley's jaw dropped. "No way. Don't tell me, she *was* Emma."

"She happened to be on the cruise, too," Darcy explained defensively. "We started dancing and, well… one thing led to another."

"You two and your Latin dancing." Riley stabbed a finger at him. "You are *not* getting back with that woman. I like Emma a lot and I know she went through hell after Holly died but she also made you miserable. She's not right for you."

Darcy disagreed. Sure, he and Emma were different in a lot of respects and they had their problems. But way down deep past the superficial stuff he still thought they were soul mates. It was just that some tragedies were so terrible they tore even soul mates apart.

"We're not getting back together. It was a one-off."

"Good," Riley said fervently. "But man, couldn't you have found another woman among the hundreds on board to sleep with?"

He hadn't wanted any other woman. Right up to the point where she'd accused him of being responsible for Holly's death. Then, oh, boy, he'd wished he'd chosen *any* other woman but her. "In hindsight, it was probably a mistake. But aside from an awkward moment when we woke up—" *to put it mildly* "—there was no harm done. Can we let it go now?"

"Sure." Riley slid off his stool. "I'd better go find Paula. Give me a packet of nuts. You know, you should offer hot food. I bet you would do a roaring business."

"You're only the five-hundredth person to tell me that." Before Holly died he'd been talking to a catering company about supplying light gourmet snacks that could be easily heated in the pub's small kitchen. After the funeral that idea had been quietly swept under the carpet. No particular reason, he simply hadn't gotten around to it again.

Riley headed off to find Paula. Darcy moved along the bar, checking if anyone needed a new drink. A cheer went up at the other end of the bar from a group of guys watching the football game. He turned away. He had to have it on because his customers expected it, but Riley was right, he didn't watch the game anymore. Like alcohol, he didn't have the stomach for it.

The door opened and a tall stranger with a shaved head entered. His solidly muscled torso was encased in a tight black polo shirt and a toothpick rolled around his mouth. He paused in the doorway, taking a few minutes to survey the room. Then he made his way to the bar. Even there, he didn't speak but studied the mugs on the high shelf and the yellowing postcards tacked to a pillar.

"What can I get you?" Darcy asked.

"A glass of '98 T'Gallant Reserve pinot noir." He said it with an almost insolent grin, as if deliberately asking for what he knew Darcy couldn't provide and relishing Darcy's discomfort.

Darcy flushed. Not much usually bothered him but this guy made his hackles rise. "Sorry, mate, we don't serve specialty wines. The house pinot is a 2010 Paringa Estate. Not a bad drop."

"I'll have a Stella Artois in that case." He slid onto a stool. "Name's Wayne Overton." He reached across the bar and pumped Darcy's hand with a grip so firm it bordered on crushing. He glanced around the pub. "You the owner?" Darcy nodded. "You've got a good business here. I always like to meet the competition."

Darcy handed him a stemmed glass with the Stella Artois emblem. "I beg your pardon?"

Wayne's grin made the toothpick stick up at a cocky angle. "I bought the old hair salon across the street. I'm going to turn it into a wine bar."

"Is that right?" Darcy took his money and put it in the cash register. "Well, we're a friendly bunch around here. It's a small town but big enough for both of us."

"That's the spirit. Keep each other on our toes, eh?" Wayne glanced around again, his gaze lighting on Tony and his bricklayer mates. "We would have a different clientele, though, wine bars being a bit more upmarket than a country-style pub. No offense."

"None taken." Darcy's smile hardened slightly. The guy was a jerk. "I take it you're new to the village?"

"Oh, I don't live here. I've got a winery with a restaurant in Red Hill. My financial planner suggested I start up another business. You know, for a tax write-off." He looked out the window onto the quiet street. "This place is a bit of a backwater."

"We like to think it has character," Darcy said.

"Yeah, real cute. I notice some big houses along the cliff and on the north side of town. There's a bit of money here."

The more Wayne opened his mouth, the less Darcy liked him. "This is a diverse community—some rich, some middling, plenty of working folk."

Wayne was in here checking out the competition. Darcy wasn't worried. He knew his clientele, who, for Wayne's information, included doctors, stockbrokers and teachers as well as tradesmen and business owners. They came for the friendly atmosphere and the familiarity of his establishment. They liked their beer and they tolerated his limited wine list.

No upstart wine bar could compete with that.

Setting aside his distaste for the guy's attitude, he stuck out a hand. "Welcome to Summerside."

CHAPTER THREE

Late February

EMMA MENTALLY ADDED UP the days and weeks since her last period as she walked briskly along the corridor of Ward 5G North. When she figured it out she stopped dead, forcing an orderly pushing a patient on a gurney to weave around her.

Six weeks.

She would definitely call that overdue. Add in the breast tenderness she'd been experiencing and the frequency of having to pee... A smile spread across her face. She wanted a baby so badly.

Tracey, filling in paperwork at the nurses' station, glanced up as Emma approached. "What are you grinning about?"

"Nothing." She leaned over a filing cabinet and pulled out a drawer, pretending to riffle through the files for a patient's case notes. She didn't want to say anything about the baby, not even to Tracey, until she knew for certain.

If she was pregnant, the baby had to be Darcy's. She'd been out with a few men she'd met online in the past four months but she hadn't liked anyone enough to do more than kiss them good-night.

Tracey reached for the phone. "I'm going to call Barb

and Sasha. Where do you want to go for drinks after work?"

Drinks were a Friday-night ritual for her and Tracey, plus Sasha, a midwife, and Barb, who was a manager in hospital administration. But alcohol would be out of the question if…

Emma stayed Tracey's hand before she could punch in any numbers. "My niece is having her birthday party this afternoon."

She hadn't planned to go even though she was invited. It was too hard. Tessa was turning three, as Holly would have been if she'd lived. The girls had been born, amazingly, on the same day. Twin cousins, she and Alana had called them. Emma had a present for Tessa all wrapped and ready to drop off at the door. But *if* she were pregnant, maybe, just maybe, she would be able to bear to see Tessa.

"We could go out for dinner instead," Tracey suggested.

"Um, I've got a tentative date for tonight. Can I confirm that before we make plans?"

"A date, huh?" Tracey grinned. "Who is it this week? The firefighter? Are you going to do the deed at last?"

"Er, no, the IT guy." There was no date. Emma kept her head down, hoping Tracey wouldn't ask questions even though in the past she'd sought her advice.

"I thought we'd decided he wasn't right for you." Tracey peered into Emma's face. "Hey, why so quiet?"

"No reason." Emma bustled about the station, moving a stack of files from one spot to another.

Tracey studied her pointless movements. "Have you been in touch with your ex since the cruise? Is Darcy why you can't go out with us?"

"Why would you say that?" Emma felt the blood

drain from her face. Tracey had an uncanny knack of tapping into what she was thinking. She didn't always get it exactly right, but close enough to be spooky.

"You're acting weird. And you never told me what happened that night on the cruise."

"Nothing happened." After confiding in Tracey about her divorce, Emma was embarrassed to say she'd slept with Darcy. She would look like an idiot. Fair enough, she *was* an idiot. All she'd admitted to Tracey was that she'd gone for a walk with Darcy around the deck. Fortunately Tracey had hooked up with someone that night and hadn't been in their cabin when she'd returned in the wee hours, upset. "We…kissed. That's all."

"Really?" Tracey said skeptically. "All that stuff you told me about how you couldn't stand him? When I saw you dancing I didn't believe it. I thought for sure you would get back together. You two were smoking hot."

"Not getting back together," Emma said firmly. "We had a great time on the dance floor but that's all we have in common anymore."

That was possibly not true. They might have conceived another baby. She would love that. They'd made one beautiful child, Holly, together and when they'd been married she'd hoped she and Darcy would have several more kids. Even if they weren't together now, she had no problem bearing his child. Once upon a time she'd loved him with her whole being and even though she knew those days were gone forever, if she couldn't have him, having his baby would be the next best thing.

Darcy wouldn't be happy, though. Huh! Not happy? That was putting it mildly. He would freaking stroke out. Oh, God, what if he wanted her to get rid of it?

She couldn't. She just couldn't. And she would tell him so in no uncertain terms. He couldn't force her—

Stop. There was no point in going up and down on this emotional roller coaster until she knew for sure if she was pregnant. She needed to know *now* or she wouldn't be able to concentrate on her work.

"You know, I do feel a bit under the weather." She lifted the watch pinned to her blue scrubs top. "It's time for my break. I'll go lie down in the on-call room for a bit."

Before Tracey could quiz her further she hurried around the corner to the supply room. Once inside, she shut the door and scanned the shelves. Every ward had pregnancy test kits. Nurses administered them when patients were not sure and had to take medications that might be contraindicated.

She grabbed a kit, stuffed it into her purse and hurried to the washroom. A few minutes later she sat on the closed toilet lid clutching the test strip. A thin blue line had formed. A half sob emerged. She was going to have a baby.

But—

Her arm wrapped protectively around her waist. The situation was far from ideal. She'd hoped that after her divorce she would meet a man she could build a relationship with, someone who would want a child as much as she did. Instead she'd gotten pregnant by Darcy, who didn't want children, and was the one man she could never have a relationship with again.

Darcy's reaction was his problem. And yes, she'd wanted to marry again but sometimes things didn't work out the way you planned. The main thing was, she was having a child. Maybe it was better that she was single. That way she wouldn't have to deal with a potential husband's opposing ideas about child rearing. This time she would be in complete control. She would be able to do everything right, take no chances.

She was prepared to raise the kid on her own. That wasn't a problem. Did she have to tell Darcy? Wouldn't she be doing him a favor by keeping him in the dark? No guilt, no responsibilities…that seemed to be the life he wanted.

She didn't need his help. As a nurse she had decent pay and conditions. She would get a year's maternity leave on half pay. Less money but more time to care for the baby. Juggling university with work and a baby might be tricky but having the master's degree would give her a better future as a single mother. There was a lot to think about but it was exciting rather than daunting. She liked working out logistics and practicalities, especially for such a wonderful reason.

Her smile bubbled to the surface. Suddenly she felt like celebrating. She exited the cubicle and pushed the test kit deep into the rubbish bin.

At the nurses' station, Tracey glanced up, clearly surprised at seeing her back so soon. "I thought you weren't feeling well."

"I'm okay. I've decided I'd rather have dinner with you and the girls instead of going on a date."

"Great, I'll round up the others." Tracey reached for the phone.

She listened to Tracey explaining to Barb and Sasha. She was grateful for her friends, for the fact they hadn't given up on her even when she was unsociable and depressed, as she frequently had been in the months following her divorce.

Emma pressed a hand to her belly. This baby couldn't replace Holly. But she hoped—prayed—he or she would be the magic bullet that would lift her spirits and allow her to enjoy time with her friends, renew her relationship with her sister and love her niece....

Not too much to ask, was it?

"HAPPY BIRTHDAY, TESSA!" Emma crouched to hand her niece a gaily wrapped present. Half a dozen little girls, their faces painted with flowers and butterflies, were seated in a circle to watch the present opening. Emma's chest tightened with a familiar ache. Holly should have been part of the circle, sitting next to her cousin.

"What do you say, Tess?" Alana stood behind her daughter, dressed in her trademark track pants and T-shirt. Her normally neat brown ponytail was fraying, no doubt a similar state to her nerves at the prospect of two hours of kiddie fun.

"Fank you, Auntie Emma." Tessa's honey-blond curls were pinned back with butterfly clips. She jiggled up and down on her pink ballet flats, making the fairy wings pinned to her tulle dress bounce.

"Go ahead and open it." Emma smiled, trying not to imagine what Holly would look like at this age. Trying not to imagine her speaking real sentences...

In the background Dave was blowing up a plastic fairy castle with a foot pump. His fine blond hair, ruffled where it was thinning on top, waved with every stamp on the pump. He must have come home from work early for Tessa's party. He'd always been great like that. Alana was so lucky.

A woman wearing a filmy dress with sparkles in her long hair and fairy wings on her back was putting away the face paint.

Tessa tore open the paper and clasped her hands. "Oh!" Inside was an extravagantly frilly pink dress with puffy sleeves and a ruffled skirt. She peeled back another layer of tissue paper to uncover a sparkly tiara and shrieked. "Mummy, look!"

"She doesn't already have a dress like that, does she?" Emma asked. "I kept the receipt."

"Are you kidding? I'm not a frilly kind of gal. Tessa's such a girlie girl. She's lucky her aunt is, too." Alana smiled warmly. "I'm so glad you could come. We've hardly seen you since…" Her gaze flicked away. They both knew Emma hadn't stepped foot in Alana's house for a year and a half, not since Holly's funeral. Oh, they met at their parents' house and in the village for coffee occasionally, but the long hours spent at each other's homes with their babies were a thing of the past.

Emma straightened from her crouch, her pain mixed with guilt. She and Alana had always been close and when their girls were born—a first child for both—the bond had grown even stronger. Together they'd charted Tessa's and Holly's every milestone, first tooth, first step, first word… When they'd realized they were getting competitive they'd had a laugh over it.

The accident had ended all that. For the first six months Emma couldn't even bear to look at Tessa, which only made her feel worse because she adored her niece. She'd hurt Alana, too, pushing her away when her sister only wanted to be there for her, and comfort her. Nor was it easy for Alana. She grieved over Holly's death, too. Emma knew she felt uncomfortable and guilty for having a daughter while Emma had none. Somehow, through feeling too much for each other, they'd ended up barely talking.

It was hard to begin again.

Alana tucked a wisp of hair behind her ear. Cleared her throat. "Cup of tea?"

Badly needing to get away from the room of little girls, Emma agreed readily. "Have you got herbal?"

"Of course. Go on ahead and put the kettle on. I'll see what's next with the fairy lady and be right there."

Emma went through the dining room to the kitchen she knew almost as well as her own. While the kettle boiled Emma admired Tessa's colorful drawings that her proud mother had stuck to the fridge. Someday, her new baby would make drawings.

Peppermint tea was steeping when Alana returned and announced they had a few minutes while the fairy lady led the children in a game. She took down tea mugs painted with stylized owls. "I was thinking. Maybe sometime you and I could go out by ourselves?"

"That would be lovely." Emma hated the uncertain note in her sister's voice, as if Emma might not want to hang with her. "I'm sorry I haven't been around. I—"

"It's okay," Alana said too quickly. She brought the mugs to the table and poured the tea. "How's work?"

Emma told her about her move to the geriatric ward and the master's degree she hoped to be starting soon. She was trying to lead up to her big news but now that she sat across the table from Alana it was surprisingly hard to say. Emma was afraid her sister wouldn't approve of her having a baby on her own. Her worry must have shown through.

"You'll manage," Alana assured her, misunderstanding. "You're so organized. You'll have every day of the week blocked out and color-coded—time for work, for study, for the gym—"

"For the baby."

Alana choked on her tea. She swallowed and stared at Emma. "The baby?"

Emma nodded, anxiously studying her sister's reaction. "I'm pregnant."

"Pregnant," Alana repeated. "That's…great. Isn't it?"

"Yes! You know I've wanted to have another baby for a long time."

"I do…but, Emma, you're on your own. Or are you? I've seen so little of you lately. Is there a father?"

What, no, *"Congratulations, Emma, I'm thrilled for you"*? She couldn't help but feel a little hurt. She and Alana were estranged, true, but they were still sisters. Alana had supported her when she was trying to convince Darcy to have a baby. Now she seemed ambivalent.

"I haven't gone through IVF if that's what you mean." Some of the tension she'd felt around her sister in the past year crept into Emma's voice.

"It's not." Alana huffed. "Do you know who the father is?"

Emma drew back. "Of course. I don't sleep around."

"Don't be so defensive. The first thing you said wasn't, I've met a wonderful man and we're having a baby. All you said was, *I'm pregnant.* I don't know if I'm supposed to be happy for you, or not."

"Fair enough. Let's both take a breath. It's been so long since we've shared personal stuff, we're bound to be rusty."

Alana refilled their cups. "Are you in a relationship with the guy?"

"No." Emma chewed her lip. "I'm not even sure I'm going to tell the father about the baby."

"What's this about a baby?" Dave asked, coming into the room. He set the foot pump on the floor next to the door to the garage.

"Can I tell him?" Alana asked.

"Sure, what the heck. Just don't go spreading it around until I've had a chance to tell Mum and Dad. Even though they're away, gossip spreads."

"Emma's pregnant and is going to raise the baby on her own," Alana informed her husband. "She won't tell me who the father is."

"I didn't say I wouldn't tell you. I just haven't told you yet. Sheesh."

Dave straightened and adjusted the silver metal-framed glasses on his narrow nose. "Even if you plan to be a single mother, it's a father's right to know his children."

Emma knew he was fervent about the issue. He'd been married before and had had to fight for access to his two kids with his first wife.

"I agree fathers have rights but…" Emma glanced at Alana and braced herself. This time she *knew* how her sister would react. "It's Darcy."

"Darcy." Alana exchanged a shocked look with Dave. "After all you went through, I can't believe you slept with that jerk. Please don't tell me you two are getting back together."

Sometimes she wished she'd hadn't told her sister how Darcy not only blamed her for Holly's death but had also flatly refused to have more children. Not that she wasn't still angry with him herself. But when Alana attacked him so vehemently she had to fight the urge to defend him. And that confused the hell out of her.

"No, it was a one-night stand. We both agreed on that. In hindsight, even that much was a mistake."

"Fathers have rights, yes, but Darcy doesn't want to be a father," Alana said. "Don't tell him. He doesn't deserve a child. You definitely don't need any more crap from him."

Crap like being swept away on the dance floor. Crap like being kissed breathless on a silver moonlit sea. Crap like being made love to as if she were a sex goddess.

Emma sighed. Making love with Darcy that night had been wonderful. But it was only a fraction of who they were together, not the whole. As well as being her closest friend and soul mate, he also had the power to hurt her more deeply than anyone else. Not that he did so on purpose, but she would have to be nuts to deliberately put herself in harm's way. "You're right. I don't need any more crap. But I still have to tell him."

"What if he wants to be part of your baby's life?"

A brief surge of hope caught her off guard. She would love to be a family again—she and Darcy and their child. She quickly tamped down the hope. Darcy had never been part of Holly's life in the way Emma had expected when their little girl was born. He was too busy with the pub, with his friends, anything but being a family man. Oh, he played with Holly and took great delight in her but he wasn't a hands-on dad who changed diapers or fed her or did any of the mundane caring things that led to real bonding—at least in Emma's opinion. Since Holly died, he never wanted to look at old photos or talk about her, something that would have given Emma comfort and helped her grieve. It was almost as if he wanted to forget Holly had ever been born.

"He can't be part of my new baby's life because I won't allow it," Emma said flatly. "But that won't be a problem. You're right…he doesn't want a child."

"Take your lawyer with you when you tell him," Dave advised. "Make sure he knows he'll have to pay child support."

"I'm not going to ask for support. Getting pregnant is

something I want—even though this pregnancy was accidental. This baby will be one hundred percent mine."

"Well, congratulations then," Dave said. "This could work out well, right, Alana?" Placing a hand on his wife's shoulder, he turned to Emma. "We're trying for another baby."

"Oh, wow." Emma leaned across the table and hugged her sister. "We might have twin cousins again."

"Hmm, yeah." Alana glanced at the wall clock above the breakfast nook. "I'd better get the cake and ice cream ready."

Emma frowned at her evasive answer. Didn't Alana want to share baby stuff with her again? This was a real opportunity for them to heal their relationship and bond over a new set of babies. She opened her mouth to speak, but Alana was heading to the counter for the pink-frosted cake and directing Dave to get out plates.

Reluctantly, Emma rose, too. "I'll go. I'm meeting friends in Summerside tonight. I might drop into the pub and see Darcy after. No sense putting off telling him."

Alana walked Emma out. Emma paused in the living room to say goodbye to Tessa, taking her away briefly from a game of Pin the Wings on the Fairy. At the door, Alana squeezed Emma's arm. "I'll go with you when you tell him if you want."

"Thanks, but this is something I have to do by myself." Emma gave her sister a hug and held her for a moment. "I would love it if you would be my birthing partner."

"I'd be honored." Alana drew back. "I'm sorry if I wasn't immediately thrilled for you. If you're happy, then I'm happy."

Emma hesitated. Alana didn't look particularly happy. Now that they'd made contact again she didn't want to be the cause of her sister's distress. "Are you worried I'm going to steal your thunder, having another baby at the same time?"

Alana shook her head. She glanced over her shoulder to see if anyone was near then clutched Emma's hand. "I don't want another baby. Dave is pushing for it. I want to go back to work. In fact, I've applied for a job at the gym, teaching group fitness classes."

"Oh, but…Tessa's three. It's a good time. In fact, you're behind schedule." Emma smiled. "You always said you wanted three children spaced two and a half years apart."

"That was before…"

"Before what?"

A hint of desperation flashed in Alana's eyes, but she didn't finish her thought. Instead she took another tack. "The longer I'm out of the work force the harder it will be to get back in. Especially in my field, where I have to be super fit. If I want to move up, maybe get a permanent position at a gym, then I need to think about my career."

Emma had been under the impression Alana chose to be a fitness instructor so she could teach classes part-time and stay home with her kids. "But I thought—"

"Sorry, Emma, the kids are finished. I've got to go." Alana hugged her. "Good luck tonight telling Darcy."

"Thanks. I'm sure it'll be fine. He'll be relieved he's not expected to do anything."

Emma walked slowly to her car. What was going on with Alana? Something was definitely bothering her. Now Emma regretted more than ever not keeping in better contact with her. It was a shame her sister had done a complete one-eighty about her plans for a family. Tessa was the sweetest kid.

Emma looked at the house. As if she'd sensed her aunt's thoughts the little girl stood at the window, waving goodbye. She was wearing the tiara. Emma blew her a kiss. Alana didn't know how lucky she was.

And now Emma was lucky, too, to be having another baby. She hoped Darcy wouldn't be too upset, but even if he was, she couldn't be more thrilled.

ANOTHER FRIDAY NIGHT at the pub, another big crowd.

Darcy held the pub door open for the departing white-haired woman in blue jeans and sensible shoes. Tony had brought his grandmother, Shirley, in for a drink on her seventieth birthday. "Happy birthday. See you next time."

"Thank you, Darcy. I had a very enjoyable evening." Shirley clutched the ten dollars she'd won from Tony's mates at the shuffleboard table.

"You're a shark," Darcy said, and winked at Tony.

"Cheers, mate," Tony said to Darcy. "This way, Gran." Tattooed arm extended, he gently steered his grandmother toward his utility truck.

Darcy glanced across the street. The lights were on in the vacant shop. Wayne was inside, reeling out a tape measure. So, it was starting to happen. Darcy wasn't against competition, but he had to admit the location of the wine bar wasn't the greatest. Why couldn't Wayne have gone to Mornington or Frankston?

Darcy was about to go inside when he noticed Emma walking toward the pub. As she passed beneath the streetlight her red hair glowed. What was she doing here? It couldn't be because she'd missed him. He hadn't heard from her since the cruise. Not that he'd expected, or wanted, to. All that angst was too much hard work.

He had to admire the graceful way she moved,

though, even walking across the road. She wore a knit wrap dress that clung to her curves and her hips swayed almost as if she was dancing. Darcy had gone to a Latin dance club in the city last week but had left after half an hour. It hadn't felt right. Now dancing was lost to him along with football and an appreciation for a fine whiskey.

Emma stopped at the curb to let a car go by. Darcy ducked inside the pub, seeking his own turf and friendly, familiar faces. Maybe she wasn't even coming here. Maybe she'd been visiting someone and her car was simply parked on this side of the street.

Emma walked through the door. Nope, guess not.

A pair of very young women slid onto newly vacated bar stools. He turned to them, grateful for the diversion. "What's your pleasure, ladies?"

"Two apple martinis," the blonde said. The brunette nodded, giggling.

Darcy smiled indulgently. "Can I see your ID?"

They dutifully pulled out their wallets and he scrutinized their driver's licenses. They were legal. Just. "Two appletinis coming right up."

Emma found an empty seat at a table next to the wall and fiddled with the drinks menu, flipping through the plastic-coated cards listing the specialty beers and ciders. She hadn't tried to make eye contact yet. Darcy knew because he kept her in his peripheral vision as he poured shots of green-apple schnapps and vodka into the cocktail shaker along with crushed ice. He made a big show of shaking the container and joking with the girls as he strained the frosty mix into cocktail glasses. They giggled some more as they sipped through tiny straws. *Eat your heart out, Wayne.*

Emma was still waiting to be served. Damn it, where

was Kirsty, or Elise, the weekend barmaid? Hefting heavy trays of beer on the other side of the pub, no doubt. Darcy lifted the partition separating the bar from the room and went to Emma's table. "What can I get you?"

"Can you sit down a moment? We need to talk."

He gave an incredulous laugh. "Em, this is the busiest hour of the busiest night of the week. Come back tomorrow morning, then we can talk. Meantime, would you like a chardonnay? It's on the house."

"No, thank you. I can't drink alcohol."

"Since when? You love your chardy." The only time she'd ever refused a glass of wine was when—

Her eyes were locked with his. Even so it took two long beats before realization hit him like a cold wet bar towel across the face. No, she couldn't be.

"That's right," she said. "I'm pregnant."

He dropped into the chair opposite. He shook his head. Blinked a few times. "Wh-whose is it?"

"Yours." She gathered her purse and started to rise. "I've told you, now I can leave."

"Hang on!" He grabbed her arm, pulling her down. "Are you positive it's mine? We used—" He glanced around and leaned closer, lowering his voice. "We used condoms both times."

A trio of guys with their girlfriends filed in, calling out hello, forcing him to find a smile and a cheery wave. Across the room a table of college students signaled for another round of beer.

"You're right, this is a bad time," Emma said. "I'll come back tomorrow."

"No." Darcy dragged a hand through his hair. "You didn't answer my question. Are you positive it's mine?"

"I haven't been with anyone else since our divorce."

Was he dreaming? Had to be. Because this was his worst nightmare ever. He spotted Kirsty and called to her. "Get Brad off his break to tend the bar, will you? Table four needs another round and I'd like a double Scotch."

Kirsty's blue eyes widened under her dyed black bangs at this unusual request. He never drank and never sat down when the bar was this crowded.

"It's an emergency," he said. "Emma, would you like a soda water, or something?"

"Nothing, thanks." She still had her purse on her lap, poised to leave.

"Thanks, Kirsty, that's all." When she'd left he turned to Emma, his fingers drumming the table. "Walk me through this."

"There's no big mystery," she said impatiently. "We had sex. I conceived. Basic biology."

A simmering rage bubbled beneath his surface calm. "You did this on purpose. You couldn't get your way while we were married. So you decided to go ahead and have a baby anyway. You played me for a fool."

"We used condoms, you dope. How can you think I did this on purpose?"

"I don't know, a little nick with a fingernail—"

She held up her nails, filed almost to the quick. How could he have forgotten? Germs lived beneath fingernails.

"Teeth?" he suggested. "You could have done practically anything while you were down there. I wasn't thinking clearly. I wouldn't have had a clue."

Emma's color deepened. "Well, I didn't."

Kirsty set his Scotch on the table, her curious gaze lingering on Emma. She'd started at the pub three months ago and didn't know Emma was his ex-wife.

"Thank you, Kirsty." He tried but couldn't keep the edge out of his voice. An edge directed at Emma.

He started to take a drink, but one whiff of the alcohol and he didn't want Scotch, after all. He set the glass carefully on a coaster. "What do you expect me to do about this?"

"Nothing. Telling you is merely a courtesy because fathers have a right to know. I'm not asking for anything. I don't want your money or your time. I don't want your interference or token parental effort. I'm going to raise this baby on my own." She looked him straight in the eyes. "Is that clear?"

"Crystal." She had it all worked out how she would manage the baby without him. Typical. She'd done that with Holly, too. Made him feel as if he was clumsy and useless. And he had to admit she was right, witness the time he'd let Holly roll off the changing table. That one incident had been a game-changer, a turning point in their little family. From then on he and Emma both accepted that he wasn't good with babies. He knew how to play with them but he didn't know how to care for them. That's how he saw it and he was pretty sure she did, too, because after that she didn't let him help.

But whether he was a good dad or not, a baby was on the way. No matter what Emma said about not wanting his money, he couldn't shirk his responsibilities. He wasn't made that way. "I'll set up an account for the child."

Money was the easy part. Worse would be the whole emotional angle he would have to deal with. Another baby. Another fragile, vulnerable, *mortal* human being he was biologically programmed to love more than his own life. He couldn't do it again. He just couldn't. The pub noise became a roaring in his ears. The walls began to close in on him.

"Darcy? Are you okay?" Emma's voice seemed to come from very far away.

Suddenly he felt light-headed. He had to get away before he passed out. Gripping the table with both hands he pulled himself to his feet. "I'll notify you of the bank details in the morning." Then he got up and walked away while he could still stand.

CHAPTER FOUR

EMMA JUGGLED SHOPPING bags full of baby things and the mail she'd collected from her box in the foyer and inserted the key to unlock her apartment door. After a nine-hour shift, then the mall, she was dying to shower, eat and put her feet up, not necessarily in that order.

She passed through the entry hall and into the small living room filled with inexpensive furniture she'd bought after the divorce. She hadn't wanted anything from the old house, no reminders of the love and family and home she'd lost. Darcy had taken the beautiful red leather couch and chairs, the handmade teak coffee table and other unique pieces they'd collected together, and crammed them into his two-bedroom apartment above the pub. The pine coffee table and hard-wearing fabric couches she owned now held no memories and if she occasionally missed her old stuff, too bad. She needed to toughen up.

She sank onto the couch with her head on a cushion and her feet on the opposite arm and leafed through her mail. It felt good to lie down for a minute. She'd forgotten how pregnancy sapped her of energy.

The Monash University School of Nursing logo stared at her from the top left corner of an envelope. She tore it open. Her application had probably been rejected. After all, she'd already started it once, before she'd gotten pregnant with Holly, and quit. Having pulled out then might go against her now. And she'd applied late. Maybe the program was already full.

But she hoped not. She was counting on this extra degree to help her provide a good future for her and her baby. She quickly scanned the single typewritten sheet. Dear Ms. Lewis, yada, yada...

Approved.

She blinked and looked again, making sure she'd seen right, then grinned. Yes! She was in. It was all happening. The master's, the baby. Everything she wanted was coming true for her.

Her smile faded. Not everything. Her marriage had fallen apart. She'd totally screwed up by getting pregnant with her ex-husband. Darcy didn't want anything to do with her or the baby. When she'd told him she was pregnant he'd looked as if he might throw up. Then he'd stood and walked away from her and hadn't come back.

Something had died inside her then, a tendril of hope she hadn't even realized she'd been hanging on to. Even though it was what she'd expected, his reaction still hurt. Money was all he was willing or able to give. Nothing of himself, no love for his own baby, no warmth for her, the mother of his child.

Well, she didn't want him. By his own admission and from her experience, he wasn't husband and father material. He *could* be, if he wanted to be. He simply didn't care about family as much as she did. Heat pricked the backs of her eyes and she pressed her fingers to them. Damn him. She'd thought she was beyond being hurt by him.

And how about his suggestion that she'd gotten pregnant on purpose? How insulting was that? Had he forgotten how quickly she'd become pregnant with Holly? She was obviously very fertile and his sperm so virile they'd done the backstroke up her vagina like mini champion athletes. On the cruise he was the one who'd started intercourse without a condom, assuming she still had an IUD.

Maybe she should have made it clear the second they'd entered his cabin that she didn't, but she'd expected he would automatically reach for protection. They were too old to be carried away by the moment. But that's what had happened. One thing hadn't changed— the attraction between them. But a relationship couldn't thrive on sex alone.

Bottom line, she was on her own. It might not be the way she wanted it but it was what she had to work with. She had to be practical not emotional, for the baby's sake.

First thing Monday morning she would contact the School of Nursing and confirm her place in the program, look at the course requirements and find out times, etcetera. Then she'd talk to the hospital about managing her hours around her classes. She didn't envisage any problem there. Barb was high up in administration, and besides being her friend, she was always encouraging the nursing staff to upgrade their qualifications.

Her stomach rumbled. Her meal of chicken salad at the food court was two hours ago. Another thing she'd forgotten, how ravenous she was all the time. She dragged herself off the couch and out to the kitchen to heat a bowl of minestrone soup in the microwave.

A week had passed since that night at the pub. Every day since she'd half expected to get a phone call from Darcy wanting to talk about the baby, but nothing. What kind of a man, even one who didn't want to be a father, walked away from that kind of news with no discussion? Oh, the next day he'd sent her an email asking for bank details so he could deposit money for the baby. She'd deleted it without replying. Thought he could throw money at the problem and it would go away. Huh!

She ate her soup then put her dishes in the dishwasher and went to have a shower. The hot water streaming over her head and shoulders gradually eased some of the tension out of her knotted muscles. She needed to let the incident go. She'd told Darcy she didn't want anything from him and she meant it. She just wished, for her baby's sake, that he cared even a little.

She turned off the tap and stepped into the steamy bathroom. Even though it was only 7:00 p.m. and still light out she didn't bother dressing again but put on a camisole and panties, ready for bed. Rubbing a clear patch on the foggy mirror she turned sideways, smoothing a hand over her flat stomach. No sign of a baby bump yet. Her breasts had started to swell, though, curving above the lacy camisole.

A knock at the door startled her. Who could that be? She wasn't expecting anyone and didn't know a soul in the building. Anyone from outside would ring the bell to be buzzed up. Pulling on a dressing gown, she went down the hall and put an eye to the peephole.

Darcy stood there, holding a fistful of purple irises and orange gerberas. Despite herself, she melted a little. Just when she was totally, completely angry and had decided she hated him, he brought her flowers.

Emma opened the door. One bare foot crept over to rest on top of the other. "What brings you here?"

He presented her with the bouquet. "Sorry I acted like a dickhead."

Wearing his button-down shirt and with his tousled dark hair, he looked younger than his forty years and sexier than he had any right to. How could she possibly feel attracted when she was so angry at him?

Hell, why was she even angry? She wasn't supposed to feel anything anymore. "Thanks," she said, accepting the flowers. Their fingers brushed. Nope, she felt nothing. That was static from the carpet, not a spark of electricity.

Darcy's gaze dipped to the neck of her robe where the top of her camisole showed. "Looks like I caught you at a bad time."

"I go to bed early. I have to get up at five." Now she was explaining in case he thought she was expecting someone. Which she had every right to do, if she wanted. Except that she wasn't, and had no plans to go out with a man in the foreseeable future. Maybe someday, after the child was a few years old she would be ready to date again, but not with Darcy's baby growing inside her.

"Apology accepted. Thanks for the flowers. Now if that's all you came for…"

She wasn't going to automatically invite him in. The apartment, even small and poorly furnished, was her sanctuary, one she'd painstakingly constructed after their divorce. Nothing from their life together existed in this apartment and that's the way she wanted it. She had to cut out all traces of the past or she would end up reliving it every single day.

"It's not." He jammed his hands in his back pockets. "Can I come in so we can talk instead of me standing out here like a delivery man? Or we could go out for coffee. Five minutes, that's all I ask." The lines bracketing his mouth deepened.

Reluctantly, she relented. It had cost him something, coming here. A baby wasn't his choice, but he was trying to make amends with her. Stepping back, she gestured to the arched opening on her right. "Take a seat. I'll put some clothes on."

She slipped into her bedroom, tugged on a pair of leggings and threw on the green silk top hanging on the back of the door. Too late she realized he'd given her the blouse for Christmas the year she'd had Holly. What the hell. She tugged it down over her hips. No sense being neurotic about this. Getting rid of all her clothes wasn't practical. Likely he wouldn't even remember, or care about the associated memories if he did.

She stood at the dresser to brush her hair. Was she trying to look nice for him? No, her hair was ruffled from the shower cap. She would have done it for anyone. She ran the brush through her hair with her vigorous strokes. She hated second-guessing everything she did. As if she was nervous.

Although if she was honest, she *did* want to look her best around Darcy. She wanted him to regret that he'd lost her. What did it matter if it was out of vanity or pride? She would hate him to think she'd fallen apart without him.

She was the organized one, the one in control of herself and her life. He was the one who always had projects planned that never got finished. Even though he was a hard worker, he tended to procrastinate. Look at the pub. He should have at least painted when he'd taken over from his dad, but had he? No. He hadn't changed a single thing regardless of how tired or worn-out the pub appeared.

Not that she cared what Darcy did with the pub or anything else.

He was perusing her bookshelf stuffed with crime novels when she came out. Only because he was too impatient to sit, not because he would ever actually read a book, God forbid. Funny how the things she'd over-looked as being unimportant when they were married had became huge deficiencies once they'd split. How could she have married a man who didn't read? Who would rather do any activity at all rather than sit qui-etly with a book?

She perched on the edge of the couch, resisting the urge to tuck her hands between her knees. "What can I do for you?"

He sat in the chair opposite, his legs sprawled and his arms relaxed. "I wanted to apologize for my reaction last week. It can't have been easy for you to come there and tell me you were pregnant, not after…everything."

It had taken him a whole week to come around to that conclusion? He had her phone number. He could have called to say this. Or emailed. Or sent her a text message. She supposed he deserved points for saying it in person.

"I hope you've recovered from your shock enough to realize I didn't get pregnant on purpose. I knew how you felt about having another child. I wouldn't knowingly bring a kid into the world whose father didn't want him."

"I believe you."

A tiny wash of relief took the tension out of her shoul-ders. Even after all they'd been through, his opinion still mattered to her and she hated to think he believed her capable of something so underhanded and manipulative. Part of what she'd always loved about him was how he looked for, and saw, the best in people.

She leaned back and smoothed out the hem of her blouse. "Why are you here?"

"I was worried about you. I wanted to see how you were."

"As you can see, I'm fine." She gestured around the

apartment. "I've got a nice place to live. I've got my job. I'm pregnant. Even though the situation wasn't planned and I'm going to be a single mum instead of having a family, I'm really happy about the baby. Everything's working out." She brightened and leaned forward again. "And I've just been accepted into the master's of nursing program."

"The master's program?" He frowned. "Are you still going to have time for that? Even when we were together and you were only nursing part-time you found it hard to juggle work and caring for Holly."

No thanks to him! She opened her mouth, wanting to snap out that she would have found studying easier if he'd helped out more, taken an active role in baby care instead of always, always going to the pub.

Yes, Darcy worked long hours and she'd been part-time—they'd needed both incomes. But that didn't stop her from resenting the time he spent at the pub. He loved socializing with customers and his friends who dropped in. Sometimes she wondered if he'd loved the social scene more than her and Holly. And though she could never prove it, and he would deny it if asked, she wondered if he spent more time there than strictly necessary to get away from the chaotic home life with a baby and then a toddler.

But she bit her tongue and said nothing. Stress wasn't good for the baby. She rested a hand on her abdomen and breathed slowly and calmly. Water under the bridge. Let it flow away and take her anger with it. "I can handle it."

"If anyone can, you will. But, Emma…" Darcy leaned forward, elbows on knees, as if finally getting around to the reason for his visit. Even then he didn't speak right away but stared at the carpet. Finally, he looked up. "Are you emotionally ready for a baby? It's awfully soon after…Holly. Are you doing this for the right reasons, or are you trying to fill a gap in your life?"

The emotional seesaw in Emma's heart that continually teetered between love and resentment tipped sharply toward the latter. What right did he have to even ask these questions? They were divorced. How dare he act as if he still cared or even had a say in her emotional welfare?

"*Soon?* It's been a year and a half. I'm thirty-five, not getting any younger." Emma got to her feet and paced the small space between the couch and the coffee table. "As for a gap in my life, yes, there's a huge gap that I want to fill. I had a family. Now I don't. I want children. You don't give up just because tragedy strikes. Or, rather, some people don't." She ignored his slight flinch. He wanted to be blunt—she would be, too. "Are you talking about me or yourself, because you can't handle the thought of being responsible for another baby?"

"I'm talking about you, of course. According to you, this doesn't affect me." His voice held a trace of bitterness.

"Only because you're adamant you don't want another child. If I thought for one second—" She broke off. Their marriage was finished. There was no point holding out hope for reconciliation simply because she was having his baby. Especially when their conflicting desires regarding babies had torn them apart in the first place.

"I'm not ready for another child. I haven't gotten over Holly yet." Quietly, he added, "If I ever will."

"You won't unless you work through your guilt."

He pressed fingers to the bridge of his nose. "I wasn't on the spot. There's nothing I could have done."

In other words, she was to blame. Is that what he was

saying? "Go ahead…you keep telling yourself that. But just ask yourself, why have you given up drinking?"

"I wanted to lose some weight, get healthier." He shrugged, apparently bewildered at her question. "Alcohol dependency is an occupational hazard in my job. I didn't want it to get the better of me."

"You weren't an alcoholic." She turned away, breathing out the tightness. "You haven't got a clue. And yet you come here and lecture me."

Silence settled over the room.

"You still cry over her," he said at last, gently.

"I will cry over her for the rest of my days." The words tore out of her. "It doesn't mean I can't love another child and have joy in my life." Her throat closed and she had to take a breath, clearing away the huge ache in her chest. Of course she was still emotional about Holly. Who wouldn't be? A mother didn't forget, ever, losing a child. But that didn't mean there was something wrong with her, as he seemed to think.

"I don't want to have these conversations anymore," she continued, her voice stronger. "I'm happy for the first time in eighteen months. I get that you don't want to be part of this. That's fine, believe me. More than fine."

"What does your family think?"

"Alana's thrilled for me."

"Really?"

"With a few reservations," Emma admitted. "But you know how cautious she is. She doesn't like any sort of risk."

"Alana, cautious? I think you're mixing her up with yourself. You don't do anything without having all your ducks lined up and ironclad safeguards that nothing will go wrong or fail. Why else do you think I'm worried about your mental and emotional state? Lots of women have a baby on their own, but for you it's risk taking. It's out of character."

He was right. Before she embarked on any new course of action she did her research. And she had. She knew babies back to front. But no amount of research could alter the fact that life had thrown her a curveball. Her baby's conception hadn't been planned, and everything that happened next would be unknown and therefore very scary.

"Doesn't that show you how much I want this baby?" The tremor was back in her voice. "What can I be *but* a single mother? I'm pregnant, with no partner."

He got to his feet, took a few paces and stopped in front of her. "Have you thought about—"

"Oh, no. You better not be about to say what I think you're going to say."

"You could consider it. It's not a bad solution."

"Not in a million years would I do that. If you say another word, I'll throw you out."

"Don't reject the idea out of hand. I know you're a private person but having other people around, especially a woman in the same situation as you, can be a support."

"A woman…?" She frowned. "Wait. What are you talking about?"

"Sharing a house with another single mother and her kid or kids. What did you think I meant?"

"Oh." She pressed a hand to her forehead and sank onto the couch. "I thought— Never mind."

He stared at her. Then shook his head as he got it. "Oh, Em, I know you better than that."

"I couldn't."

"I wouldn't want you to," Darcy said quietly. "I thought you knew me better than that, too."

She turned to the window and gazed out at the view

of the bay, the merest glimpse of blue between the trees. Okay, the thought of terminating the pregnancy had crossed her mind—once—in the dark hours of the night when she was feeling scared and vulnerable and *alone*. She'd lain awake wondering how she was going to manage on her own. But that was just night terrors. By morning her fears had evaporated and she'd once again felt happy knowing she would be a mother again.

Darcy picked up a plush teddy bear from the carpet. The bag of baby things she'd bought earlier had fallen open. Emma hadn't been able to resist even though it would be months before the baby was born. All Holly's toys had gone to a church bazaar. He smoothed the bear's fur. "I want you to be happy, Em."

She nodded, not trusting her voice. His good wishes meant a lot to her. But she was so mixed-up, one minute angry with him, the next minute wishing they could still be a family. She had to get *that* notion right out of her head.

"What did your parents say?" Darcy asked.

"I sent an email but I haven't heard back yet. They're on the road, somewhere near Darwin, out of phone range." She sighed. "You know them. No doubt you can predict their reaction."

"Your mother will be excited but your father will worry about you. He didn't have anything good to say when your cousin had a baby on her own a couple of years ago."

"What about your family? What's their reaction?" He was silent. "Oh, my God. You haven't told them yet."

"It's only been a week. I haven't seen them."

"Your father is in the pub every week."

"Yeah, well, I need to think about how to tell them.

They took our divorce pretty hard." Darcy ran a hand through his hair. "This whole situation is unexpected."

"It's not going to get any easier. Just tell them." She paused, suddenly understanding his reticence. "You know they'll be thrilled. You're just afraid they'll pressure you to reconcile with me." Was he also afraid he might be tempted? "Don't worry. I'll set them straight on that score." The last thing she wanted was to reunite only because their families wanted it.

"I'll talk to them soon." He studied her face. "You look tired. I'd better go." Then he paused. "Before I do, is there anything you need?"

Oh. The electrical outlet in the nursery wasn't working. But she couldn't ask... "No, I'm good. Thanks."

"Your eyes flickered. What is it?"

"It's all right. I'll call an electrician—"

"Those guys charge an arm and a leg and take a week to come. Where is it?"

"If you really don't mind... The socket in the spare room sparks when I plug something in."

"I'll have a look." He offered without hesitation which was to his credit, given she hadn't exactly welcomed him into her home. That was the great thing about Darcy; he was always ready to lend a hand to anyone who needed it. Including her.

"This way." Emma reached for the bags and carried them across the foyer and down the short hall to the second bedroom. She was practical but some things, like electrical problems, were beyond her. His steady footsteps behind her were comforting. She shouldn't like that he was taking charge. But she did.

DARCY FOLLOWED, half wishing he hadn't agreed to look at the outlet because he had to get to the pub. But Emma needed his help. She was one of the most competent people he knew, but like a lot of women she didn't know how to handle tools. That wasn't being sexist, simply stating a fact. Even though they weren't together he still felt responsible for her. Holly had tied them together and now this baby was another link. He had mixed feelings about that. He couldn't imagine life without Emma in it. On the other hand, how would he ever move on if he kept seeing her?

The new-paint smell hit him as he stepped in the doorway. He stopped dead, his gaze sweeping the room. The walls were a pale yellow below a frieze of colorful balloons. He took in the white-painted cot, matching dresser and changing table.

This wasn't a spare room. It was a nursery.

He hadn't been prepared for baby furniture. Or for the tightness in his chest. Or the flash recall of Holly, her bright hair and gurgling smile, as she played peeka-boo through the bars of her crib.

He didn't usually allow himself to think about her. Holly was gone. Never coming back. There was no point in torturing himself. Love and happiness were ghosts. They flitted in and out of his life, haunting him with memories and taunting him with unfulfilled dreams.

"Darcy?" Emma was looking at him strangely.

He shook his head, banishing the image. "Sorry, were you saying something?"

"It's this socket next to the dresser. I want to put a lamp here for when the baby wakes in the night." Emma dropped the bags on a toy chest with a padded lid that doubled as a bench seat. "When I tried to plug it in, the outlet crackled."

"Have you got a screwdriver?"

"In the laundry room. Hang on a tick." She hurried out of the room.

Darcy pushed aside the bags and sat on the toy box. Though he tried to block the memory of Holly, traces lingered like cobwebs in the dark corners of his mind. In the weeks before she'd died, she'd started climbing out of her crib. Emma had wanted to get her a child's bed. She'd been after him to go look for one. He hated malls and had put her off, and put her off. In the end, he'd gone shopping with her—not for a bed but for a coffin.

He pressed fingers to the inner corners of his eyes.

"Will these do?" Emma entered and handed him a set of screwdrivers in a folding plastic case.

He grunted, not trusting his voice, and kneeled to unscrew the faceplate. Carefully, he prodded the wires with a fingertip. "The connection is loose. If you can turn the power off, I'll tighten these wires."

"I think the switchboard is in the residents' garage. Tell me which switch to flip and I'll do it."

"The main breaker. It should be labeled. I'll go." Anything to get out of this room so he could breathe. He was on his feet and heading out the door in seconds.

"You'll need the key to get into the garage." She came after him and fished in her purse for a set of keys. "Are you okay?"

"Fine." He swallowed, hating that she'd seen him react to the baby things. It made him feel weak.

He went to the garage, flipped the breaker then came back up, using her keys to get into the apartment. Tightening the wires took only a few minutes. He'd learned a few basic skills of the trade from his older brother Dan, an electrician. They came in handy when things needed fixing around the pub.

As he worked, he could hear Emma in the kitchen,

moving around, running water. It was almost like the old days, at their home. Doggedly he pushed those thoughts away, too, and turned on the flashlight Emma had set on the carpet by the outlet. Nostalgia was a trap that would be easy to fall into, but it didn't make the bad stuff go away. The fighting and the tears, the words that could never be unsaid. Those memories were burned into his brain, too.

He put the faceplate on and put away the screwdrivers. Then he went out to flip the breaker on and returned a few minutes later to the aroma of fresh-brewed coffee.

Emma appeared in the foyer as he shut the door. "Do you want a cuppa? It's decaf."

"No, I have to get to the pub." Seeing the strain in the faint lines of her face he forgot about himself and his feelings. "Anything else I can do?"

"No, that's it." She straightened her shoulders and smiled. Then she touched his arm. "I really appreciate this. Thanks."

"It's nothing. Look, Em, I don't agree with what you're doing." Her smile faded. "But I am going to support you and the baby."

"You don't have to. I've decided I won't name you as father on the birth certificate. That way Child Services won't be able to come after you for support payment."

That took his breath away. It hadn't even occurred to him that she wouldn't name him as father. Knowing there would be a blank line where his name should appear…well, he didn't like the idea one bit. Nor did he like the idea of the baby seeing that blank line when he or she grew up. It was almost as if Darcy didn't exist. Or that he'd abandoned the child.

"You can raise the baby any way you want," he said. "It's yours. I won't interfere. But I *will* do the responsible thing for any child of mine." She opened her mouth to protest and he raised a hand to stop her. "I'll do it because I want to and because it's right, not because Child Services tells me I have to."

"You can't have it both ways, not being an active father and also getting to have a say in whether you're named on the birth certificate."

She had him there. "Clearly you hold all the cards," he said tightly. "You do what you think best."

"Darcy, I wish…" She spread her hands. "I don't even know what I want to say. I'm sorry it has to be this way."

He wished it didn't have to be this way, too. He'd give anything to turn back the clock if only he knew how. He would even go on that damn picnic if it meant he could do over that day and Holly would still be alive.

"Don't say anything." His voice turned gruff. Something—nostalgia, again?—made him lean in and kiss her on the cheek. Feeling her soft skin beneath his lips, breathing in the clean scent of her, he wanted to slide his hands inside her silky blouse—the one he'd given her that Christmas—and feel the heat of her body. He wanted to angle his face and put his mouth on hers and deepen the kiss.

But he didn't. If the past wasn't enough to stop him, now he had the future child to deter him, as well. There could be no going back for him and Emma, no second chance. He would not touch her or kiss her or any of the things his body was begging him to do.

"I'll see you." When, he had no idea. He made himself step back, turn the door handle and leave. Walking away from her right that minute felt like one of the hardest things he'd ever done.

He punched the button on the elevator at the end of the hall. Damn thing must be broken. The light seemed to be stuck two floors above on five. He hit the button again. If he had to stand here one more second, he might turn around, take her in his arms and make the second biggest mistake of his life—the first being sleeping with her after their divorce.

But he wouldn't. Seeing the nursery had brought up sad memories, but it had also reminded him that sex had consequences. Like careless teenagers he and Emma had been caught. Hopefully they were both smart enough not to compound their mistake by thinking they could get together again.

The elevator still wasn't moving. He spun on his heel and pushed through the emergency door to the stairwell. His footsteps echoed off the concrete walls as he clattered down and down.

The days of wine and roses and Latin dancing were truly over.

EMMA CLOSED THE DOOR behind Darcy. Dissatisfaction nagged at her, but it was worse than a near-miss sexual encounter. It had been a near-miss emotional connection. She'd wanted so badly for him to hold her close the way he used to, and tell her he loved her and that everything would be all right. She craved it so badly, it scared her.

Instead he'd retreated. No doubt he'd done so out of honorable intentions. She could picture each step he took away from her. Fifteen paces to the stairwell—because he would be too impatient to wait for the elevator once he'd found out how slow it was—then down three floors and out to the lobby. Another ten paces and he would be out of the building, heading to his truck.

With every step he took away from her, the tug in her chest grew. She wanted to run after him and beg him to come back. Was she wrong to want the father of her child and the love of her life to love her and love their baby? Maybe this pregnancy was a sign that they should try again. Maybe the joy a baby brought would lift them out of their impasse and set them on the path to a brighter future—together.

Yet even as she longed to reunite with Darcy, she knew it would be a terrible mistake. He didn't want a role in the baby's life. He hadn't even protested when she'd said she wouldn't name him as the baby's father. That proved how detached he was. It was wrong and sad. Even though he hadn't been a hands-on father with Holly there had never been any doubt he loved her.

Emma stroked a hand over her belly. If only he could love this baby. She pictured him holding her and pressing his hand on her stomach to feel the baby move, love in his eyes and in his smile. Talking about baby names, planning where to live. They'd always dreamed of building their own home, somewhere with a big yard and lots of trees—

But it wasn't going to happen. She was being weak, giving in to wishful thinking. She would only make herself unhappier by allowing herself to hope.

Pushing those thoughts out of her mind she went to the nursery. She plugged in the lamp and pressed the switch. Light spilled through the darkening room, and she pulled the curtains against the coming night. He'd only fixed an outlet, but it was an act of caring.

When they'd been married, she was the one who made sure bills were paid on time, who got the groceries and cooked the meals. Darcy kept the pub going, remembered everyone's birthday in both their families and maintained the house and cars. And they'd looked after each other. They made a good team. She missed that.

She emptied the shopping bags of baby clothes,

folded the clothes neatly and laid them in the dresser. She'd bought more than she'd planned on, in sizes up to twelve months. She started to rip the tags off then paused. Maybe she should leave them on just in case.

She used to go through life thinking nothing bad was ever going to happen to her. And then it had. So many things could go wrong—miscarriage or stillbirth or even an accident to herself.

Again, she pushed the unwelcome thoughts away. She didn't want to dwell on the negative, not when she had so much that was positive to look forward to. She started to walk out of the room then stopped in the doorway to survey the nursery. She'd painted, bought furniture, even put up a frieze. What were those if not acts of faith?

She went back to the dresser, took out the baby clothes and tore off the tags. Nothing was going to go wrong with this baby.

CHAPTER FIVE

"HEY, MUM." Darcy kissed his mother on the cheek and breathed in cinnamon and nutmeg from the apple cake she was baking.

The kitchen of his parents' four-bedroom brick home in the older part of Summerside could be called cluttered and untidy. Darcy saw it as lived-in. Growing up here with his two brothers and his sister, he'd gotten used to a lot of stuff lying around. Now the toys and drawings and games belonged to the grandkids that spilled in and out as if this was their second home. A framed photo of Holly sat on the windowsill. Every time he came here his gaze went to it, then quickly away.

Marge wiped her floury hands on her apron and pulled Darcy into a hug. She held him at arm's length to look him over. "I made a roast. You're going to take the leftovers home with you."

Did he really look like he was starving? Darcy liked himself a bit leaner, but everyone was making a big deal of him dropping a few pounds.

"Who else is coming today? I haven't talked to anyone in a few weeks." Chloe, his parents' tan-colored poodle cross, jumped up and licked his hand. He ruffled her ears. "Hey, girl."

"Dan and his family. Possibly Mike." Marge tipped the chopped apple into the bowl of batter.

"Where's Dad?" While his mother's back was turned,

getting the cake pan ready, Darcy sneaked a taste of the spiced batter.

"In the backyard." Marge turned and shooed him away from the counter. "Don't think I didn't see you dip your finger in the bowl."

"When I was a kid I really believed you had eyes in the back of your head." He sat on a stool at the counter and reached for a scrap of apple peel, taking a bite to delay the moment. "I've got some news."

"Emma's pregnant." Marge poured the batter into the pan and scraped every bit out with a rubber spatula.

"How did you know?" He should have asked Emma who else she'd told besides her family. For some reason he'd assumed no one, but that was probably naive.

"My friend Lydia works at Target. She served Emma the other day when she was in buying a ton of baby things. Lydia reckons there's no way she'd buy that much for a friend, or even for her sister." Marge eyed him sympathetically. "Do you know who she's with? Who the father is?"

Darcy shifted uncomfortably on his stool. He hadn't told his family about hooking up with Emma on the cruise. There hadn't seemed to be any point. Half a dozen times in the pub he'd been on the verge of telling his father about the pregnancy, but he was usually busy and Roy was always surrounded by his mates. By the time Darcy found a moment to himself, his dad had gone home.

"As a matter of fact, I'm the father." He quickly held up a hand. "And no, we're not getting back together. It was an accident."

Marge shook the spatula at him. "You're too old for that kind of accident."

"Don't lecture me, Mum. How's Dad's hip?"

"Don't change the subject. But since you asked, he's been moved up on the waiting list. We're expecting a call from the hospital any day for him to have the operation."

"That's great. How's his blood pressure?"

"It's come down a touch. He'll be all right." She opened the oven door and slid the cake inside. Then she faced him across the counter. "What's going on with you and Emma?"

"Quite honestly, I don't know. We're not unfriendly, but it's tense at times. I want to pay support but she doesn't want me to have a role in the baby's life." He shrugged uncomfortably. "But then, I never wanted another child."

"Now that it's happening you have to deal with it." Marge wiped up the mess on the counter. "You two should try again. A baby might bring you together."

"I know people who think that will work, but I wonder how often it's successful in practice."

She dropped the peel in the compost container then looked at him, her eyes filled with hope and fear. "I want to know my grandchild, Darcy. Is she going to allow me and your dad into her life?"

There was no reason for her not to, but with Emma he never knew. "I'll talk to her."

"Or I could. Do you mind if I call her?"

"If you like." The ramifications of this baby were still sinking in. Whether he was an active father or not, his child would be at the center of a web of family ties. And there wasn't a damn thing he could do about it. Not that he wanted to keep his mother away. She and Emma used to be close, and she was a wonderful grandmother to Dan's three kids, Mike's two and Janine's four. Holly had adored her.

Darcy slid off the stool. "I'll go say hi to Dad."

If the kitchen was an example of his mother's haphazard housekeeping, the backyard was a testament to his father's obsessive tidiness. The grass was trimmed to precisely two inches high, the edging done every week like clockwork and the flowering shrubs neatly pruned.

His father was leaning on the fence, holding up an azalea cutting and demonstrating how to plant it to his neighbor Hal, a stockbroker in his early fifties.

Darcy walked over, picked up his dad's cane where it had fallen in the grass and propped it against the fence. "Hey, Dad." He lifted a hand to the neighbor. "Hal."

His father turned and saw him. "Hal, this is Darcy, my youngest. He runs the pub now."

"Nice to see you again. We've met, Dad." Many times. His father was over eighty and getting forgetful along with the creeping deafness and the dodgy hip.

"Hey, Darcy." Hal gave Roy an indulgent smile. "I'll let you go. Thanks for the tips."

"Don't forget this." Roy handed the cutting over the top of the fence. "Mind you water it well."

Darcy put his arm around his dad's shoulder and gave it a squeeze. He handed him his cane and adjusted his pace to Roy's slower limp as they walked toward the shed. "How are you feeling?"

"Fine, fine," Roy said, wincing at a misstep. "Never better."

"It'll be good to get that hip replaced."

"Ah, there's no hurry. Come and see my new power drill." Roy told Darcy about his new project, making and selling birdhouses at the craft market, as he led the way inside the garage he'd made into a garden shed cum workshop. Floor-to-ceiling shelving along one wall stored gardening implements, woodworking tools and miscellaneous items Roy had taken out of the pub when he'd handed it over to Darcy.

Darcy duly admired the power drill then perched on a sawhorse while his father tidied his potting table. How many times as a kid had he worked in here with his dad while they chatted companionably about everything and nothing? He'd always imagined doing something similar with Holly when she got a little older. It was another experience he wouldn't have with Emma's baby.

"I guess Mum told you about Emma."

"Nice girl, Emma." Roy wiped his secateurs then hung them on a hook on the wall. "I wish her luck with the baby."

"You know I'm the father." He paused. "And Mum thinks we should get back together."

His father looked at him over the top of his glasses. "Doesn't matter what your mother or anyone else wants. What matters is between you and Emma. That's all I'm going to say on the subject."

"Thanks." The vote of confidence was nice to hear. His father was right—he and Emma had to work through this themselves. He was also grateful his dad wasn't interested in hashing over the situation because he had other things he wanted to talk about.

"Did you hear about the wine bar going in across the street from the pub?"

"Wine bar? What the hell is a wine bar?"

"Fancy wines at inflated prices, basically. Also competition for the pub."

"You're not worried, are you?"

"Nah." He paused. "But I wonder if I should get the place painted. Freshen it up a little."

Roy climbed onto a step stool, and from the top shelf he brought down a dusty roll of blue-tinged paper. "I was cleaning up the other day and found these. They're the original architect's drawings for the pub. It was supposed to have a garden room. Pretty avant-garde for those days, for a country pub. Guess the first owner thought so, too, because he never had it built. Or else he was short of cash." He handed the drawings to Darcy. "Anyway, you might find them interesting."

Darcy tapped the dust off the roll and unfurled the plans on the workbench. "Looks like there's supposed to be a proper kitchen, too."

"Leaving that out was a mistake. Every country pub serves up a Sunday roast at the very least and most do counter meals during the week. Course, those days are over, and we're not exactly a rural area anymore."

Darcy glanced at his dad. "Do you think I should revamp the old girl?"

"You do what you think best. Wine bar might be a flash in the pan. Lots of places come and go."

"Not the Summerside pub." Darcy rolled the paper and handed it to his dad. "I like the pub the way it is."

Roy waved the plans away. "Keep them. They're a curiosity if nothing else."

Darcy shrugged and tucked the roll under his arm. He saw nothing wrong with the pub, and besides, he had too much on his plate to think about major renovations. Even though he'd voiced concerns to his dad, he couldn't seriously see how a wine bar could hurt his business to the point where he would have to take such drastic action.

He'd always thought someday he would pass on the pub to whichever of his children wanted it, the way his father had handed it over to him. But what if he didn't have any more children? What if Emma's baby—who he wasn't to have any part of—was destined to be his only living offspring?

The legacy of the pub started to feel pretty hollow.

OVER THE NEXT few days Emma registered for her courses and obtained approval from the hospital to work part-time in the evening to allow her to attend classes. She was going to be very busy but planning was key to success. And if she was busy, she wouldn't have time to pine for what she didn't have, like a partner.

She'd been alone before. She could handle it, that wasn't a problem. She simply missed what she and Darcy had had, especially now that the baby was coming.

Instead of dwelling on what might be missing, she created a spreadsheet on her laptop and blocked out time for classes, study and work, color-coded for easy identification. Everything else—exercise, chores, socializing—filled the small allotments of an hour here and two hours there.

By the end of the week, she was all organized. She'd even bought her nursing textbooks for the coming semester. She couldn't wait. She loved caring for patients, but study challenged her brain in ways she didn't get in the day-to-day routine around the wards.

The phone rang. Absently, she picked up. "Hello?"

"Hey, it's me," Alana said. "How are you doing?"

"I've just been planning the next twelve months." With the phone tucked beneath her chin, she rearranged an entry.

Alana chuckled. "You're doing a spreadsheet of your life, aren't you?"

"Go ahead and laugh but it's how I'm going to get through this year."

"Make sure you factor in time for the gym." An undercurrent of excitement bubbled through Alana's voice.

Emma glanced at the green-shaded exercise squares. Not as many as she would have liked, but her free periods were limited. "I've allocated a couple of slots a week for that. Why?"

"Because that might be the only time we see each other from now on—"

"Oh, my God! You got the job." Emma saved her document then leaned back in her chair.

"Yes! I'm the new fitness instructor at Brett O'Connor's gym right here in Summerside. I start next Monday doing three days a week."

"How does Dave feel about this?"

"He doesn't know. And I'm not going to tell him."

"Alana Jane. You can't keep something like this from your husband."

"Actually, I can. I'm telling Dave that I've renewed my gym membership. Tessa can go into the day care there while I teach my classes. Tessa won't know if I'm attending a class or leading one. It's perfect."

"I meant, you can't lie to Dave. You have to tell him the truth. You guys are so solid. You talk about everything and don't let disagreements cause cracks in your relationship. You're my marriage role models. If you two can't tell each other the truth, then I don't know what to think."

"We are solid, at least we were until we came up against this one sticking point—me getting pregnant." Alana's voice trembled. "Honestly, Emma, it's bringing our marriage to the brink. You haven't been around so you don't know. I don't *want* to lie. But I'm just not ready to have another baby."

Alana's situation was the reverse of her and Darcy.

She wanted the baby and he didn't. It was all very well for her to urge Alana to open up to Dave but that hadn't worked for her and Darcy. Still, she hated to see her sister's marriage put under this stress.

"What about the money you make? How are you going to explain that?"

"I'll set up a separate bank account in my name. When I've saved enough for a nice holiday, I'll tell him. Hopefully when I wave tickets to Tahiti in his face, he'll think differently about me working."

Maybe. As a chemical engineer working for the government Dave earned enough that Alana could stay home with the kids but not enough for luxuries like holidays and a new car. He might be glad of a trip, but Emma couldn't imagine him easily forgiving the deceit.

"And in the meantime he thinks you're trying to get pregnant? How does that work?"

"I get lots of great sex. Oh, please be on my side, Em. Don't go ratting me out to Dave."

"I wouldn't. But I think you should tell him."

"And I think you shouldn't have a baby on your own. So we're even."

Emma was stung into silence by her sister's blurted rejoinder. It was easy for Alana, speaking from the comfort of a stable marriage. "If you really mean that, maybe you shouldn't be my birthing partner."

"Oh, Em, I'm sorry. I don't know what I'm saying these days."

Emma struggled to set aside her hurt feelings. She'd been without her sister for too long, and she didn't want the rift to get any wider so she would overlook this. There was no question where her loyalty lay, even if her sister was misguided.

"If you need me to do anything—look after Tessa

or whatever—I'll be there for you. Just don't ask me to lie to Dave."

"Never. Thank you. And I *so* want to be your birthing partner. Please don't cut me off."

"I won't. So will you have another child at all?"

"Someday, maybe. You must have passed the first trimester by now. Are you showing yet?"

Emma lifted the hem of her T-shirt and smoothed her hand over the slightly curving skin. She'd only had a touch of morning sickness this time and it was almost over. "I'm starting to get a baby bump. Probably no one else would notice, but I do."

"Are you going to find out what gender it is?"

"No, I don't care. As long as it's healthy it doesn't matter if I have a girl or boy." Emma picked up an empty teacup from the coffee table and carried it into the kitchen. "Hey, how about you and I go to dinner and a movie one night, just us girls?"

"I would love that! Let's make it Friday. It's the only day Dave doesn't work late and can look after Tessa." Alana hesitated. "Are you sure you can spare the time?"

Emma felt bad. She was guilty of the thing she'd resented about Darcy, not making time for family.

"Of course I can." She went to her computer and clicked to the first spreadsheet. Virtually every day was blocked in solid. But if she shaved off an hour from study time and an hour from the gym and went to bed a couple of hours later... Damn, she had to get up at six o'clock Saturday morning for work. She glanced around the room at the mess she needed to clean up. She hadn't done housework all week.

What the hell. Vacuuming could wait and sleep was overrated. "Friday would be great."

She hung up and focused on her spreadsheet, making small amendments here and there. Just a few more minutes at this then she might start reading her textbooks. It had been years since she'd studied theory, and a refresher would stand her in good stead once classes started in a couple of weeks.

The phone rang again. She was never going to get finished. If it was Tracey, she would tell her she'd talk to her at work tomorrow. "Hello?"

"Emma, it's Marge." Her ex-mother-in-law's voice was gentle, hopeful, caring. Quietly assertive. Only she could wrap so much emotion into a few words.

Emma hadn't seen or talked to Marge in months and then only in passing when she ran into the other woman in the post office. "Darcy told you."

"I wanted you to know that if ever you need anything, you can call on me." She paused. "It takes a village to raise a child. Or at the very least, an extended family."

"So I've heard." Emma sighed. Marge had been wonderful when she'd had Holly. And she agreed with Marge's saying, *We women have to stick together.* But if she took her up on her offer, she would get sucked into the Lewis family. Which she loved, but it would mean frequent contact with Darcy. As much as she cared about Marge she didn't think she could handle that if she and Darcy weren't together.

"Um, thank you," Emma added. "That's really kind of you. I'll let you know."

There was a short shocked pause as Marge absorbed her brush-off. "All right, dear. I'll be here."

"Say hi to Roy for me."

"He'll be pleased you thought of him."

Emma ended the call, feeling guilty. Marge cared about her and had always been supportive. Whereas Emma was being a wee bit selfish for wanting things her own way. She was doing it to protect herself, but that didn't make her feel any better.

July, midwinter

DARCY STOOD IN the doorway of the pub and watched workmen unload red velvet couches and chairs, antique coffee tables, long gilt mirrors and old-fashioned oil paintings. The wine bar was going to look like a brothel.

For months builders had worked feverishly on the site. They'd gutted the interior then replastered, painted, put in new flooring and lighting. In spite of all that activity, part of Darcy hadn't really believed it was going to happen. And yet, tomorrow was the grand opening.

A flyer drifted along the sidewalk with a gust of wind. It was an advertisement offering free finger food and fifty percent off all drinks on opening day. Darcy picked it up and stuffed it in the overflowing garbage bin. The damn things had been littering the town all week.

Fifty percent. His profit margin was already almost as low as he could go and stay in business. But he was confident his loyal customers wouldn't let him down. They came to him for the atmosphere and out of long habit. And okay, because until now his was the only watering hole in town. He wasn't afraid of a little competition. *Bring it on, wine bar.*

Tomorrow was also, by coincidence, Emma's birthday. He got out his phone and started scrolling through electronic birthday cards. Nothing jumped out at him as appropriate for an ex-wife-pregnant-with-his-child with whom he had irreconcilable differences.

He hadn't seen her since the day he fixed her outlet, though he knew his mother had called. He'd phoned once or twice, just to see if she was okay. She'd kept the conversation brief, saying she didn't have a lot of time to chat, but she'd sounded upbeat, not as if she was missing him. Or needing him. Well, why would she? She was going to have her baby and that's all she wanted.

His thumb slowed on the scroll button. She used to rag on him for sending e-cards. Okay, he would send her a real card. He clicked his phone off and poked his head inside. "Kirsty, I'll be back in five minutes."

He headed across the road to the newsagent. There he perused the racks for something funny but unsentimental. He didn't want her to think he was pining after her. They used to go out to a nice restaurant on her birthday. This year he imagined she would do something with her girlfriends or her sister.

Or was there a new guy in her life? Was that why she never had time to talk? It didn't seem likely she was seeing anyone, but of course it was possible. What kind of man would want to hook up with a woman pregnant with someone else's kid?

A generous, caring guy who could look past circumstances and see Emma for the jewel she was, that's who. Emma was pretty special. The fact that she hadn't found someone before the cruise said more about the men on offer than about her desirability. Darcy had no right to be jealous. He wanted her to be happy and to have the family she was so desperate for, even if he couldn't be that guy for her.

He picked up a card with a cartoon elephant on the front. The caption inside read something about never forgetting her birthday. She would be seven months along now. Would she take that elephant the wrong way?

In the aisle behind him, he overheard a couple talking

while they looked at magazines. "…wine bar…Friday," the woman said.

Darcy's ears pricked up. Friday was the opening.

"I drink beer," her male companion protested.

"…boutique…imported beers." Her voice was softer so Darcy couldn't catch every word. But he heard enough.

Darcy turned around and casually glanced through the racks of cards behind him. The couple looked to be in their late forties, smartly dressed. They were interested in cooking and photography judging by the magazines they were leafing through.

I serve imported beer, too, he wanted to tell them.

"…free finger food," the woman went on. "…flyer… discount. Tanya and Jerry…meet us there."

"Sounds good. We'll do it." The man shut his magazine. "Are you ready? I want to get to the bank before it closes."

Wayne Overton's flyers were clearly working. Too preoccupied to care about the birthday card anymore, Darcy carried the one in his hand up to the cash register, paid for it and wrote a quick message to Emma. His journey to the pub after dropping the envelope in the mail took him past the wine bar. He picked up another of the flyers from the gutter along the way. This time he hung on to it. He had a thing about littering, especially in his town.

Wayne was setting out a sandwich board on the footpath. His shaved head gleamed in the sun and he wore a black polo shirt revealing a thick gold chain around his neck. "G'day. How's it going?"

"Getting ready for your big opening, I see." Darcy glanced through the big plate-glass window at the finished decor. He had to admit, now that it was finished, the effect was appealingly lush and decadent, like a fin de siècle Paris bistro. "The place looks very… comfortable."

"If the customers are comfortable, they'll stick around longer, and drink and eat more."

Darcy handed him the flyer. "I found this down the road. There are quite a few of them floating around."

Wayne waved it away, completely missing his point. "Keep it. Come on by opening night. First glass of wine is on the house for local business owners."

Darcy crumpled the slip of paper in his fist. "Thanks, but I'll be working, keeping *my* customers happy so they don't all end up at your wine bar."

Wayne laughed. "Hey, you're a funny guy. I can see we're going to be friends." He started to go inside then paused. "Not a lot of parking around here, is there? Mostly just lining the street."

"It's not usually a problem at night. There's an overflow lot farther down, next to the dog park."

"I don't want people to have to walk too far, especially if it's raining." He tipped his head, a calculating gleam in his eye. "You've got parking behind the pub, don't you?"

"It's a small lot." And it was his. He'd bought the land, had it paved and marked, and he maintained it for his customers. "It fills quickly with pub customers."

"Right." Wayne cocked a finger and pointed it at Darcy. "Gotcha."

Darcy stepped away. "I'll let you go. I'm sure, like me, you have plenty to do."

He walked back to the pub fuming. The man's friendly-like-a-shark demeanor was annoying. What really got Darcy's goat was Wayne's shifty and calculating account of the way he'd come to Summerside for a tax dodge and was deliberately going after a rich clientele.

Really? Darcy brought himself up short. Wasn't that how successful businessmen operated? Not him, of course. He wasn't cutthroat. He liked to make a living doing a job he enjoyed and seeing his customers happy.

Maybe that wasn't enough anymore. For the first time, he had to admit, he was a tad worried.

THIRTY-SIX YEARS OLD. She was practically Methuselah. Emma splashed cold water on her face after work, resisting the urge to flop on the couch and watch trashy reality TV. In spite of her fatigue, she really didn't want to miss her birthday party.

Going to the new wine bar in Summerside was Alana's idea. Emma didn't feel right about patronizing Darcy's competition. Not that he had anything to worry about. The pub did a roaring business, if his constant presence there when they were married was anything to go by. Besides, Darcy wasn't worried. He never worried about anything.

She, on the other hand, worried about everything. And she had good reason to. What had possessed her to begin a master's degree *and* continue to work while she was pregnant? The hospital was okay with her taking time off for the birth—that was part of maternity leave. But university continued regardless of major life events like having a baby. She had three exams at the end of the month and a major term paper due the same week the baby was due.

Add in that she was as big as a house and tired to boot and life was catching up with her. All she wanted to do was crawl beneath the covers and go to sleep for a week. Instead she had to put on makeup and something nice to wear and go out to a wine bar on opening night. She couldn't drink. It would be crowded and noisy. What was Alana thinking?

She sighed. Alana was no doubt thinking Emma and her friends would love the wine bar. Her sister had gone to a lot of trouble to make Emma's birthday special. Tracey had let it slip there was a cake, prearranged with the owner to be delivered to their table while the jazz pianist played a cool rendition of the birthday song.

As wonderful as it sounded, it all felt like too much. Too many people, too much noise, too much entertainment. There would be a million people there besides her small group of friends and her sister.

But she couldn't let Alana down. They'd grown close again in the past six months, spending regular evenings together, just the two of them. Alana seemed as committed as Emma was to repairing their relationship. They even went grocery shopping together. Emma loved the time they spent by themselves, plus it meant she didn't have to lie to Dave about Alana going to work.

When she'd talked to Alana earlier in the week her sister had hinted at some news. She wouldn't go into detail over the phone, and Emma couldn't tell if she was excited or anxious because she was whispering so Dave didn't hear her.

Emma dried off and went into her bedroom to dress. Darcy's card stood on her dresser along with the rest of her birthday cards. An elephant. Was that a not-so-subtle allusion to her size? Even if not, it was a bit tactless but he probably didn't intend to be mean. When she'd been pregnant with Holly he'd loved her round figure, telling her she was sexier than ever. But he'd been in love with her then. Now he sent her cartoon cards with no more sentiment than a kindly uncle. His occasional phone calls left her with a longing for more contact. They made her feel so weepy and upset that she invariably cut them short.

When she arrived at the wine bar, the street parking was completely full. She cruised past the brightly lit bar. Despite the coolness of the evening, people spilled out of the open door onto the sidewalk with their glasses and small paper plates piled with finger food.

She circled the block twice and finally went around the rear of the pub. Even though the lot was restricted to pub-goers she was pretty sure some wine bar patrons must be using it. Cars were double-parked. She couldn't recall that ever happening before.

She squeezed her turquoise Holden Barina into a tiny space between the last spot and a gum tree. Hopefully Darcy would cut her some slack on her birthday.

Hurrying around the building, she pulled her scarf closer against the chilly wind. She glanced inside the pub as she passed the door. She should tell Darcy what she'd done, but he was serving a customer. Besides, her friends were waiting and she was already late, so she kept going.

Alana, Barb, Sasha and Tracey were already inside when she arrived. They all hugged her and fussed over her, making sure she had a seat and a glass of nonalcoholic wine that tasted as good as the real thing.

Emma relaxed on the plush comfortable couch. Surrounded by friends, with delectable tapas appearing regularly, her fatigue and her worries fell away.

The evening flew past. The piano was just the right soothing tinkle in the background and the atmosphere convivial without being overpowering. Then the cake came out and the entire room sang to her.

Emma smiled and swallowed and blew her nose. It

was okay to feel a little weepy. She was hormonal, after all. Her sudden attack of the blues had nothing to do with the fact that the only person missing of the people she cared about—besides her parents—was Darcy.

TONY SLID ONTO ONE of the empty stools at the bar. "That new wine bar's going off like a frog in a sock."

"So I noticed." Darcy would have to be blind and deaf not to notice the happy wine-quaffing revelers across the street. He reached for a beer mug and filled it at the draft spigot with Tony's usual drink, Tasmanian Tiger lager.

"They're making a bloody mess," Tony said. "The little paper plates they're serving food on are all over the place." He reached for his draft, took a long sip then wiped his mouth with the back of his hand. "I'm surprised you're not complaining."

"Things will settle down after tonight." But it was annoying. Litter from the wine bar was being blown onto his side of the street and collecting against the brick wall of the pub. Twice now he'd gone out to clean it up.

Half of his parking lot was taken up by wine bar customers. He'd noticed it when someone had complained about being blocked in. What was he going to do, call the cops and get everyone pissed at him? It was the wine bar's opening night and he was making allowances, but this better not continue.

Even Emma had parked there. He knew her turquoise Barina by the dainty metal chimes dangling from the rearview mirror. That she'd chosen to go to the wine bar on her birthday instead of the pub didn't exactly shock, but it stung a little. She hadn't even stopped in to say hello.

The pub, normally packed on a Friday evening, was only half-full. Business was so slow that Kirsty, Elise and his weekend bartender, Brad, were able to handle the drinks by themselves. Just as well. For once Darcy wasn't in the mood to chat or make jokes or entertain his customers with his cocktail-making skills.

Instead he sat at a table with his laptop and opened up his online banking account. He'd accepted that it was too soon to pay child support. After all, the baby wasn't even born yet. So he'd started a college fund and was making regular payments into that. He'd never set up a college fund for Holly. Why was he doing it for this baby? Out of guilt, to make up for not being a husband to Emma and a proper father to the baby? Or was he simply trying to have a connection with Emma?

He couldn't stop thinking about her and about the night they spent together on the cruise ship. Before he'd run into her, he'd hoped and expected that the cruise would ease his way back into the dating scene. Instead it had the opposite effect. He hadn't been with anyone else since that night. He'd lost interest in flirting. If a woman he met in the bar or at a friend's house got too interested, he politely moved away. It was driving him crazy. The last thing he wanted was to be hung up on his ex-wife.

Emma walked into the pub around eleven o'clock. Even knowing she was seven months pregnant, Darcy wasn't prepared for the sight of her round swollen belly, clearly defined by her blue dress. Her face had rounded, too, softened by the few extra pounds she'd gained in pregnancy. Nor was he prepared for the way she made him feel protective and resentful at the same time.

"Hey, Emma." He closed his laptop. "It's nice of you to patronize my establishment, especially tonight when I'm competing with the wine bar opening."

A pink flush crept up her neck into her cheeks. "I,

uh, I've just come from there. Um…someone's blocking my car in your parking lot. A black Hilux with lights across the roof."

"You parked in my lot and went to the wine bar."

"Darcy, I'm sorry. I know it was shabby of me." She pushed back the red hair curling loosely about her shoulders. "The venue was Alana's choice. She organized the party. I shouldn't have parked in your lot. I just…" She waved a hand, looking beautiful and tired, as if at any moment she would be on her knees with fatigue.

Darcy pulled out a chair at his table. "Sit down. The Hilux is Tony's. I'll get him to move it. If you give me your keys, I'll bring your car around. I see a parking spot has opened up."

"You don't have to do that."

"It's not a big deal." He dragged another chair over. "Put up your feet."

Emma sank onto the chair and slipped off her shoes before settling them on the other seat with a sigh. She handed him her keys. "Thanks, Darcy."

Darcy found Tony at his usual corner table in the back of the room with his girlfriend. "Tony, can you move your truck? You're blocking Emma."

"Sure thing." The tattooed brickie dug in his jeans pocket for his keys. "Emma doesn't usually come in here. Are you two back together?"

"No." He didn't elaborate. Many of his regulars knew Emma and knew about the divorce. But this new development—her having his baby and them not being together—didn't reflect well on either of them, in his opinion. He didn't like to think of her as the subject of gossip, even though she, not he, would undoubtedly get the sympathy.

Not that she needed anyone's sympathy. Emma was

the most confident, organized person he knew and if anyone could successfully raise a child by herself, it would be her. But some people might not see being a single mother as something to celebrate. Frankly, despite his respect for Emma's parenting skills, he was one of those people who thought kids should have two parents.

On the other hand he didn't agree with continuing a relationship for the sake of a child, either. His brother Mike had stuck out an unhappy marriage for ten years before finally splitting up with his wife. Before that, the tension hadn't been good for him, his wife or for their kids.

Cool winter air penetrated Darcy's light pullover as he wove his way through the jammed-in cars. His lot had parking for twenty cars. There had to be thirty in here. He could imagine the double-parking offenders saying to themselves, *Darcy's so easygoing—he won't mind.* And they could be forgiven for thinking that. Every year at the annual Summerside Fete he opened his parking lot to all comers and even got one of his staff to act as a parking valet, purely out of community spirit. But making it easier for Wayne to take business away from the pub? There was a limit to his altruism.

Emma was sipping chamomile tea when he got back from retrieving her car. He sat and slid her keys across the scarred wood table. "How are you feeling?"

She slanted him a wry look over her mug. "As big as an elephant." His sheepishness must have shown because she smiled. "I appreciate the thought behind the card." She pressed a hand to her chest and stifled a burp. "I didn't think you would mark the occasion."

"You're still my friend, Emma." And the mother of his child. Children. "Have you been eating spicy food?"

"Buffalo wings." She groaned. "I know they're bad for me but I can't help myself."

"So the food wasn't very good?" he asked hopefully.

"It was fantastic. They had all these different types of tapas, all free. Chorizo sausage—" she burped again "—frittata, shrimp fritters, patatas bravas, artichokes with jamon."

"Naturally you had to try them all."

"I *am* eating for two. Spicy tapas aside, the heartburn seems worse this time around. I never had this much trouble when I was pregnant with Holly."

"Oh? Remember the time we drove up the coast highway to Byron Bay and we stopped for fish and chips?"

Her face lit at the memory of the trip they'd taken when Emma was four months pregnant with Holly. They'd been young and deliriously happy, eating their simple meal on the beach while the sun set. They'd talked till the stars came out, planning their baby's future. Later, they'd made love in the tent to the soft shush of the waves lapping the sand.

Emma's smile faded, as if she was now remembering all the bad stuff that had happened since then. "You're right. I got indigestion pretty bad that night."

"You didn't answer my question. Is everything going okay with you and the baby?"

"Fine. Everything's fine."

"You look tired."

"I'm always tired these days. But honestly, I'm fine." She grimaced again and pressed a hand to the top of her round belly.

"That heartburn must be bad."

"It's not that. She's kicking. Ow. Right under the rib cage. Thanks Ivy."

"You've named her Ivy. Do you know it's a girl?"

She'd named her without his input. That made him feel strange…and kind of uncomfortable to have that taken away from him. But he'd made his decision. He couldn't have it both ways.

"Ow. Yup. I haven't had any tests, but I'm pretty positive she's a girl. And a feisty little thing."

So Emma was going by intuition. Or was that wishful thinking, a desire to turn back time and have a little girl again? As Darcy watched the material over her baby bump rippled. What would it be like to press his palm against the hard curve of her belly and feel the baby moving beneath her skin? His baby.

"Do you want to feel?" Emma asked.

Yes. No. I don't know.

"Nah, that's okay." He clenched his fist in his lap, resisting the urge to reach out. There was no point getting attached to this kid, since he wouldn't be part of its life. Emma and the baby were a unit, the same way she and Holly had been. He was on the outside, as usual. This time, though, he had the sense to know that was for the best.

"I've been adding to the baby's college fund. After it's born I'll pay a fortnightly sum straight into your bank account. You need to give me your account details soon." He glanced over her stomach. "It's not that far away, right?"

"A month and a half. But Darcy—"

"I'll let my parents know, too. Birthday, Christmas, if anyone can't think of a present for the baby—"

"Darcy! Slow down and listen for a change. Why are you doing this? Do you think you can let yourself off the daddy hook by throwing money at the baby?"

"According to you, I'm not on any hook."

"You're not. But I know you and your sense of responsibility. How can I convince you that the baby and I don't need you?" She covered her face with her hands. "I don't mean that the way it sounded, ungrateful and harsh. But you don't want another child. And I don't want you to feel obligated in any way."

"Emma, I know *you*. You have this need to prove you can be a supermum, able to do it all and then some. You think you have to be perfect. You don't. Let me help. I can be like a…a silent partner."

"I don't want a silent partner. It's all or nothing. And I know you can't give me and the baby your all, so it has to be nothing."

"Why? Why can't I contribute so I know he or she is okay?"

"I love that you're so responsible, but it's not only about responsibility. It's also about being present in my child's life. What if one day you wake up and realize what you're missing and decide you *do* want to be a father? Fine, I let you into our lives. But then maybe after a while you won't be able to handle being a father anymore, or we can't work out our problems, and then what? You don't get to opt in and out when you feel like it. This is my child. I'm taking sole responsibility for it. I'm not trying to prove anything. I'm doing this because I want to protect my child's emotional future."

He stared at her. *My child.* How many times had she said those words in that little speech? Three, four? She was staking her claim. She hadn't made the decision to raise the child by herself because he wasn't stepping up. She was doing it because she really, truly wanted to raise the child without him.

The implications sank in. Even if he did want to be part of the baby's life, she wouldn't ever let him. He'd wanted it this way, so he had no right to feel hurt, or angry at her selfishness. But it was depressing, thinking she had to protect her child from him.

Grimly he nodded, acknowledging he had no choice but to accept her decree.

CHAPTER SIX

August, late winter

EMMA STEPPED OUT of her car in the hospital staff parking lot into the pouring rain. Damn. She'd forgotten her umbrella. Not only that, her shift started in five minutes and it took ten minutes to waddle to the back entrance and hike her swollen body up to Ward 5G North.

Head down, she set off between the rows of cars. She was always late these days. Late for class, late with her fifty-page term assignment and now late to work.

She was supposed to have gone on maternity leave a week ago but the geriatric ward was overflowing with an influx of pneumonia patients during these last days of winter. To top it off, Tracey was off work with a bad case of flu and another nurse was on annual leave, so Emma had volunteered to work a few extra days to cover the ward. The other nurses had made allowances for her through morning sickness and absences due to ultrasounds and other tests. She owed them.

But it had been hard getting up this morning. She'd spent a restless night, unable to get comfortable, plagued by Braxton Hicks contractions.

She tried to step over a puddle because it was too much trouble to go around it and missed. Cold water seeped into her shoe as she splashed down. Her stomach tightened so painfully she had to stop and pant through it. Damn Braxton Hicks. Three more weeks to her due date. The birth couldn't come soon enough as far as she was concerned. She was a fat cow, and the baby had dropped and was pressing uncomfortably on her groin.

She'd barely started walking again when she had another contraction, sharper and tighter than before. She bent double, struggling to make sense of the spreading wet stain on her white stockings. Not blood. Rainwater? Oh, God. Amniotic fluid. This was it. It must be. Her water had just broken. Not Braxton Hicks but the real deal.

No! She couldn't have the baby now. She still had that paper to write. She was supposed to be on duty.

"Stop it, Ivy. Don't do this to me." A hot flush sent heat into her chest and face. She stood there trembling, her legs spread wide for support.

What was she going to do? The parking lot was deserted, the hospital entrance still three hundred yards away. Another contraction hit. She bent over again and clasped her arms over her belly. Rain streamed down the back of her neck. Well, wasn't this just bloody inconvenient? She had to stop it right now. She didn't want to have this damn baby, after all.

"Excuse me, madam, do you need some help?"

Emma glanced up. A dark-skinned man with square black glasses touched her elbow. She recognized him. He was a urologist. "What does it look like? I'm having a fricking baby. But it's not due yet and I'm not ready for it. If you could help me inside, I'm sure the doctors can stop it for me." Why was he looking at her so strangely? Slowly and clearly she enunciated, "I'm. Not. Ready. To. Have. The. Baby. I want to put it off for a week, preferably two."

Another contraction hit her. She moaned. "Maybe if I sit down, it'll go away."

The doctor whipped out his phone and punched in a number. "E.R.? Send an orderly out to the staff lot with a wheelchair immediately. I'm with a pregnant nurse who's in labor. If I'm not mistaken, she's already in transition."

Emma sank to a crouch. A groan ripped out of her. "Tell them to hurry."

Two HOURS LATER Emma gazed into the dark unfocused eyes of her brand-new baby. Her hair was plastered to her forehead and temples with sweat, she felt as if she'd run a marathon and her peritoneum was so sore she couldn't move.

None of that mattered. Her baby was here. Her beautiful baby. Her *boy.* He'd been checked over by the doctors, bathed by the nurses and swaddled tightly in a pale blue blanket.

"You're not Ivy. But you're perfect." She tucked her little finger beneath his starfish hand. Her heart clutched as his tiny fingers curled around hers. "What am I going to call you? I wasn't prepared for a boy. And I definitely wasn't ready for you to come three weeks early."

She wasn't ready in any sense of the word. Not with regard to her university courses, with her work—even the nursery wasn't finished. "I was waiting for a pram to go on sale next week. It's a beauty, with big silver wheels."

"How's mum and bub?" Sasha bustled into the room, beaming. "I'm so glad I was on duty when you came in. We're getting a bed ready for you in a semiprivate room. It won't be long now." She strapped the blood pressure cuff around Emma's arm and pressed a switch to inflate it. "Have you called Alana yet?"

"I will soon. She'll be sorry she missed the birth." As soon as Emma spread the word, she would be inundated with family and friends. Which would be wonderful—she couldn't wait to show off her baby—but first she wanted a few precious moments alone with him.

Sasha made a note of the blood pressure on Emma's chart and stuck a thermometer under her tongue. "What are you going to call him?"

"Don't know," Emma mumbled around the thermometer. "Got any suggestions?"

"I always think using a family name is nice. What's your dad's name?"

"Percy." She made a face. "I've always liked the name William. If Holly had been a boy that's what Darcy and I were going to name her."

"That's a good name. Does it have any significance?"

"It's Darcy's middle name."

Sasha's eyes narrowed. "I'll hunt up a baby name book at the nurses' station." She rolled a bedside table with Emma's purse on it within reach then left the room.

Emma pushed back her gown and put her baby to her breast. His mouth opened and closed and his tiny fist hit out blindly. "Come on, little guy." She guided her nipple but although he mouthed it, he didn't latch on. "Don't worry. Not every baby can do that right away. We'll figure it out."

She reached for her purse and found her phone. Darcy answered on the fourth ring. She felt suddenly nervous and couldn't speak.

"Emma? Are you there? I can see your caller ID."

"I—I just wanted to let you know I had the baby a couple of hours ago."

He was silent for three long beats. She could hear the clink of glasses in the background. Maybe he wasn't sure if he heard right. "I said—"

"Was there a problem? Is that why you delivered early? Are you all right? And...and the baby?"

"I'm fine. The baby's fine, too. I don't know why he came early. Sometimes they just do."

Again, there was a brief silence. *"He?"*

"Yes. I had a boy." She paused. "I thought I would call him William. Not necessarily after you. I just like the name." No response. She stroked her sleeping baby's hair where it was stuck to his temple. The skin there was nearly transparent, traced with fine blue veins. "Darcy? Did you hear what I said?"

"I heard you." His voice was gruff.

"Labor was really quick." Briefly she related events, not sure if he wanted to hear this. But he listened as she told him about the parking lot and the urologist and being whizzed into the delivery room with no time to call Alana, her birthing partner. "The main thing is the baby is healthy. He's seven pounds, two and a quarter ounces. His hair is thick and dark. The first growth falls out but I think he's going to take after you—"

"Thanks for calling, Em. Sorry, but I have to go now. A big group came through the door and I'm here on my own."

"Sure, okay. I'll let you go." She clicked off and slowly lowered the phone. There was no reason to be disappointed at his reaction. What had she expected—that he would jump up and down in joy? He'd let her know from the beginning the baby meant nothing to him. And *she'd* made it clear he wasn't welcome in her son's life.

She softly stroked the baby's dark hair, still streaked

with traces of white wax. "I know you're going to be a strong little man, William. You'll need to be."

She frowned. William sounded too formal for a baby. "Will?" Better, but still too grown up for a small boy. "I'll call you Billy. Yes, that suits you."

She trailed the back of her finger along his downy cheek. She wished Darcy were here. A father should see his son being born, and hold him in his first hours.

"It's just you and me, Billy. Your father is a good man, but he won't be around for you. Don't worry— you've got grandfathers and uncles. We'll be fine on our own."

A lump formed in her throat. Huskily, she added, "I'll be such a good mother it won't matter that you don't have a dad. I'll do everything for you that a mother and a father would do. I'll care for you and play with you…."

Work to pay the bills, and study to ensure their future. She would do it all because she wanted to and because she had to. Her baby was not going to miss out on a single thing simply because his father wasn't around.

DARCY HUNG UP the phone after saying goodbye to Emma. He'd lied about the large group coming in— although he was alone, the pub was empty. For reasons he couldn't explain to himself, hearing her talk about giving birth had been too much.

He carried on with the task of replacing the soft drink canisters, his movements mechanical. The steel containers clanked against each other, the sound overloud in the empty pub.

He had a son named William. Of course Emma had named her baby after him. She wouldn't do that by coincidence. She was big on family connections and most of the names on her side of the family were odd.

She hadn't asked him to visit. That was good. He didn't want any tugging on his heartstrings to sway him into making the mistake of thinking he could try to be a father, even supposing Emma would relent and let him. But she wouldn't. And he didn't want to risk it. He'd screwed up with Holly. He didn't want to do the same with this baby.

Emma had sounded elated on the phone. Elated and tired and a bit wistful. Shame she hadn't had anyone with her for moral and practical support. Giving birth was hard work. Of course she would be tired. And emotional.

Carrying an empty canister in each hand, he went out the rear door of the pub and stood them against the building where the delivery truck could pick them up. Across the empty parking lot, through a thin stand of trees, he could see a boy's soccer team practicing on the public playing field. Parents, mostly fathers, stood on the sideline or in the bleachers, calling encouragement to their sons. He would never be one of those dads, supplying orange segments and lobbying the coach for more field time for his boy.

He would never hear his son's first word or see him take his first steps. He would never know the feel of small arms circling his neck or a chubby cheek pressed against his. He would never watch his son graduate from high school or get married.

He would never do all those things with Holly, either. But here he had another chance and he wasn't taking it. Wasn't allowed to.

Suddenly he was filled with a sense of loss so overpowering he almost fell to his knees on the oil-stained pavement. Loss and shame that he couldn't step up in any meaningful way for his son. What kind of a man didn't acknowledge his child?

Emma wasn't letting him in. And for good reason. He'd told her he didn't want another child long before they'd hooked up on the cruise. Nothing had changed. They were still divorced and had no intention of getting back together. Making a lame attempt to be a husband and father again against his better judgment wouldn't do Emma and the baby any good. He would only prolong the emotional fallout of his failed marriage. The baby was better off with her.

He dusted off his hands and went inside. Emma was still his friend. He could at least send her flowers. Or even better, take them to her in person.

Even though it was the middle of the afternoon, he locked up the pub and hung the closed sign on the door, something he hadn't done since Holly's funeral. At the local florist he picked out an arrangement of yellow roses and pink carnations and drove to the Frankston Hospital.

Holly had been born here. Stepping off the elevator onto the maternity ward he was hit by déjà vu so overwhelming and painful he wanted to turn right around and go back to the pub.

Instead he clutched his bouquet tighter and walked around to the nurses' station, peering into rooms as he went. Some mothers were sleeping, their babies in a bassinet at their bedside, others were holding court with family and friends. So many mothers, so many babies.

Emma's laughter rang out from a room two doors away. He stopped and listened, drinking in the sound of her happiness. For a moment some of her joy found its way into his heart. He'd done that for her, given her the baby she so desperately longed for.

He paused outside the doorway. Emma was sitting up in bed, her hair tied back in a ponytail. Her eyes shone as she chatted with Alana, who was perched on the bed. Dave, holding Tessa, stood with his back to the door. A nurse stood next to him—Emma's friend Sasha, probably, judging from her shoulder-length blond hair—and he recognized dark-haired Barb in a black skirt and red jacket at the foot of the bed.

There was no bassinet. The baby must have been taken to the nursery. The tightness in his chest eased a little. Was that relief that he didn't have to see his son?

He raised his hand to knock and then paused as Emma made a quip about some get-together they'd all obviously attended in the recent past, and everyone laughed. Darcy lowered his hand. He didn't belong here. He wasn't part of her life anymore. He didn't know what she was talking about, and quite likely none of these people would welcome him. Alana had been openly hostile to him when he'd run into her at the grocery store not long after the divorce. He didn't know what Emma had told her, but she clearly regarded him as the enemy.

He didn't want to make Emma uncomfortable by barging in and ruining her party. Darcy spun on his heel, wanting to get away before they saw him. At the nurses' station he passed over the bouquet of flowers. "Give these to Emma Lewis, thanks."

As he walked off he realized he'd automatically given her married name. He had no idea if she still used it or had gone back to her maiden name. Hopefully there weren't any other Emmas on the ward.

Where were the damn elevators? All the corridors looked the same. He came to a junction and went right. He found himself in front of the floor-to-ceiling glass walls of the nursery filled with rows of bassinets.

He picked up his pace to hurry past then found himself slowing. And stopping. With his fingers pressed against the glass like any doting father, he looked in, scanning the sleeping babies for a head of thick dark hair. One look to satisfy his curiosity, and then he would go.

There, was that him? No, the name tag on the bassinet indicated the baby was a girl. A nurse came into the nursery and moved through the rows. She wheeled away a bassinet near the window.

And there he was, in the bassinet behind. William James Lewis. His son, bearing his name. Even though he'd been warned, seeing the name tag threw his emotions into unexpected turmoil.

She should have consulted him *before* she'd used his name. William. They'd planned to call Holly that if she'd been a boy. Back then he'd wanted a boy so badly. Then Holly came along and instantly he hadn't cared a jot that she was a girl. He didn't think it was possible to love another human any more than he'd loved his daughter.

To have a son now, when his marriage had broken down and he couldn't handle the thought of being a father again, seemed like fate had played a cruel joke on him. Surely Emma could have found another name, one with no connection to the past.

He was about to leave when the baby opened his eyes, yawned and blinked. Despite himself Darcy was mesmerized. The baby seemed to be looking directly at him. Even though he didn't think the baby could focus yet, it still gave him a funny feeling. He had to leave. Now.

His eyes blurring, he walked swiftly away. Seeing his son had confirmed what he already knew—he didn't want any contact with the child. Emma probably thought he was coldhearted. The opposite was true. He would bond too easily with this child.

With Holly, he'd wanted to be a father so badly, but he'd never quite measured up. The pub took up much of his time, and even when he'd been home he couldn't seem to manage the basics of baby care. Toward the end of Holly's life he'd actively avoided times of the day when she was most demanding—dinnertime, bath time, anytime he could screw up somehow, the way he had that time he'd tried to change her.... He'd failed Emma and he'd failed Holly. He didn't want to do that with William.

Holly's death had brought him face-to-face with unimaginable pain, made all the worse by knowing he had a hand in it. He never wanted to go through that again.

October, Spring

"HEY, ALANA," Emma said into the phone. She paced the living room with a fussing Billy over her shoulder. "Would you be able to look after Billy tomorrow afternoon for a couple of hours? I need to get some work done on my term paper."

"Sorry, I can't," Alana said. "Brett asked me to work full-time while Janet is on holiday. I can't say no. He's really under the gun. And this is my big chance to show him I can act in an assistant manager role as well as lead fitness classes. Sorry."

"No worries. Thanks, anyway. I'll manage." She tried to keep the desperation out of her voice. She'd just got home from school. Billy was wet and hungry but she'd wanted to talk to Alana before her sister got busy with dinner. With a new baby there always seemed to be a dozen things that had to be done at once. She was hungry, too. Her nerves were shot, her apartment was a mess and to top it all off, she was coming down with a cold.

"I could babysit tomorrow night after dinner," Alana offered.

"No way. Dave and Tessa need you in the evenings. I'll be fine."

"If you're sure…"

"I'm positive."

"Is your milk coming in any better?"

Emma jiggled Billy and kept pacing. He was only two months old and although with Holly she'd loved the infant stage, with Billy she wondered when he was ever going to grow up. "No. I don't know what's wrong—other than that he won't latch on properly. He's feeding every two hours and not satisfied. I'm having to supplement with formula." Plus her nipples were cracked and burning, and nursing sessions invariably ended in tears—both his and hers.

"Put him on the bottle. Why go through that?"

"I'm not giving up. I nursed Holly till she was a year old and I'm going to do the same with Billy."

"Does he still have colic?"

"Yes," she said tersely, not happy at the reminder. Every night at ten o'clock when she was ready to fall into bed, Billy woke up and cried for three or four hours. Nothing settled him. She'd tried everything. And she was so sleep-deprived she felt like a zombie.

She changed the subject. "Have you told Dave about your job yet?"

"Not yet. I'm really enjoying the work. And I can't bear to have another fight about expanding the family. He's pressuring me."

Emma winced, hearing herself in the description of Dave. Had she made Darcy feel as desperate as Alana sounded? "If you talked to him, told him how you feel, I'm sure he'd understand. Tell him you've been a full-time mum for three years and you just want to feel like you're your own person again. Find a compromise."

"Like you and Darcy, you mean?" Alana sighed heavily. "Sorry. I know you mean well but you giving me marriage advice when your own marriage broke down…"

"I know but…" Emma hesitated. The difference was, Darcy hadn't talked about his feelings because his resistance to another child was wrapped up in his grief over Holly. Still, she'd made mistakes, too. "I wish now I'd tried to compromise with Darcy instead of pushing to have a child right away. I should have waited." Easy to say in hindsight. At the time she hadn't seen any other course of action open to her.

"Why didn't you?"

"I panicked when he said he didn't want another child *ever.* That made me feel I had to convince him now or I'd lose all possibility of having a family."

"That sounds horribly familiar. Hang on." Tessa whined in the background for something to eat. "I'd better go."

Emma said goodbye and carried Billy to the nursery and laid him on the change table. He continued to cry as she peeled off his sleeper and wet diaper. "Shh, it's okay," she ground out, unable to muster even forced cheerfulness. "Soon you'll be dry and fed and you'll be happy. Please be happy. One of us should be."

Dispassionately, she went through the motions of caring for her baby, but the truth was, her heart wasn't in it. It wasn't only the breastfeeding that had gone wrong. He might as well be a stranger's baby for all the love she felt. If only she could breastfeed him properly, she was sure the bonding would come. And the joy. At the moment she wasn't enjoying Billy at all. She felt guilty for not being a better mother and guilt made her resentful.

He wasn't an easy baby. And she hated not being her usual self-sufficient, capable self. Nor did she like asking her sister and her friends for help. Everyone thought she was this amazing superwoman—student, nurse and mother.

Marge had offered her services, anytime. She and Roy had come to see the baby in the hospital, but there'd been no contact since. Emma felt badly about that, but how could she call on Marge when she'd cut Darcy out of Billy's life?

Darcy hadn't even come to see his son. That hurt, even though it was her fault he'd stayed away. She'd been so adamant she would do this on her own and he wouldn't be involved. So she certainly couldn't call on him for help.

Which was fine because she could handle this. She sat in the rocker in her bedroom and put Billy to her breast, wincing at the pain as he tried to latch onto her cracked nipple. He gave up after a few seconds and cried harder. "All right, damn it. I'll give you a bottle."

She went out to the kitchen, fighting tears, and prepared a bottle, grabbing an apple from the fruit bowl for herself. These days she didn't even have time to shop for groceries or eat properly.

Billy took the bottle with no problems, the little sod. Emma stifled a yawn even though it was only five o'clock in the afternoon. Her books and laptop on the desk taunted her with the work she should be doing. If this had been Holly, she could have put the baby to bed for a nap and had plenty of time to do her term paper. Billy was completely different in every respect to Holly.

The rest of the evening was a blur—feeding, bathing and changing Billy again. Emma ate toast and peanut butter because she was too tired to make dinner. Finally she put Billy to bed and sat at the dining table to work on her paper.

Around ten o'clock she was rubbing her eyes, more than ready to call it a night. Maybe, just maybe, tonight Billy would sleep through. No sooner had she thought that than he started to wail. Like clockwork.

She hurried into the nursery, flipping on the Blinky Bill koala lamp on the dresser. Billy's scrunched face was red and angry, his little fists clenched and waving.

"Shh, sweetie, it's okay." She scooped him up and positioned him over her shoulder, ready to begin the hours of walking the apartment. Nothing she did seemed to help. He would nurse greedily, then cry some more. Sometimes he threw up everything he'd eaten, making him angrier than ever and hungry all over again. Emma was worn-out.

In her dressing gown and sheepskin slippers, eyes open only enough to see where she was going, she paced a well-worn route from Billy's room, past the stack of library books three weeks overdue; through the living room and the piles of clean laundry waiting to be ironed and folded; past the dining table, where flowers were rotting in the vase; into the kitchen, where dirty dishes and takeaway food cartons were piling up in the sink and down the hall to the nursery.

"Please stop crying, Billy," she murmured, even though he was wailing too loudly to hear. His hot cheek, sticky with tears, was pressed to hers. "I wish you could tell me how to help you."

She'd tried every remedy in the book and then some. Nothing worked. Doubts were creeping in about her fitness as a mother. Was she wrong to work and study? Did he cry because he sensed her fatigue and it made him anxious? Was it something she was eating that got into her milk and upset his tummy? How much longer would this go on? Was it retribution for having a baby on her own?

Okay, that was crazy. When she was rational she knew she wasn't being punished for choosing to keep her baby and raise him on her own. But in the wee hours, when she was dead on her feet and knowing she had to get up again at 6:00 a.m., her mind played funny tricks on her.

She started another lap of the apartment.

Yes, Holly had been a dream by comparison with Billy. And Emma had taken six months' maternity leave with Holly. But this time, the hospital had reduced maternity pay due to funding cutbacks and Emma had needed to return to work early. Not only that but she had the added load of her studies. Which she loved. She wasn't giving that up.

She felt like a bad mother, a bad person. Selfish for wanting to do it all, resentful of Billy for not being as easy as Holly and guilty for even thinking mean thoughts about him.

Billy was her responsibility, and no one else's. That's the way she wanted it. But she'd never expected it to be this hard. She'd sacrificed her marriage because she wanted another baby. Maybe she *was* being punished—

Her foot came down on a magazine on the floor and slipped out from underneath her. With a strangled cry she held Billy up, out of harm's way and went down hard on her rear end. Stunned, she sat among the mess, the wind knocked out of her and pain shooting up her spine.

Billy was so startled he stopped crying. Emma broke into semihysterical laughter, and rocked back and forth, as much to distract herself from the pain as to comfort him. "Oh, Billy. Mummy's going crazy."

He made a gurgling sound. She eased the blanket away from his face and he gave her a gummy, toothless smile. His first smile. A milestone that ought to fill her with joy. It didn't.

She felt no love gazing into his adorable face. Instead she had nothing but fatigue and anger and resentment for this creature who had turned her life upside down.

"Oh, Billy." The tears spilled down her cheeks. "It's not you—it's me. It's because I'm so tired."

His face crumpled and he let out a cry. *Here we go again.* Leaning against the wall amid the rubble, she opened her nightgown and put him onto her breast, wincing as he latched on.

More tears leaked from her eyes, not from the physical pain. On some deep level she knew she must love him but she didn't feel it. She adored children. The best thing she'd ever done was be a mother to Holly. And now this. She didn't understand it. She'd heard of other women not being able to bond with their children but never thought *she* would experience this…nothingness when she held her son.

She had to believe she would change. But when? Until then, she would care for him because she had to. And try to hide the fact that she was the worst mother ever. What would Darcy think if he knew? Oh, he said he didn't want a child, but he would be horrified if he could see her now, dreading every minute she had to spend with her baby.

CHAPTER SEVEN

"DARCY, PHONE FOR YOU," Kirsty called above the noise of the pub. She picked up a tray and headed off to deliver the drinks.

Darcy finished serving a customer and moved down the bar to pick up the landline. "Hello?"

"Your father's going into the hospital for his operation." His mother sounded breathless, as if she was in a hurry. "We're leaving in a few minutes."

"When's the surgery?"

"Tomorrow morning. He's in Ward 5G North."

Darcy glanced around the pub. Not too busy but then it rarely was on a Monday night. "I'll try to get in later to see him. Thanks for letting me know." He hung up.

Emma worked on the geriatric ward now. Could he call and ask her to check on his dad if she was on duty?

No, that was the sort of thing you could ask a wife but not an ex.

Anyway, she'd only given birth two months ago. She would still be off on maternity leave. He hadn't seen or talked to her since the day her son had been born. But not a day had gone by that he hadn't wondered how she and the baby were doing. He wished he could pretend William didn't exist but that wasn't in his DNA. He thought about his son every single day, as soon as he woke in the morning and the last thing before he went to sleep at night.

An hour later Darcy stuffed a bottle of beer and a packet of chips in his pockets, left Kirsty in charge and headed to the hospital. He followed the green line down the corridor to Ward 5G North.

At the nurses' station Emma and her friend Tracey had their heads bent over a computer. She turned away to cough then reached for a tissue to blow her nose. He stayed back a little, waiting for them to finish so he could ask where his dad was. They hadn't noticed him.

Emma's hair was clipped up, exposing the tiny mole on her neck he used to like to kiss. She laughed at something Tracey said, and Darcy smiled involuntarily. He used to think the whole world lit up when she smiled. He caught himself and his smile faded. On second thought, he didn't want to talk to her, after all. He slipped unnoticed around the corner and went off to find his father.

Roy was in a room with three other elderly men. Darcy's mother sat in a chair at Roy's bedside. They were watching a game show on TV. Darcy paused in the doorway, taking in the reality of his big bluff father looking far too frail plugged into an IV drip.

"Mum, Dad." Darcy kissed his mother on the cheek before taking a seat on the opposite side of the bed. He squeezed his dad's hand then deposited the beer and the chips on the swing-arm table that held the remains of a half-eaten dinner.

"Thanks, son." Roy yelled at the TV, "Lake Louise." Satisfied he'd gotten the answer right, he turned to Darcy. "No need for you to come down here. I'll be home in a couple of days."

"He was mad at me for calling you. He didn't want you to see him in the hospital," Marge said in a stage whisper.

"I'm not deaf, woman."

Darcy twisted the cap off the beer and handed it to his father. "Here, get your gob around that. Of course I'm going to see you the night before a big operation."

Marge frowned. "Darcy, I don't think beer—"

"I have until ten o'clock to eat and drink before I have to fast for the anesthetic." Roy took a sip of beer. "As for the operation, it's simple. Replace the ball and socket joint. A mechanic could do it."

"Maybe you'd like your mate Ralph to perform the surgery," Darcy suggested dryly. "He probably still has all his tools." He opened the packet of chips and set it where his dad could reach them.

"What's this, a party in Room 17?" Emma wheeled a trolley into the room. "Time for your meds, Roy. Sorry, but they don't go so well with alcohol." Tsking good-naturedly, she plucked the bottle out of his hand. Her gaze cut to Darcy. "You should know better."

Behind the disapproval there was a hint of a smile but also a wariness when she looked at him. Up close he could see how worn-out she looked. Her voice was hoarse as if she'd been coughing a lot. Again, she reached for a tissue and had to excuse herself to blow.

"Have you got a cold?" he asked when she was done and rubbing her hands with sanitizer from a small container she'd pulled from her pocket. He was conscious that his mother was hanging on every word, every look that passed between them. His dad was still calling out answers to the game show. "You shouldn't be working if you're sick."

"I'm okay." She didn't seem to know where to look so she checked the watch pinned to her chest. "Family hours are nearly over."

"I'm going." Darcy rose so his mother could have a few minutes alone with his dad. "See you tomorrow after your operation, Dad. Don't give the nurses a hard time. Mum, call me and let me know how it goes."

"I will," Marge promised.

"Tell the boys at the pub I'll be back next week," Roy said. "I'll challenge them to a footrace around the block."

"I'll let them know to start training." Darcy touched Emma's arm as he passed. "Can I have a word?"

"Sure." She set a paper cup containing pills on Roy's tray and poured him a glass of water. "I'll be right back," she said to Darcy's mother. "You could help him take those if you like."

He waited for Emma a few steps down the corridor, well aware Tracey watched him from the nurses' station. He acknowledged her with a nod and turned away.

Emma came out of the room striding briskly. Her steps slowed as she approached. "Before I forget, thanks for the flowers. I meant to send a note but things got crazy."

He was momentarily thrown. "Flowers?"

"The ones you brought the day Billy was born."

"Billy. So that's what you're calling him." Darcy moved to the side of the corridor as a couple went by. "How is he?"

"He's wonderful!" she said brightly. "Such a good baby. He smiled for the first time the other day."

"That must have been great."

A shadow momentarily dimmed her animated expression. Or it might have been the fluorescent lights flickering. Emma gave another brilliant smile but it didn't erase the lines of strain around her eyes. "It was amazing," she enthused. "I recorded it straight into the baby book."

"I'm surprised you're at work. Shouldn't you be on maternity leave?"

"The hospital cut maternity pay. I could use the extra money so I've come back part-time." Darcy's mother came out of Roy's room. Emma stepped back to let her go past. "Good night, Marge. I'll take good care of him. Don't worry."

"Thank you, dear." Marge's smile turned wistful. "I would love to see the baby sometime."

"Uh, yeah, sure. When I get my term paper finished. I'm flat out at the moment." Emma brushed wisps of hair back from her eyes. "I don't even have time to get my hair cut."

Marge glanced at Darcy then to Emma. "I'd be happy to babysit for you."

"That's really nice of you. But I've got it under control, honestly. He spends so much time at the day care when I'm at university that I like to have him at home when I can."

Marge bit her lip, struggling to hide her disappointment. "If you need me, just call." She hugged Darcy and walked quickly away toward the elevators.

Darcy waited until his mother was out of carshot. He glanced over at the nurses' station. People were moving through the open area—orderlies, visitors, nurses—but no one was paying attention to him and Emma.

He turned to her. "Would it have hurt you to give her some time with her grandson? I don't understand. You say you have everything under control but it sure doesn't sound like it." As she pulled a tissue out of her pocket, he added, "And you are sick. You shouldn't be working."

Emma stiffened, her chin lifting. "In case you've forgotten, we're divorced. You don't get to tell me what to do."

"I'm not trying to tell you what to do. I'm asking you to be nice to my mother. She's the baby's grandmother, after all. Your mother's not around. My mum would be happy to stand in for her."

Emma didn't reply.

Hell. He wanted to shake her. He wanted to kiss her. He missed her like crazy. Everything was so messed up. He couldn't stand that she was working too hard and wearing herself out. It wasn't necessary. "I offered you support payments. You didn't have to return to work yet."

"Oh, I get it. You're afraid I'm not taking good enough care of our son. You're afraid I'm neglecting him."

"What? Did I say that? I don't think that at all." He drew back. "You're a terrific mother—"

"I love him, okay? I love him to bits," she added fiercely. "So you can just stay out of it."

"Emma?"

"I'm sorry." She took a deep breath and wrapped her arms around herself. "We've had this conversation already. I'm too tired to do it again."

A tense silence sizzled between them. Emma glanced at the nurses' station, at Roy's room. Darcy knew she had tasks to do, but he didn't want her to leave on a negative note.

"I came here that day, the day he was born." He didn't know why he was telling her this. "There were so many people in your room, I didn't stay."

She softened fractionally. "Did you see him?"

Darcy nodded. Remembering the difficult emotions he'd struggled with that day, it was hard to talk about his son without feeling like a jerk. He went back to trying to help Emma. "You're working too soon. Plus you're studying, too. And looking after a baby. You don't need to do all that. You could accept my help and stay home longer."

"I'm coping."

"Are you? Your eyes are all red as if you've been up half the night. All the time I've been standing here, you've had a crease between your eyebrows. And your voice is too tight.... You seem like you're about to snap."

"Could that be because you're criticizing me? You should go. This is my workplace. I don't have time for personal conversations."

"It's not criticism. It's the truth. But for some reason you don't want to hear it."

She stabbed a finger in his face. "You see me *one* time in months and you think you know what's going on with me. Let me tell you, you don't have a clue."

"I don't know the details of your life right now, but I can guess. And I can see you're upset and uptight. You are usually calm and in control."

"I have a new baby. And yes, I'm juggling work and school. It's hard. Tell me something I don't know."

"You don't know how to let people help you."

"Money," she said contemptuously. "That's your idea of help. I don't need money. I need practical assistance! I need someone to change a diaper, to help with the feeding, to give me a night off from the crying baby." Tears sprang to her eyes. "Just one goddamn night without the crying. Is that too much to ask?"

"Whoa." Darcy stepped closer and put a hand on her shoulder. "I know you wouldn't want *me* to do anything with the baby but if you need help so badly, why didn't you take up my mother's offer?"

"She's too...close to you. I know she has a right, but I'm not ready." Emma blotted her eyes with the already-soggy tissue. "I'm still mad at you basically. I wish you could be who I want you to be and I'm angry that you can't. Or won't."

Darcy let out a breath. This was emotionally exhausting for both of them. "I obviously struck a nerve a minute ago. Is the baby being difficult?"

"His name is Billy, remember?" She shook his hand off. "He's just being a baby, doing what babies do. Cry, eat, sleep, cry, eat, sleep, cry, cry." Her voice had risen in pitch with each word. Suddenly she seemed to notice and stopped, her face paler. "I didn't mean to say that. He's fine. I wasn't asking for your time."

"My mother—"

"I like your mother a lot, but she would be subtly working to bring us back together for the sake of Billy. We both know that's not a good idea."

"Something we agree on." Darcy took a step back. "Okay, I'll go. Try to take it easy. I'm sure you're doing everything the baby needs and more. I was only saying you need to make sure you get enough rest or you'll get really sick. And then what?"

"Thanks for stating the obvious." Again Emma touched the corners of her eyes with the soggy tissue.

Ah, jeez. She *never* cried. Now she'd done it twice in the space of minutes. It undid him. "Don't, Em." He put his arms around her and drew her to him.

"I'm on duty. You can't hug me." She tried to push him away.

"Well, I *am* hugging you. What are you going to do about it?" He tightened his embrace. She didn't resist but she didn't go into his arms, either. "I'm sorry if I was harsh. I didn't mean to make you cry."

"I'm not crying. I've got a cold."

"What was I saying? You're making yourself sick trying to do it all. Even you aren't superwoman."

"I suppose you're going to tell me some platitude like everything's going to be all right." She sniffed.

"It will be. Somehow." He laid his head on top of her hair. For three long precious seconds he simply stood there and breathed her in.

Then before he could kiss her, she pulled away. Just as well. It was better they kept their distance. She and the baby were a package deal. Take one, take the other.

"If you change your mind about the money, you know where to contact me."

He turned and walked to the elevators. Emma had revealed a lot, either deliberately or accidentally. She wasn't coping. The baby was difficult. But what was Darcy supposed to do about it? She didn't want him in their life. He had no reason to feel guilty because he wasn't doing more. She had no right to expect his practical help and he doubted she would take it if he offered. Something fundamental was broken between them, and a baby wasn't going to fix it.

TYPICAL. DARCY SWOOPS IN, pats her on the head, tells her she's doing a great job then disappears to the pub. No one could push her buttons like him. Why did they keep hurting each other? Why did he try to appeal to her emotions when what she needed was practical assistance?

You told him you didn't need or want him in your and Billy's life, remember?

Emma forced her focus on her work. She didn't have time to stand around brooding. She was in the middle of her evening rounds. She went into Roy's room.

"Sorry, I got sidetracked with Darcy for a minute," she said to Roy. "I see you've taken your pills. We'll do your blood pressure now." She strapped the cuff around

his upper arm and set the machine. "How are you feeling?"

"Fine," Roy said. "Aside from this bum hip of mine."

"Which will be fixed up in no time." Emma noted
the systolic and diastolic measurement. His blood pressure was a little high. "I see your surgery is scheduled
for tomorrow morning."

"Have you got your tomatoes in yet?"

He was avoiding talking about his operation. After
years on the wards she recognized the tactic among patients afraid of surgery. She and Roy used to be buddies,
swapping plants and gardening tips, and she had a soft
spot for him. "I'm in an apartment. I don't have room
for a garden." Nor the heart for it, either. She'd lost that
along with Holly.

"Nothing beats the taste of homegrown."

"That's true." She wrapped the cords around the
blood pressure cuff and replaced it on the trolley. "How
many plants have you got this year?"

"A dozen, three of the cherry variety." Roy tipped
up the chip packet and the last one fell into his palm.
"Funny you calling your baby William when you and
Darcy have split up."

"You shouldn't eat that salty stuff with your blood
pressure." She stuck a thermometer clip on the end of
his finger. "How come you planted your tomatoes so
soon? You always told me to wait until the first week
in November."

"I had to get them in before I went into hospital.
Marge wouldn't get around to it if—"

"If what?"

His face settled into a frown that made his jowls
droop even more than they ordinarily did. "You got a

balcony? Tomatoes grow great in pots. I don't even know where you live now. Darcy shouldn't have let you go."

"I'm in Mornington. It wasn't a question of Darcy letting me go." He'd walked out on her. Sure in hindsight she could see that maybe she drove him to it, but their problem was they hadn't agreed on the things that really mattered—Holly, how they saw themselves as a family, what their plan was for the future. Emma managed a tight smile. "I believe it's called irreconcilable differences."

"I've seen plants that have been cut back to nothing, burned by summer drought, ripped out of the ground—you name it. You stick them in good rich soil, give 'em plenty of water and some nourishment and they survive, even thrive. Nothing can't be fixed with a little TLC."

"You've been reading Marge's romance novels, haven't you?" Emma recorded his temperature and removed the finger clip. Then she squeezed his hand and held it. "Don't worry about the operation. Hip replacements are routine these days. You'll be back in action in a few weeks."

Roy started to bluster about how he was fine, then his gaze flicked to hers. "The doctor was in earlier—the one who's going to knock me out. She told me I'm at risk because of my blood pressure."

"They have to warn people. It's a standard caution. You're going to be fine. I promise."

"What if I cark it on the table?"

"I'll water your tomatoes," she said lightly.

"Will you bring Billy around to see Marge?"

"Oh, Roy."

"Promise me."

If only he knew how much she would have loved for Billy to be part of the big, boisterous Lewis family, under the right circumstances, that is, if she and Darcy were together. He would have lots of cousins, including a boy nearly his own age. But how could she attend Lewis family gatherings when she and Darcy weren't together? And Darcy was unlikely to take Billy on his own.

Nevertheless, she couldn't leave Roy hanging. "I promise."

A flurry of activity at the door made her turn around.

"Good afternoon." Dr. Avery Pritchard swept into the room, his white coat flapping. "How is our patient today?"

Emma handed the doctor Roy's chart on which she'd written her observations. "He's doing well, Doctor."

"Excellent." He turned to Roy. "I'm Dr. Pritchard. I'll be doing your hip replacement tomorrow morning. It's a straightforward procedure...."

Emma wheeled out her trolley with the meds and blood pressure equipment, leaving Roy with Dr. Pritchard.

She wished Darcy wanted to be a part of his son's life as much as Marge did. He was keeping himself at arm's length with offers of money. She got that he was devastated by Holly's death, but that was in the past. Billy was here and now. She didn't care for herself, but for Billy's sake she wished Darcy would let Billy into his life. How awful to think of her son growing up aware that his father lived nearby but didn't want to know him. Besides everything that had gone wrong between them over Holly, she couldn't ever forgive Darcy for that.

WHAT THE HELL was wrong with Emma? Darcy turned his truck out of the hospital parking lot and headed to Summerside. She was in trouble, forced back to work early. Why wouldn't she let him help her by contributing financially? What was so wrong with him easing his conscience in that way? It was almost as if she was punishing him for not wanting to be a father to Billy.

She was really punishing herself. And the baby.

So be it. It wasn't like he had a ton of spare cash to throw around. He'd done his monthly bookkeeping last night and business had fallen off since the wine bar opened.

He parked in front of the pub and got out in time to see two of his regular customers coming down the street—Greta, a hairdresser, and her boyfriend, Larry, a gangly apprentice baker. If it weren't for people like Greta and Larry, who came in a couple of times a week, he would really be hurting. They didn't drink a lot—they nursed a couple of beers and socialized—but he could count on them.

He lounged in the doorway, enjoying the first mild evening in months—spring was definitely here at last—and waited to greet them with some of that personal service he hoped would be the salvation of his pub.

Greta paused to peer into a boutique window. Larry tugged her away, waving a piece of paper in her face. Instead of coming straight to the pub, they crossed the street. Darcy's stomach fell as he watched them walk into the wine bar.

He swore quietly. If even these two abandoned him, he was in trouble. Surely they couldn't afford the wine bar prices. In about thirty seconds they'd be out the door again, over to his pub.

Hands on hips, he waited. Three minutes ticked by. Greta and Larry didn't come out of the wine bar—but four more people went in. Wayne must be giving out more discounted drinks. It was almost as if he was try-ing to put himself out of business. Except that his strategy was drawing huge crowds. Customers were flocking to his joint and not to Darcy's pub. Greta and Larry weren't his only customers to defect in recent months. Oh, people still came to the pub, too, just not as often.

Thoroughly disgruntled, Darcy went back inside. He stood in the doorway and surveyed the room, much as Wayne had a few months ago. In contrast to the wine bar's colorful furniture and paintings the wood-paneled pub looked dark and, to Darcy's now-jaundiced eye, less than inviting.

Light. He needed more light in here. More windows and modern light fixtures. Maybe he ought to get a draftsman or a builder to look over those architect's drawings for a garden room. Alternatively, if he didn't want to go the whole hog he could paint, put in new carpets, buy those tall tables and stools....

"What's the matter, boss?" Kirsty said, going past with a tray of drinks. "Is your dad all right? His friends came in and then left again. Complained they couldn't play a proper game of darts without Roy."

"He's doing okay." At least the wine bar had yet to put in a dartboard or shuffleboard.

A garden room with glass walls on three sides would solve the light problem. If he put in a kitchen, he could offer simple meals and snacks.

Garden room. Kitchen. He was talking about a major project. Suddenly it seemed daunting. If he and Emma were still together, he could have talked it over with her. She was great with practical stuff. And she had excellent color sense. Darcy couldn't afford an interior decorator but Emma would know how to match carpet shades with seat covers.

"What do you think of the decor in here, Kirsty?"

She shrugged. "It's cozy, warm. It's a pub."

If he changed the atmosphere to attract new customers, would he lose the ones he had? Hell, he was already losing them. He couldn't sit still and do nothing while the wine bar stole his business.

If he did do major renovations, he would have to take out a sizable loan. Could he afford to do that?

Could he afford not to? Going into debt was a gamble, but if he didn't do something he was in danger of going under, maybe not this year but possibly next. But possibly the wine bar really would be a novelty that would wear off. When people got tired of the red velvet couches they would come back to his pub.

What if they didn't? The wine bar had been open nearly four months now and was busier than ever.

He'd been complacent, secure in the knowledge that his was the only bar in town. Circumstances had changed. Now he had to try harder. Maybe he should be grateful to Wayne for forcing him to lift his game. If he was going to go bankrupt, he might as well go out in style.

The pub was his livelihood, his home away from home, the place where the people he cared about hung out. He'd lost his wife and daughter. He'd lost his interest in Latin dancing and football. Since he'd split up with Emma the pub had become the center of his life. Hell, it had become his *whole* life. He lived in the upstairs apartment and worked every day behind the bar. All he had left was the pub. It represented everything that was important to him—his connection to family, friends and the community. If he lost it, he didn't know what would happen to him.

He didn't want to find out.

EMMA STRUGGLED TO fit the tubing onto the intake nozzle of the breast pump. Who made these stupid tubes so small? Dirty dishes were stacked in the sink and on the counter. Her dishwasher had broken and she hadn't cleaned up in days. Her cold had worsened in the night and she longed to crawl into bed. But she was on duty at the hospital this morning and she wanted to be there when Roy went in to surgery. First she needed to try to pump enough milk for Billy to take to day care.

The phone rang.

"Perfect." She put the tubing down and fished among the clutter for her phone. "Hello."

"Hello, darling. How's everything?"

"Hi, Mum." Emma forced a cheery note into her voice. "I'm good. Where are you?"

"At a roadhouse in some tiny town in the outback of Western Australia. Your dad's tanking up the car and I'm waiting for our food order. How's my gorgeous little man?"

Emma glanced over at Billy, strapped into his car seat. He was quiet for once, playing with the plastic keys dangling above him. At times like these she felt the best about him, that is to say, neutral.

"He's smiling. And holding his head up. He's definitely going to have dark hair, although I think his eyes might be blue-green like mine."

"You can't tell at this stage. They won't be set for months yet."

"Mum, I've only got a few minutes. I'm getting ready for work." Emma tucked the phone between her chin and shoulder and picked up the breast pump to have another attempt at assembling the pieces.

"That's okay. I just wanted to say hi. I wish we weren't on this big long trip when you had the baby."

"You were here for the first two weeks." There, was

that right? Emma gave an experimental tug on the tubing. It came off in her hands.

After the birth her parents had flown home. During their stay Billy had been a model baby, sleeping most of the day and only waking at night to be fed and have his diaper changed. Emma had blithely urged her parents to resume their trip. A week after they'd left, Billy had developed colic. Two and a half months later he was still crying every night for hours.

"If you need me, say the word and I'll fly back," her mother said. "I don't feel right leaving you, and I don't like missing out on his early months. The first two weeks were wonderful, but he'll be doing so much more now."

"He'll still be small when you're here at Christmas."

She couldn't let on she was struggling. Her mother had been a rock when Holly died. Emma had also leaned on her when her marriage was falling apart. Her mother would return to Summerside in a heartbeat if she thought Emma needed her. However, her parents had planned and saved for years to travel around Australia in a campervan. They deserved this trip, and Emma wasn't going to spoil it for them.

"I tried calling Alana, but she's never home," her mother said.

Emma pushed at the tubing, finally easing it over the nozzle. "She's got a new job—" The words were out before she could take them back.

"She's working? She didn't tell me that."

Uh-oh. "It's new. Might not last. Don't say anything to Dave. She hasn't told him yet."

"She hasn't told him? Why not?"

"It's a long story...."

"And you don't have time right now. Okay, I won't

keep you much longer. How's your milk supply? Alana told me you were having trouble."

"I'm fine, really." She glanced at the wall clock. "Sorry, Mum, I have to go."

"I talked to Marge yesterday. She told me about Roy's hip operation."

"You talked to Marge? Why?" Giving up on a quick end to their chat, Emma sat at the kitchen table, pushed up her top and attached the pump. She flipped the switch and gently squeezed her breast, hoping for a trickle, something, so she wouldn't have to give Billy formula again.

"Why wouldn't we? Darling, we're friends. And we're grandmothers together. Of course we talk."

"What else did she say—about Billy?" Emma pressed her fingers to her throbbing sinuses. Here it came. Would it be a gentle reproach or a stern lecture about allowing Marge access? If her mother were here, they could talk things out but she wasn't and Emma didn't have time to explain over the phone. It was all building up, becoming too much, her job, her studies, Billy and now the family.

"She said how adorable he was, how precious for his age. What a wonderful mother you are."

Marge had covered for her. That was so like her, un-selfish, concerned and caring. And Emma had repaid her by not finding time for her to see her grandson. Just then Billy began to cry. Emma felt like crying, too. She was completely, utterly inadequate in every way.

"Mum, I really have to go. I'll talk to you later."

She had to pull herself together and carry on. Billy needed her to be strong. But it was increasingly hard when she felt as if her life was spiraling out of control.

WEDNESDAY NIGHT WAS slow, too. So slow Darcy got out the architect's drawings and unfurled them on the bar.

He could do a lot of the work himself, things like painting and ripping out old carpeting. Dan could do the wiring and Tony could do the brickwork. They would cut him a deal and he'd rather give them the business than some stranger.

The aspect that worried him most was the interior decorating. It wasn't a top priority till the structural work was complete but now that he'd decided to move ahead he should at least start thinking about it.

He'd visited his dad in the hospital that morning before the pub opened. On his way home he'd swung by some paint and upholstery shops to pick up color samples and fabric swatches. He spread them out on the bar next to the architect's plans, arranging them in different combinations, trying to visualize them incorporated into the pub's decor. But he couldn't mentally transform the tiny scraps of color into chair seats and walls. His brain didn't work that way.

Riley came in dressed in civvies and pulled up a stool. "What's all this? Are we redecorating our dollhouse? Cooper's Pale Ale, thanks. Make it a pint."

Darcy pulled a pint of ale and blotted the foam. "This is what I like to see, Summerside's finest, keeping the streets safe from crime."

"Even the senior sergeant is allowed to have a drink when off duty." Riley glanced at the rectangles of color and fabric. "What's with the samples?"

"I'm giving the old girl a makeover. What do you reckon?"

Riley shrugged. "I like her the way she is, but then I'm not competing with the new kid on the block."

"Have you checked out the wine bar's liquor license?"

Darcy was only half joking. "The owner seems to me like a shady character."

"You want me to shut him down, I'll shut him down." Riley grinned as he sipped his beer.

"Not good enough. He would reapply and be back in business." Darcy leaned over the bar and dropped his voice. "You must know some crims who would torch the place. Put me in touch, then look the other way and five percent of my takings are yours."

Riley chuckled. "Yeah, that'll be a big help when Paula nails my ass and puts me in jail. Seriously, have you got a plan?"

"I'm fighting fire with fire." Darcy nodded to the chalkboard above his head listing a dozen new wines by the glass. "And the makeover. Hope it's enough. Speaking of renovations, how's the extension on the police station coming along?"

"Slowly, but it's getting there. I'll be glad when I don't have to dust my desk for sawdust every morning."

Darcy rearranged the swatches once more. "Which do you like best, the green and brown together or the peach and blue?"

"Mate, you're asking the wrong person, but I'd say neither."

"Paula makes quilts, doesn't she? She must be good at fabrics and color combinations. If I took these over to your house one night, would she give me some advice?"

"I'm sure she would—if she was around. She went up to Tinman Island for a couple of weeks to visit John and Katie and Tuti."

John Forster, who'd given Darcy half the cruise ticket, used to be in charge of the police station until he'd left to take up a position on a remote island in tropical North

Queensland with Katie, his new wife, and Tuti, his half-Balinese daughter from a previous relationship.

"I had an email from John last week. Sounds like he and Katie like it up north."

"He's glad to be back on active duty. Paula called today to report in. Katie's working on her third children's book, and Tuti's learning to boogie board. Apparently they can't keep her out of the water."

"Excellent," Darcy replied distractedly. He leaned his elbows on the bar and studied his color swatches.

Riley sipped his beer. "Emma did a good job decorating your old house. Have you asked her?"

"She's got too much on her plate. Anyway, neither of us is interested in getting involved again." Darcy pulled himself up. No one had mentioned getting involved. Was that a Freudian slip?

"I was talking about decorating. But now that you mention it, you two have a child together. It doesn't get much more involved than that."

Darcy stared at Riley. What was this backflip on Riley's part? "You were against me having anything to do with Emma. You said she was bad for me."

"I'm not talking about you and Emma. I meant you and your son."

"Oh." A muscle in Darcy's jaw twitched. "I tried to offer her child support and she wouldn't hear of it."

"Money isn't the only thing a kid needs."

"I'm not father material." How many times did he have to say it? "I'm never around. I'm not good at the hands-on stuff. I make more work for Emma when I do try to help. No, I don't want to screw the kid up. Having no father is better than having a bad one."

"I don't believe for one second that you don't care about your own kid. Even if Emma doesn't want you to play an active role, you don't have to accept that. And you weren't a bad father to Holly."

"I wasn't there for her enough. I wasn't competent enough to do things for her, change her diapers, feed her, bathe her. I was the playmate. Kids need more than that."

"Nobody's born knowing how to care for children. You have to learn. You were absent for Holly because you had to work, but when you were around she thought you hung the moon and the stars. I saw you. You were a great dad. In fact, I remember thinking that if I ever had a child I hoped I could be as good a father as you were."

"If by *good* you mean I gave a lot of horsie rides, yeah, I was a great dad. Can we drop the subject?" Darcy didn't want to get into this. There were some things he didn't tell even his best mates. Like the fact that when he'd been changing Holly and she'd fallen off the changing table she'd landed on her head on a wood floor. She hadn't gone unconscious, in fact, she'd barely cried and hadn't seemed fazed in the least. He'd rushed her to the hospital where Emma had met him. Holly had been checked out by a doctor and pronounced fine.

He'd felt so badly afterward that he'd driven Emma nuts asking if Holly was acting normally, if she was on course for being at the right developmental stage for her age. Emma hadn't reported anything amiss, but Darcy had always been waiting for the injury to manifest itself in some horrible, irreparable way.

Now Holly was gone and there was no point telling this particular story. But the experience had frightened the hell out of him as a new father.

"I saw Emma the other day at the gas station," Riley said after a moment.

"How was she?"

"Not great. She has a bad cold or the flu. She could barely talk…she was too busy coughing up a lung."

"I told her that would happen. What about the baby? Is he sick, too?"

"I peered through the car window because *I* haven't seen the mystery kid yet. Even though I was godfather to your first child. His nose was running but that could have been because he was crying."

Darcy didn't want to feel a tug at his heart. But he did. Damn it, of course he cared about his child. Billy was a little over two months old. He must be starting to smile, and doing other stuff. He, Darcy, was missing out on all the stages of his child's life.

He swept up the paint and fabric samples and put them in a big manila envelope. He hated to think of Emma trying to cope with everything and being sick, as well. It was one thing for her to play around with her own health, but she had no right to put his son's health in jeopardy. "I'm going to go see Emma and Billy."

Riley sipped his beer. "I thought you might."

CHAPTER EIGHT

DARCY STABBED EMMA'S doorbell outside her apartment building a second time. She was taking ages to answer. Maybe she wasn't home. Maybe she was feeling better and had gone out. But he didn't think so.

"Hello?" she croaked over the intercom.

"It's me. Can you buzz me through?"

"This isn't a good time, Darcy."

He couldn't tell her he knew she was sick or she would deny it up and down. But if she thought he needed her—if she thought anyone needed her—Emma wouldn't refuse.

"I'm renovating the pub. I was hoping you could give me some advice on the color scheme."

There was a long silence. Darcy kicked a pebble off the mat, took two paces away and came back. Pressed her bell again. "Emma, are you still there?"

"Come up." She pressed the buzzer.

Darcy didn't know what he'd expected but the sight that met his eyes when Emma opened her door left him speechless. She had deteriorated significantly in the two days since he'd seen her. Her eyes were red-rimmed, her hair lank. Thick wool work socks protruded beneath her quilted dressing gown. She held a tissue pressed to her pink, chafed nose. Her movements were slow and stiff, as if every joint and muscle ached.

"You look like death warmed over."

"I've got a spring cold."

"I'm no doctor, but I think what you have is more than a cold." He glanced over her shoulder into the apartment. It looked as if a bomb had exploded in a clothing factory. There was laundry everywhere, on the furniture, on the floor, not all of it clean.

Without waiting for her to ask him in, he walked into the living room. Nursing textbooks and papers covered the dining table, along with dirty dishes and used coffee mugs. He peeked into the kitchen. More dishes were piled on the counter and in the sink. The garbage was overflowing. He discreetly sniffed. Dirty diapers. Food left out on the counter.

This wasn't like Emma. She was an immaculate housekeeper. Even when Holly had been a baby the chaos had been controlled. At times the house might have been untidy but Emma always kept things clean. He'd tried to do his share of housework but she preferred to do it herself so she knew it was done to her standards. Now, her living space looked like a homeless person's nest under a bridge. Magnified a hundred times.

In the nursery, the baby was crying. Emma paid no attention. She blew her nose on a tattered damp tissue.

Darcy stepped out of the kitchen into the hall. "Aren't you going to pick him up?"

"Why?" she said listlessly, shoulders slumped. "It won't make him stop crying."

Okay, this was truly worrying. Emma loved being a mother. She was a nurse. She would never neglect her child, especially one who was sick. He'd seen her give out bandages for a kid who scraped his knee in the park, and dispense cough drops to an elderly woman at a bus stop. Strangers in need got her attention, but she left her baby to cry piteously? Something wasn't right.

"Does he have a cold, too?" Darcy asked.

Her eyes closed and she nodded.

Darcy could hear the tiny heart-rending cough in between wails. "Have you taken him to the doctor?"

That got a spark out of Emma. Her eyes blazed to life. "Of course I took him. Do you think I'm a bad mother?"

Was that a note of hysteria in her voice? Before this he would never have considered that possibility for a second. But now she was ill and crumbling under too great a workload.

Darcy headed for the nursery. Billy was lying on his back, red in the face and hacking between wails.

"Oh, my God, Emma. How could you leave him like this?" Darcy picked the baby out of the cot. His sleeper was damp from sweat and a leaking diaper and stained with vomited milk. Darcy had no idea where to begin with a baby in this much distress. Emma had always taken care of Holly when she was sick.

Darcy held him out to her. "You need to clean him up. Feed him. Give him medicine. Give him whatever it is he needs."

Emma rocked the baby and patted his back but her motions were mechanical. She didn't hold Billy close or make a real effort to comfort him. "Shh, Billy. Be quiet. Please."

"You should have called someone if you couldn't cope. Alana, or one of your friends."

"I can cope," Emma said shrilly. "Of course I can cope. As soon as I get over this cold I'll be fine." She started hacking, deep rattling coughs that Darcy felt in his own chest.

Or maybe that was the ache from seeing Emma and his son in such a pitiful condition. What was going on? Was she having some sort of nervous breakdown as well as being sick? Was she suffering from postnatal depression? Should he take her to the hospital?

"Where's your phone? I'm calling Tracey." Another nurse would at least know what to do. *He* should know what to do. It bothered him that he didn't.

"Tracey's in Bali."

"Alana, then. Or who's your other friend—Sasha?"

"Sasha's at home taking care of her kids, who are sick, too. Alana's working. Anyway I don't want to risk her catching this. She can't afford to be sick, and she certainly wouldn't want Tessa to get it." Emma jiggled the baby and coughed away from his face. "Don't call anyone. We'll get through this, won't we, Billy?"

She wasn't being rational. He had to call someone. Darcy walked through the apartment, searching for her phone amid the clutter. He finally found it by calling her on his phone. The ringing came from inside an empty pizza box on the kitchen counter. He quickly scrolled through her contacts list and found Barb's number. It rang and rang.

Emma stood in the doorway, still holding Billy awkwardly away from her. "If you're calling Barb, she's in meetings every day this week. It's the end-of-year performance reviews for her staff."

Darcy hung up before the call went to voice mail and called his mother. *Please, please let her be home.* She'd retired years ago from her job as an accountant, but she did a lot of volunteer work. The phone picked up. *Thank God.* Someone to take responsibility.

"Emma's sick with bronchitis, or something," Darcy said. "The baby has it, too. What should I do?"

"Have they been to the doctor?" his mother asked.

"Yes, but she's really sick. She can't look after herself let alone the baby. All her friends are away or sick or working."

"Then I guess it's up to you."

"Um, I was hoping you could help."

"I would love to look after the baby, but your father was discharged from the hospital this afternoon. He's not mobile. Plus I need to change the dressings on his surgical wound every few hours."

"Oh, well, that's good he's out. I saw him this morning but he didn't mention he was going home."

"He's getting forgetful," Marge said.

While they talked, Darcy gathered up dishes and took them to the sink. His shoe stuck to the floor. The whole place was unhygienic. "I've got a pub to run. And I don't have a clue what to do with a two-month-old."

"Babies aren't that difficult. They need food, clean clothes, dry diapers and love. I'm sure you can handle that." She paused. "Your father's calling me. Sorry, love, I've got to go." And she hung up.

Darcy went in search of Emma. She was slumped on the couch, eyes closed, mindlessly rocking the baby. She hadn't changed him and seemed to be making no attempt to feed him. Billy had worn himself out and his cries were sporadic, punctuated by hiccups.

Darcy felt Billy's forehead. It was hot. Fever or de-hydration, he had no idea. Emma must be really sick to let the situation get this bad.

The baby wasn't his responsibility. Emma had told him so repeatedly. She didn't *want* him to be involved.

He kicked a pile of laundry out of his way. Had she thought about this scenario when she decided to have a child on her own? What if he hadn't come by? What if someone else had found her and called Child Services?

They might take Billy into custody, possibly foster him out temporarily. Emma would hate that.

Or what if no one had come by and something seriously bad had happened to Billy?

Someone *had* come by. Him. It was no good telling himself he wasn't responsible when he knew full well he was. He felt ashamed of himself for calling his mother. Fine to ask for advice but to try to palm off his kid…it was wrong. He had to step up. It was only temporary, till Emma got better.

Gingerly, he reached for the baby and took him out of Emma's slack arms. "Go have a shower while I change him."

She blinked at him then gazed blankly at her empty arms. "You wanted to talk about decorating."

"Shower. Now. That's an order." His mouth set in a grim line, Darcy held the soaking-wet baby out from his body and strode back to the nursery. From the recesses of his mind he recalled something Emma had said when Holly was sick. *It's a good sign if the diaper's wet. It means she's not dehydrated.* So Billy being soaked through was a *good* thing. Yeah, right.

Darcy laid the baby on the change table and held him firmly in place with one hand on his tummy while he studied the situation. The sodden sleeper was a one-piece with snap closures. How hard could this be? It wasn't like he'd *never* changed a baby's diaper. Before that terrible day when Holly had fallen, he'd been in charge while Emma was out shopping. Back then Emma had laid out everything in the order in which he would need it. However, judging by the jumble of wipes, pins, powder and other unrecognizable stuff on Billy's dresser, this time he was going to have to wing it.

"Don't worry, kid. I'll get you clean and dry in a jiffy."

Billy started at the sound of his deep voice. Then cried louder. Darcy began to peel the wet clothing off a small squirming body. Ugh. The baby's undershirt was soaked, too. Emma was using cloth diapers. No wonder everything was wet. Exactly how long had it been since she'd changed him? He thought of asking and rejected the idea. She probably didn't know. Emma was a nurse and a mother, but right now she was in crazy town.

With relief, he heard the shower running. At least she wasn't so far gone she couldn't clean herself. How long had she been ill and trying to cope on her own and patently *not* coping? He felt sick to think about it. While he'd been preoccupied with the pub she'd been floundering by herself with only the occasional delivery from the pizza place for sustenance.

With two fingers Darcy dropped the soiled sleeper directly into the garbage. "Hope that wasn't your favorite outfit, kid."

He could see how Emma would go batty if she had to listen to that crying night and day. Why hadn't she called him? Yes, he'd told her he wanted nothing to do with the baby and she'd insisted over and over that Billy was *her* baby, her responsibility. But surely she knew she could count on him in an emergency.

He almost gagged when he tore off the sodden diaper. Oh, man, this child needed a bath. He listened. Emma was still in the shower. This was going to be tricky.

He put the diaper in the pail and wrapped Billy in a towel he found lying on the floor. When Holly had been tiny Emma had bathed her in the kitchen sink. Darcy carried the baby to the kitchen and surveyed the basin filled with dirty dishes and scraps of food. Not an option.

Now what? How had he come to be standing in this filthy apartment with a crying baby in his hands? Darcy felt a little like howling himself. All he'd wanted when he came over here was to make sure Emma was okay, get a peek at his son and go on his merry way content in the knowledge that she was happy, had what she wanted and he didn't need to feel guilty about a thing. He'd expected her to be under the weather, not having mental problems.

This was partly his fault. By not insisting he take an active role he'd pushed her into trying to do it all herself. The stress had been too much for her.

There was no point casting blame when he had a cold, wet, hungry, *naked* baby literally on his hands. The kid needed a bath. He explored the rest of the apartment. No laundry room. Great. The crying was really starting to get to him. How did the baby keep that up? His throat must be so sore. Which no doubt made him cry even more.

"Your mum won't be too much longer, kid," Darcy muttered, pacing the short hall. "Then we can get you cleaned up."

How long had she been in there? Must be over ten minutes. Emma didn't waste water. Even after the drought had ended she still limited her showers to two minutes, four if she washed her hair—

Oh, no.

She wouldn't. Would she?

Darcy banged on the door, his heart racing. "Emma! Answer me."

All he heard was the sound of running water.

He flung open the door and stepped into the steamy

room. Behind the frosted glass shower door Emma stood naked and motionless, hands at her sides and her face turned into the spray.

Thank God. Oh, thank God. Darcy's knees crumpled. He sat on the edge of a bathtub separate from the shower. She hadn't heard him call out or come in, wasn't even aware of his presence in the bathroom. She was lost somewhere in her head, hiding under a waterfall. He could hear her singing to herself, faint and tuneless.

He wasn't leaving this room until the baby was bathed. Suddenly that seemed of vital importance. Surely he could manage that, if nothing else. Billy was half-asleep, exhausted by crying and illness.

Clutching him to his chest, Darcy leaned over the bathtub and ran the water, testing the temperature with his elbow. Why the elbow? He'd always wondered that. The elbow had to be one of the least sensitive places on the human body. And a baby's skin was ultrasensitive. But maybe he had that wrong. When Holly had been born, Emma had given him a stack of baby-rearing books which he'd never read.

Why would he read about babies when playing with Holly was so much more fun? He'd been an expert on getting her to giggle and blowing raspberries. Not so much on, say, when to start a child on solids. Emma took care of all that. He only breezed in for a couple of hours, got Holly hyped up, as Emma would say, then went to the pub. If he didn't do anything that mattered, then he couldn't screw up.

When the tub held a couple of inches of warm water Darcy unwrapped the baby and carefully lowered him in. Billy woke up and flung both arms out, his eyes wide and his mouth gaping. Snot hung from his nose in two yellow-green ribbons. He began to cry. Of course. What other response would a baby have to a bath?

Slippery little devil, too. He wriggled and twisted, slipping out of Darcy's grip and flipping over with his face below the water. Crap! Darcy grabbed him and whipped him out and upside down to drain any water that might have filled his nostrils. Darcy was sweating in the humid room and he could smell his own fear.

"What are you doing?" Emma asked.

He glanced over his shoulder. The shower had stopped and he hadn't noticed. Emma stood directly behind him, naked and dripping, watching his clumsy handling of her precious baby with a curiously detached expression. Even though she was shivering with the cold she made no move to dry herself or wrap up in a dressing gown.

She'd completely lost it. Non compos mentis. He'd been thinking he would bathe Billy, make sure Emma fed him, clean up the apartment and leave. Now he realized there was no way he could leave her on her own.

In a detached fashion another part of his brain registered her body. Her belly was still slightly rounded from childbirth, her breasts were full and the nipples bright red. Even postpartum she was sexy. Ordinarily he would feel lust seeing her fresh from the shower without a stitch on. But with her in this state it was wrong, like lusting after someone not capable of rational thought.

He averted his gaze. Even looking at her was wrong because he was doing so without her informed consent. Instead he concentrated on Billy, holding him firmly in one hand while he cleaned him with a soapy cloth, gently getting in between the crevices and folds.

"You'd better dry off and put some clothes on," he said. "Then get ready to feed him. He feels hot."

"I have no milk."

Darcy glanced over his shoulder again. She'd made no move to dress. "What have you been feeding him?"

"I have a trickle. And I'm supplementing with formula." She cupped her breasts, wincing when she touched her cracked nipples. "He won't latch on properly so the milk hasn't come in the way it should."

Darcy pulled the baby from the water and looked around for a towel. "Pass me a towel? And put something on, for heaven's sake."

She pulled her dressing gown on over her still-wet body. "I'll see if I can find a clean towel in the hall." Off she went as if everyone kept their clean linen on the hall carpet.

Meanwhile Billy was shivering and whimpering. Darcy couldn't wrap him back up in the dirty towel. Poor little sod. He unbuttoned his shirt and tucked the wet baby inside next to his bare skin, pulling the shirt over his back as far as he could. Billy stopped wriggling. He stopped crying. He snuggled in as if he belonged there.

Oh, man. Darcy could feel a tiny heart beating next to his. He glimpsed himself in the foggy mirror, a frazzled-looking man with a huge lump in his chest. And he didn't mean the baby.

EMMA SIFTED THROUGH the piles of clothes for a clean towel. She really ought to tidy up a little. But hey, it wasn't like Darcy had never left a dirty mug on the coffee table. She held a towel to her nose but her sinuses were too blocked to tell if it was clean or dirty.

She picked her way across the living room and drew the curtains to hold the towel up to the window. She was surprised to see daylight. What time was it? The clock on the TV read seven o'clock. Was that morning or evening?

Had she dreamed that moment in the bathroom when she'd stepped out of the shower naked in front of Darcy? Had that really happened? Maybe she'd imagined it. The past few days had been a blur. Once, she'd woken in the dark, delirious with fever, and thought she'd seen hundreds of dwarves in medieval tunics marching off to the mines with pickaxes over their shoulders.

Maybe she'd hallucinated Darcy, too. She listened. She could hear him in the bathroom, clearing his throat. Thank God. She hadn't gone completely off her rocker. But now she cringed to think he'd seen her postbaby flabby stomach, stretch marks and heavy breasts.

Forget about her appearance, it was her emotional state she was worried about. She had to hold it together. She couldn't let Darcy know how close she was to losing control. There must be no repeat of her earlier outburst. Cool and calm and organized, that's what everyone said about her. And she was, really she was. This— She glanced around the room as if seeing it for the first time, and was horrified. This wasn't like her.

At least Billy was quiet for once. When he cried and cried and cried her brain short-circuited, and she couldn't think. The cold/flu/bronchitis—whatever it was she had—made her head ache like it was going to explode.

"Did you find a towel?" Darcy stood in the doorway, his shirt half-open revealing olive skin flecked with dark hair. For a moment she couldn't figure out what the bulge in his shirt was. Then she saw it move and whimper. A fleeting revulsion made her look away.

Billy was her baby, the child she'd wanted so badly she'd basically sacrificed her marriage to have. She didn't love him. She wanted to, and Lord knows, she'd tried. Sasha, who knew all about maternity matters, had told her that sometimes it took time, that once he was nursing well, the love would fall into place.

What about women who didn't nurse, who fed their babies formula from the beginning either because they couldn't, or didn't want to, nurse? They still loved their babies and bonded with them. What was wrong with her? Billy was a squalling bundle of noise who was driving her insane. Oh, she took care of him, made sure he was fed and clean—or at least she had before she got so sick—but the horrifying truth was staring her in the face—she was an unnatural mother. What kind of woman didn't love her own child?

"Here." She thrust the towel at Darcy, hoping he wouldn't expect her to take the baby.

"You need to dry off yourself." He pushed aside the clutter on the couch and sat with the towel spread over his lap. Then he gently extricated the baby from inside his shirt and laid him on the towel.

Emma curled up in a chair by the window and watched, winding a piece of wet hair around and around her finger. This was the first time Darcy had handled Billy. Even though he was awkward, how could he not want to be a father? What chance did her poor baby have with a mother who couldn't, and a father who wouldn't, love him?

Darcy had found a clean diaper and was trying to put it on Billy. Not surprisingly, he was doing it wrong. She could count on one hand the number of times he'd changed Holly's diaper.

"You've got it backward." Emma covered her mouth to hide a smile. There was nothing funny about it except that Darcy looked sweet, his forehead furrowed in concentration, his big hands surprisingly gentle.

Darcy glanced up, flushed and scowling. "Maybe you'd like to do it. Make sure it's done right."

"No, no, you're doing fine." Her hands went up as if warding off the child. She noticed and dropped them back in her lap where they twisted themselves into knots. "The tabs wrap toward the front, is all."

He eyed her narrowly for another moment then flipped the diaper around. Then he turned his attention to the clean sleeper. As he tried to stuff a foot inside, Billy snapped awake. He glanced up at Darcy and started crying.

"He's hungry." Emma instinctively wrapped her dressing gown tighter around her. She wanted to nurse him but her nipples were sore and bleeding. Every time he latched on, the pain made her tense up and her milk wouldn't let down.

Darcy abandoned the sleeper and wrapped the towel around the baby. He started to rise. "I'll bring him to you—"

"No." Emma shrank away. Seeing the shock in Darcy's eyes, she quickly made excuses. "I have germs. It wouldn't be good for Billy."

"I meant you could hold him while I get a bottle ready." Darcy's frown deepened as he studied her.

"Oh. Okay. I could do that." Emma reached for Billy and laid him across her lap. She felt no desire to comfort him. She wasn't capable of giving comfort. Once Darcy got the bottle he would probably leave again. What could she do to make him stay? She was afraid for Billy's sake. But she couldn't tell Darcy how she felt. He would be so angry. He'd told her having a baby was a mistake.

He hadn't wanted it and now he'd been proven right. He would hate her and resent Billy....

Tears leaked from her eyes and dripped onto her baby. His wriggling had loosened the towel and his bare legs kicked free. Suddenly she realized how cold it was in the apartment. She was shivering herself but that could just be her cold. If only she could go to bed and all this—the baby, the apartment, her solitary life—would go away and she would wake up in her old house, wrapped in Darcy's arms and Holly sleeping down the hall....

The tears flowed faster. She was so weak. When had she become so weak?

She looked at Darcy and pleaded silently, *Please don't leave me alone with this baby. I might do something terrible. I might* not *do something and that could also turn out to be terrible.* Darcy looked so stern, so angry, as if he was disgusted with her for screwing up their lives and being such a miserable mother.

"Emma, can you hear me?" He had a hand on her shoulder and was gently shaking her. "Do you have formula?"

"What? Oh, in the cupboard to the right of the stove."

"Once he's fed we're leaving."

"What? Who's leaving? No! Where to?" The words came out in a squawk and she put a hand to her sore throat. Was he taking Billy away from her? She was a mess, but she wasn't giving up on her baby. Her brain was too muddled to make sense of what was going on.

"I'm taking you and Billy to my place." He swore under his breath. "God knows how I'm going to look after you both, but I'll figure it out."

"No, Darcy." She rallied the last crumb of her strength and dignity to protest. "Thank you for bathing Billy. I can take it from here. You don't owe me anything."

"I'm not walking away from you when you're this sick. Maybe you should even be in the hospital. When we get you to my apartment I'll get Dr. Maxwell to check you out." He cupped her cheek in his warm palm, his fingertips slightly raspy, and his voice was low and rumbling. So gentle she could weep. "Don't worry, Em. Everything's going to be all right."

Emma closed her eyes. She wanted to believe him so badly. And for the moment she did. He'd saved Billy from her. Thanks to him, their baby was going to be all right.

Darcy went into the kitchen to hunt for formula. She was beyond caring whether a clean sterilized bottle was on hand. Normally she wasn't the sort of woman who relied on a man. But just this one time she would let Darcy sort it out.

CHAPTER NINE

DARCY BUMBLED HIS way through sterilizing the bottle in the microwave and preparing the formula. Luckily the unit was sitting on the counter with the instructions written on the lid. No doubt Emma could do it in a fraction of the time, but for once she was biting her tongue. She probably didn't mean to make him feel inadequate around children, but her sheer competence was hard to measure up to.

In the living room, Billy was fussing. Darcy hurried. He didn't think it was a good idea to leave him with Emma for too long. He tipped a measured amount of formula powder into the bottle and mixed it in with the boiled water. Even he knew that was going to be too hot. But how did he test the temperature—with his elbow again? No, the wrist, stupid. He splashed a few drops onto the inside of his wrist. Way too hot. With ice from the freezer he made an ice bath and plunged in the bottle.

Then he went to get Billy. He stopped short.

Emma's eyes were closed, her head resting against the high back of the chair. Her limbs were loose, but even in sleep her hands curled protectively around Billy, tightening reflexively when the baby squirmed too much. She might be sick and behaving oddly, but she was instinctively a good mother.

"Come here, little mate." Darcy carefully eased the baby off Emma's lap. Her fingers fluttered, grasping the air, and she moaned in her sleep. With his free hand he captured hers and laid them back in her lap.

Darcy sat on the couch with Billy tucked in the crook of his elbow. He was still crying fitfully. If Emma could sleep through that, she was even more exhausted than he'd thought. Right up until this moment he'd actually hoped she would wake up and feed the baby. Now he knew that was wishful thinking.

He tilted the bottle over his inner wrist to double-check. The drops that fell on his skin were pleasantly warm. "Right. Here goes. Insert nipple A into mouth B."

Gingerly he touched the bottle to Billy's tongue. Instantly Billy stopped crying and started sucking urgently. "Whoa, steady on, little guy. No one's taking this away from you. If you eat at that rate, you'll give yourself gas."

With the baby nursing in his arms and Emma asleep in the chair, silence settled on the apartment. Dusk darkened the room. Darcy leaned over and switched on the table lamp. In the glow, Billy's tear-filled eyes gazed up at him reproachfully as if to say, *It took you long enough to get here.*

With a fingertip Darcy wiped away the moisture from his hot cheek. "I know, buddy. But I'm here now."

He gazed at his infant son and his chest bloomed with a nameless ache. Was that love? Surely that was impossible. How could he feel an instant bond with a baby he didn't even want? But it brought home to him how much joy had gone out of his life. First Holly, then Emma.

Billy stopped sucking. His eyes closed briefly and his chest heaved with a gusty sigh. Then he opened his eyes again and resumed feeding. He gazed up at Darcy sleepily, his eyelids heavy. Trusting. Darcy held out a baby finger and Billy casually wrapped his tiny fingers around it and hung on. Darcy's vision blurred.

"Just don't get used to me being around long-term because that's no part of your mother's plan."

EMMA WOKE UP in her marriage bed. Wonderingly, she smoothed her fingers over the handmade coverlet of muted greens traced with dark red she and Darcy had chosen together from a market stall in Mornington.

Just for a moment she wanted to believe the past couple of years were nothing more than a horrible dream. She closed her eyes, picturing Darcy in the kitchen making coffee and Holly softly babbling to herself in her room down the hall. In a moment she would get up, pick Holly out of her cot and head to the kitchen for breakfast. Outside, a warm spring sun would be shining and the sliding doors open onto the deck where bees were busy in the flowering shrubs. Darcy would kiss her and tell her that instead of watching the grand final football game with the guys he would rather go on a picnic with her and Holly—

The baby cried.

The dream evaporated.

Her eyes opened. The pillow next to hers was plump and empty, the other side of the bed not slept in. The furnishings were familiar, but the room itself, white walls and dark wood trim, she'd never seen before.

Where was she? Through the window she could see a huge gum tree and the flat roofs of buildings. Oh, right. Darcy's apartment over the pub. He must have brought them here. Muted sounds drifted up through the heating vents, the clink of beer glasses being stacked, the quiet murmur of conversation, the TV.

The nightmare of reality came flooding back. Her fever, Billy's colic, her unfinished term paper...

Billy was crying in the room next to hers. She had to get up. Somehow she had to find the strength and the will to nurse him. She pushed the coverlet back and swung her legs over the side of the bed. Her head spun as she weakly pushed herself to a sitting position. Her thin camisole was damp with perspiration and her pulse was racing. Every joint and muscle ached.

Darcy had been amazing yesterday—was it yesterday?—bathing Billy and feeding him. She never would have thought Darcy capable of such—well, she couldn't call it competence, but he'd managed, somehow, and done so with surprising tenderness. No, she wouldn't have thought that possible given he didn't want anything to do with Billy. Yet in a crisis he'd stepped up.

Billy's cries became louder, more insistent.

Today would be different. She couldn't rely on Darcy to keep on taking care of Billy. He needed to be downstairs in the pub, tending to his customers. The pub would be his first priority, as always.

"I'm coming, Billy." Stifling a groan, she slowly pushed herself off the bed and stood, swaying dizzily. She tried to take a step, stumbled against the nightstand and fell onto the bed. Head bowed, knees on elbows, she tried to gather the strength for another attempt.

Miraculously, the crying stopped.

Huh? Billy *never* stopped once he'd started, not until he was picked up and fed. Sometimes not even then.

Something must be wrong. Maybe he'd fallen, though she hadn't heard a thump. Where had Darcy put him to bed? Oh, God, maybe he'd choked. Maybe—

The door opened. Darcy had Billy in his arms and was feeding him from a bottle. "How are you feeling?"

"Okay." She was so startled to see Darcy with the baby she hardly knew what she was saying. Penetrating the fog of her illness was a sharp stab of joy at seeing Darcy holding his son. Never in a million years would she have chosen to get this sick, but maybe her illness would have a silver lining.

"Can you manage him for a while?" Darcy said. "It's lunchtime and Kirsty hasn't come in yet."

She nodded and climbed beneath the covers. He walked over and laid Billy in her arms, taking a moment to adjust him properly. With his head bent close, she could see the tiny whirls of dark hair on the back of his neck.

She shouldn't notice such things about Darcy. It only made it harder that they weren't together. Dropping her head weakly on the pillow, she turned to the baby in her arms. "Hey, little guy."

"Here, let me help you sit up." Darcy stacked another pillow behind her shoulders and brought over a couple of cushions lying on a chair to support the arm that held the baby. "Better?"

"Much, thank you." She looked into his dark eyes. With his face close to hers, the look that passed between them felt intimate. Mother, father, baby. Man and woman. Familial images were mixed up with sexual feelings—all emotions she wasn't supposed to be having.

Quickly she gazed at Billy, sucking noisily on the bottle. Her breasts felt heavy and her nipples tightened with a prickling sensation. If Darcy hadn't been there she would have tried to nurse, but she felt shy in front of him. Not so much about baring her breasts but baring her inadequacy as a mother if Billy refused to latch on. "I don't know what I'd have done if you hadn't come by last night."

"Last night?" Darcy perched on the foot of the bed. "I brought you and Billy here two nights ago."

She stared, mentally calculating. "I've been asleep for nearly thirty-six hours?"

"You weren't asleep the whole time. Some of it you were awake but delirious."

"Oh, my God. I don't remember a thing. It's no wonder—" She broke off. She'd been about to say, "No wonder I feel so weak."

As wonderful as it was to be taken care of, she couldn't stay here. She was under no illusion that just because Darcy had stepped up when she was too sick to care for herself, let alone Billy, that he wanted her and the baby in his life. No doubt he couldn't wait till she was well enough to go home and he wouldn't have to be bothered heating up bottles and mopping her fevered brow.

"No wonder I have no idea what day it is." And that meant she'd lost another precious day when she should have been working on her term paper.

"I called Alana and uh…told her…where you were." Darcy was looking at her chest. "Do you want a cloth?"

Emma glanced down. Oh, dear. Even with her low milk production, two days without nursing had left her breasts full. Now they'd let down and the leaked milk rendered her white camisole transparent, revealing her swollen nipples. Her cheeks flamed with embarrassment.

She glanced at Darcy and was surprised to catch his gaze flare with heat. Her nipples tingled, releasing more milk. The transparency spread, exposing the whole of her breasts. Darcy didn't move a muscle but his pupils widened, making his eyes even blacker. She was anchored by the baby, unable to deal with the sexual undercurrent and too weak to even tug the sheet up to her armpits. "A cloth is probably a good idea."

Darcy strode out of the room. A minute later he pressed a clean white terry cloth in her hand. "It's a bar towel but you know, kind of appropriate."

For mopping up spilled drinks. Smiling, she tucked the towel over her wet camisole. "Thanks. Go, tend your bar."

"When Kirsty gets in I'll bring you something to eat. You should drink some water in the meantime." He nodded at the glass on the bedside table he must have put there earlier.

"You don't have to wait on me." He cocked an eyebrow and she lowered her gaze. It was patently obvious that she couldn't help herself.

He pressed the back of his hand against her forehead, his fingers as cool as water. "You're still hot, and I can hear your chest rasping every time you breathe. Sienna Maxwell's coming over on her lunch break. She came the first day and prescribed antibiotics. She wants to see how you're doing now."

Emma began to protest that she didn't need a doctor but Darcy shook his head. She knew she had a tendency to ignore minor illnesses on the assumption she was fundamentally healthy and would get better on her own. Clearly that strategy hadn't worked this time. And Billy should be checked, even though he appeared better than two days ago.

"Okay." She eyed Darcy curiously. "Did you look after Billy all by yourself for two whole days?"

"My sister helped. In fact, she did most of the caring. She had a couple days off so she slept on a cot in the baby's room while I took the couch. She just left a few minutes ago, had to go to work."

"I see." He left the room and Emma lay back on the pillow. It was foolish to feel disappointed. Darcy had never claimed to be good with babies. Playing with them, yes, but he avoided the hands-on work. For a few minutes she'd begun to hope he'd started to bond with Billy. God knows, her poor child needed someone. She knew that on some level she loved Billy. Where was the warm, fuzzy feeling she was supposed to feel when she held her baby?

A tiny frown creased Billy's brow as he concentrated on sucking. He seemed to glare at her above the bottle as if to say, *You're a nurse. You should have known better than to get so sick and not ask for help.*

She was still bone-tired and weak as a kitten. Emma reached for the water and drank thirstily. Next to the glass was her phone. She checked for messages. There were a dozen or so awaiting her attention. In a little while she would call Alana, but at the moment she didn't feel up to talking to anyone, not even her sister.

She could still feel Darcy's touch on her forehead. Had she imagined his fingers lingering in a brief caress? Darcy might be helping her and Billy, but only because he was a good, kind, generous man who couldn't bear to see anyone suffering. It didn't mean he would fall in love with her again. Or with their son. She knew how good Darcy was at guarding his heart.

She adjusted Billy more comfortably in her arms and pushed the blanket back from his face so it didn't get in his way. Then she closed her eyes. A few moments' rest…

She must have slept because the next thing she knew,

Darcy knocked on the bedroom door then eased it open. "Emma, Sienna's here."

"Come in." Billy was sleeping still, snuggled into her arm. She and he must look the picture of a perfect mother and baby. Only she knew how false that was.

Dr. Sienna Maxwell entered and placed her black bag on a chair. She removed her navy suit jacket, revealing a crisp white blouse tucked into a navy skirt. Her mass of red curly hair was pulled back into a ponytail.

"I'll leave you to it," Darcy said.

"Can you wait until I've examined Billy and then you can take him with you?" Sienna said.

"Sure." Darcy sat on a chair in the corner, his hands linked between his knees.

Sienna opened her black bag and got out her stethoscope and blood pressure cuff. She perched on the edge of the bed. "Hey, Emma. Let's have a look at this little man and see what he's fussing about. Then we'll check you out. You're looking better than you did the other day."

Emma relinquished her hold on Billy. "He always fusses. Mostly at night when he's colicky. But with this cold he's even worse."

Sienna undid a few snaps on his sleeper, inserted a thermometer beneath his armpit and held his arm in place while she listened to his chest. Billy woke up and immediately began to fuss. Sienna checked the temperature then turned him over and listened to his back. She shone a penlight into his eyes, passed her fingers gently over his fontanel and peered down his throat.

Sienna hung her stethoscope around her neck. "He's congested and a bit dehydrated, but his temperature is down. It is just a cold and not a secondary infection."

"That's good."

"Keep up his fluids, supplementing breast milk or formula with cooled boiled water with a solution to replenish his electrolytes." She wiped the baby thermometer and put it away in its case. Then she strapped the blood pressure cuff onto Emma's arm. "Darcy said you were having trouble nursing him. How's your milk supply?"

"Not great. And now with this cold I'm afraid it's drying up."

"Cold?" Sienna shook her head. "You have pneumonia. Get some rest, give the antibiotics another day or two to kick in fully and your milk will likely come back. Sometimes these things resolve themselves with time. Is there anything else you wanted to ask about with regard to Billy?"

Emma hesitated. She hadn't told anyone she hadn't bonded with Billy. She especially didn't want to say anything in front of Darcy. Being a mum was such a big part of who she was that not to be able to bond with her son was...well, it simply wasn't her.

Sienna noticed her hesitation. She took Billy from Emma's arms and held him up to Darcy. "I think your son needs a change, Daddy."

When Darcy had left the room, Sienna asked gently, "Now, what's troubling you?"

"I don't feel anything for my baby. I don't love him." Emma's words gushed out, along with a few tears. "We haven't bonded. I don't know what to do. I think if I could nurse him it would help but since I have to supplement my breast milk with a bottle..." Her voice wobbled. "I feel like such a failure."

Sienna laid a hand on her arm. "You must know that sometimes mothers don't bond with their infant right away. It's not your fault."

"I know." But she didn't know. There was no certainty in her at all. She was terrified. As a doting mother she hadn't been able to keep Holly safe. If she didn't love Billy the way she was supposed to, what chance did he have? "What if I never love my child?"

Sienna unstrapped the cuff and smiled gently. "That's not even remotely possible. Don't be so hard on yourself."

"I don't feel anything for him." Tears welled and she blinked them back. "Nothing."

"You're sick and run-down. Darcy told me you've been working as well as studying. And also raising Billy on your own. That's a lot of pressure right there, let alone trying to bond with a difficult baby."

Emma was silent. Everything Sienna said made sense, but she was sure there was more to it than that.

"Did you want this baby?" Sienna asked.

"I did. I *do*," Emma insisted. "But now that he's here… Maybe I blame him for my marriage falling apart. Not *him* because my marriage failed long before he was conceived. But my wanting him. But then it's not his fault. It's mine. Oh, it's all so confusing."

Sienna put a hand on hers and gave it a comforting squeeze. "My son Oliver is fifteen now and I love him more than life. But when he first came along, I resented him. He wasn't planned and I made the mistake of marrying his father because I thought it was the right thing to do. It took years for me and my ex-husband to realize our mistake." She smiled cheerfully. "Luckily it took a lot less time for me to bond with Oliver."

"How long?" Sienna asked, sniffing.

"I can't really remember. I was in med school at the time. A few months at least."

"I wanted Billy. I knew I was raising him on my own."

"You don't need to make sense of your feelings right now. Your first task is to get well. Your body is telling you to slow down. I recommend you take some time off. Rest and recover. Once you're feeling better your milk will come in. And if it doesn't, that's not the end of the world. Babies survive on formula."

"And the bonding?" Emma sniffed.

"With time, you will more than likely feel love for your baby. And if you don't, a qualified counselor can help. The important thing is not to give up."

"Oh, I won't ever give up." How could she when Billy depended on her? "Thanks, Sienna."

She felt better having spoken her fears aloud. Sienna's calm, practical manner put her problems in perspective and made them manageable. Get better. Then sort out her emotions. She and Billy were going to be okay. She had to believe that. She *did* believe it.

DARCY CARRIED BILLY into the second bedroom where he'd set up the cot and changing table. He placed Billy on the table but the baby wriggled, and he didn't feel comfortable with him up so high. So he moved the changing pad to the floor and knelt beside him.

He'd felt like a fraud when Sienna called him *Daddy*. That was going to change from now on—whether Emma liked it or not. It was clear to him that he needed to be around for backup in case something happened to her. She was right, money wasn't enough. Whether *he* liked it or not, he *had* to be hands-on.

Speaking of hands-on, how the hell was a guy supposed to change a diaper when the kid was wriggling and squirming? "Hold still, mate."

Why was his baby's name so hard for him to say? He'd seen a documentary years ago about India. In some parts of the country infant mortality was so high people didn't name their babies until they were six months old in case the child didn't survive. Was that what he was doing by not calling Billy by his name—subconsciously preparing himself for the worst?

Darcy didn't want to be morbid—it wasn't his nature. But Holly's death had shaken his belief that nothing truly terrible would ever happen to him, or anyone he loved. The belief wasn't logical, but it was how most people lived, by trusting they would survive.

Billy gazed at him, vulnerable and yet so trusting. He couldn't protect himself, and his mother was temporarily out of action. He was relying on Darcy. It was a huge responsibility, one Darcy had never really taken up with Holly. Suddenly he realized how important parents were to their children. How important Emma had been for Holly, doing everything for her, making sure she survived and thrived.

"Billy. Hi, there. It's me..." He swallowed. "Daddy."

Miraculously, the baby stopped squirming, looked at him and smiled. Darcy stilled, and for a moment he simply held his son's gaze. Then Billy kicked his legs. Darcy cleared his throat. "Don't get too used to this, buddy. Me taking care of you is only temporary. Now hold still. I'm going to change your diaper."

Step one, remove the sleeper. He undid the snaps and pulled the baby's legs out, then his arms and set the clothing aside. Step two, remove the diaper. Darcy held his breath and peeled back the tabs. Okay, this was a full load. "Bear with me, Billy. I know I changed you once, but that doesn't make me an expert."

He hadn't realized until Billy had come to live with

him, and Emma wasn't taking care of him, exactly how absent he'd been for Holly. After she'd rolled off the change table he'd been extra nervous around her. Emma had never again asked him to do a thing for Holly. Even though Holly hadn't been injured, Emma had quietly and competently done it all herself.

She hadn't trusted him. The conclusion was inescapable. He hadn't realized until now how angry and useless that had made him feel. Not that he'd expressed that anger or tried to assert himself. He didn't trust himself with a baby, either. Emma was a nurse, after all. She knew better than he did about these things.

Well, he was learning now. And she didn't have any choice but to trust him.

Step three, clean the critter off. Darcy grabbed a dozen or so wet wipes and swabbed the decks. He eyed the nether regions for signs he'd missed anything. Nope, that should be good enough for now. Later he would give him a bath. That, he was an expert on.

Billy smiled and made a gurgling noise. With only his undershirt on, his bottom was bare. He kicked his feet in the air. Darcy couldn't help but laugh. "You like that fresh air and freedom, don't you, kid? Does it feel good getting those wet pants off?"

He glanced around. Sienna was still in the next room with Emma. No one was about. He leaned over and blew a raspberry on Billy's stomach. It made a big fat farting noise, the kind that appealed to guys like him and Billy.

Billy kicked harder. He laughed out loud. Darcy blew another raspberry on his tummy. There was no doubt he was enjoying playtime as much as Darcy. "You want another one? Do you, Billy? Here we go. I'm coming to get you…." He brought his face closer. "One." Closer… "Two." And closer… "Three—"

A spray of pee hit him in the cheek. "What the— Ew!" Billy giggled merrily, spraying Darcy, the bedspread and the wall. "Think you're pretty smart, don't you?" Darcy blindly reached for a towel or a fresh diaper.

A towel was thrust into his hand. "Is this what you're looking for?" Sienna asked, amused.

"Thanks. Little bugger got me good." Darcy wiped himself off.

"I'll finish changing Billy if you want to go clean up." Sienna moved into his place next to the table. "Then we can talk about Emma."

"Thanks." Darcy went next door to the bathroom. He ripped off his shirt and sluiced water over his face and upper body. *Talk about Emma.* That sounded ominous. How sick was she? What if it was serious? His hands stilled, water dripping from his hair and face. For a fractured moment he didn't recognize himself. Who would he be without Emma in the world?

Then he shook the water from his eyes, blinked and reached for a dry towel. One minute he had only himself and his pub to worry about. Now Emma was lying sick in his bed, and a son he hadn't wanted was under his direct care. His life had been turned upside down. But, strange as it seemed, he wouldn't have it any other way. At least when they were both under his roof he could look after them.

He tiptoed into his room to get a clean shirt from the closet. Emma was asleep, her cheeks flushed but the rest of her skin pale against the vivid red of her hair. A lock had fallen over her eye. Softly he smoothed it away and felt the unnatural heat coming off her skin. The niggle of worry he carried for her intensified. Her lips were slightly parted and each breath she took in through her mouth rasped softly.

He went out and closed the door quietly. Next door, Sienna had Billy dressed in another one-piece sleeper of mint-green. When he saw Darcy his arms pumped up and down. Without hesitation, Darcy reached for him. "Let's go into the living room."

The window looked out over the soccer field, empty today. How long ago that day seemed when he watched the boys playing and felt the pain of his decision not to be a participating father. Funny how things worked out.

He and Sienna settled opposite each other on the red leather couches. "How bad is she?"

"She has viral pneumonia with a secondary bacterial infection," Sienna said. "The sputum and blood samples I collected at my first visit confirm that diagnosis. Make sure she takes the full course of antibiotics. She needs complete bed rest for at least a week, though knowing Emma I suspect she'll be up and about earlier. She should have sought treatment sooner."

"I thought so," Darcy said. "From what I gather she's been working too hard and not taking care of herself."

"From what you gather?" Sienna repeated delicately. "I know you and Emma aren't married anymore, and you have your own lives. But surely through your contact with Billy you would have seen her condition deteriorate."

"It slipped past me." To his relief, Billy began to cry, derailing the conversation. He was ashamed of not being a father to his son, even though Emma had wanted to raise the child on her own. He'd been *glad* she'd pushed him out of the baby's life. But no way did he feel comfortable confessing that to Sienna.

Billy continued to cry. What was wrong with this

kid? He'd been fed and changed. Darcy jiggled Billy on his knee, hoping to distract him from whatever was bugging him. The baby only cried harder. Great, now what? Jiggling was his only strategy. He glanced at Sienna who was discreetly looking at her watch, probably thinking about getting to the clinic. In a minute she would go, leaving him all alone with a crying baby.

Darcy got to his feet and began to pace. "Do you have any idea what's wrong with him?"

"He probably needs to burp."

"Ah, of course." Darcy eyed her desperately. "And what do I do for that?"

"Put him against your shoulder and pat his back. Or lay him across your knee—" She broke off at his awkward movements. "You haven't cared for him much, have you?"

Darcy fumbled the howling baby into place against his shoulder. "I—I'm busy with the pub."

"If you're that busy, then I strongly recommend Emma go into the hospital where she'll get total rest and proper care."

"What about Billy?"

"He would go in with her. The nurses would look after him."

Here was his out if he wanted it, with no shame involved. Darcy walked the floor, patting Billy lightly on the back while he cried. He knew and trusted Emma's nursing friends, but he didn't like the idea of his son being in the hands of strangers with Emma not able to keep an eye on him. "Which nurses?"

Sienna shrugged. "Whoever's on duty. All are more than capable. You don't need to worry."

Billy continued to fuss. No doubt any one of those nurses was more capable than he was. "Would Emma recover if she stays here or does she require hospital-ization?"

"The hospital isn't essential. I only suggested it to make it easier to care for Billy. Providing Emma's comfortable and is allowed to rest, she'll be fine."

Darcy paced some more while the baby cried in his ear. No one would blame him if he followed the doctor's recommendation and let Emma and the baby get professional care. Or, he could send Emma to the hospital and keep Billy. However, he knew she wanted to nurse the baby. She couldn't do that as effectively if they were miles apart—even if Darcy was prepared to ferry pumped milk back and forth several times a day. And even if Emma couldn't care for Billy, she would want to stay close to him.

"Emma and Billy will stay here with me." He spoke loudly to be heard over the sound of Billy's crying.

"Are you sure?" Sienna said. "The antibiotics appear to have kicked in, but Emma's not going to be much help for a few days."

No, he wasn't sure. In fact, he was terrified at the thought of being in sole charge of Billy. And running a pub. And organizing renovations. What if he ended up like Emma, sick in bed?

She would nurse him back to health. He knew that as surely as he knew his own name. She would do it for him.

"I can manage. Piece of cake." Just then Billy gave a loud burp and abruptly stopped crying. Darcy felt the tension drain from his shoulders. "Thanks for the vote of confidence, mate. I hope I'm worthy."

CHAPTER TEN

"ALANA'S HERE," Darcy said from the bedroom doorway later that same afternoon. "Are you well enough for visitors?"

Emma blinked awake from a light doze. Then stared. It looked as if Darcy had Billy strapped to his chest in a baby carrier. First feeding him, now carrying him around. Was she hallucinating?

"I'm not a visitor. I'm family." Alana, all five feet of her, ducked beneath Darcy's arm.

Before Emma could decide if she was in her right mind, Darcy left the room.

"Hey, sweetie, how are you?" Alana waved a hand in front of her face. "Are you with me?"

Emma struggled to sit up. "Better. Still a bit weak. Was Darcy carrying Billy in a sling?"

"Yeah, wild, eh? Who would have thought he knew how." Alana sat on the bed wearing her gym gear, a cropped sports top and Lycra three-quarter-length pants. Her feet, shod in new trainers, dangled off the side of the bed. "I would have been around before this, but your gatekeeper barred all visitors till now."

"Darcy?"

"Who else? I can't stay long. I've got to teach a pump class in twenty minutes."

"How's the job working out?"

"Fantastic. Janet's back so I'm off managerial duty

but I've graduated to teaching five classes a week. Brett's talking about a possible sixth."

A U2 ring tone sounded. "That's mine." Emma glanced around. "Where is it?"

Alana fished the phone out from behind a box of tissues on the side table, glancing at caller ID. "It's Dave. He rang me a few minutes ago but I was driving and couldn't take it. Why would he be calling you?"

Emma took the phone. "Hey, Dave."

"Is Alana with you?" Dave's normally mild-mannered voice held an edge. "I just called the gym. Tessa's there but she's not. And she's not answering her phone."

"She's—" Emma began.

Alana frantically waved her hands in Emma's face, mouthing, "No."

"She's up to something behind my back, isn't she?" Dave said.

"I think you should talk to her—"

"I would but she's never home. She said she wanted to go to the gym to get her figure back. I thought, great, she'll feel better and be healthier for when she gets pregnant again. So I didn't mind that she was spending all her time there. Now she looks amazing but she never wants to have sex. *Why is that?*"

"Uh, Dave, I'm not comfortable with this conversation." Emma glared at Alana, who was pacing the floor and chewing on her thumbnail.

"She's having an affair, isn't she?" Dave was building up a head of steam. "She's stashing Tessa at the gym's child care center while she has her fling."

"No, Dave, she's not having an affair."

Alana stopped pacing, eyes wide. She looked sick.

"Then where is she?" Dave roared.

"Right here." Emma handed Alana the phone. "Talk to him." She sank into the pillow.

"Hey, baby," Alana said sweetly. "I just stopped in to see Emma before I went to the gym." She paused to listen. When she spoke again, her voice hardened. "I'm not making excuses. I didn't bring Tessa here because I didn't want her to be exposed to Emma's germs. No, I'm not having an affair—"

Dave's angry tone, if not his precise words, came through the phone loud and clear. Emma shut her eyes, wishing she wasn't privy to her sister's marital spat.

"If you must know, I'm working at the gym," Alana snapped. "That's right. As a fitness instructor. I don't care if that means I won't get pregnant. I don't want another baby. So there." She hung up.

"That answers my question of whether you'd told him or not," Emma said. "Why'd you leave it so long? You've made things worse."

"I didn't want to say anything until my probation period was up and I'm hired on permanently."

"That's what, three months? Oh, Alana." She shook her head. "At least now it's out in the open. You two can start talking about the issues."

"There's nothing to talk about." Alana resumed her pacing, her ponytail swinging. "He's adamant he wants more kids. I'm equally adamant I don't."

"Tell him you need more time. Find a compromise. You could work for six months and then try for a baby."

"Time won't make any difference. This has been going on for over a year. Maybe we should just call it quits."

"You're risking your marriage for a job? I can't believe that. You can work for the rest of your life, but you're getting close to an age when you won't be able to have more children."

Alana stopped pacing and sat on the end of the bed. "You don't understand, either. I love Tessa with all my heart and soul, but frankly, I've had enough of being at home with a small child. The career thing has a clock on it, too. I'm a fitness instructor. I can't stay out of the workforce too long or I'll be so old that no one will hire me. And if I can't get a toehold in a gym then there's no hope of moving up the ladder to a management job like the one I was doing to cover for Janet."

"You always wanted three children, just like me." She'd been counting on Billy having a little cousin playmate. Not quite twin cousins, but close enough.

"I've changed my mind." Alana fidgeted as though gathering her thoughts. "Tessa's finally getting to an easier stage. She's toilet trained and she'll be going to kindergarten next year. I'm starting to have a life again. To start over with the whole infant thing—the diapers, being up all night and tired all day... Seeing what you're going through with Billy confirmed everything I was thinking."

"I've had a tough time with Billy, but the newborn stage passes. And Dave helps out a lot, way more than Darcy." Although to give Darcy credit he was doing it all now.

"Dave helps when he's around, but he works long hours. Most days he comes home and Tessa's been fed, bathed and is ready for bed. His dinner is made, the house is clean and I'm starved for adult company but he's ready to veg in front of the TV. Reading a child a story before bed isn't the same as being with the kid 24/7."

"You could work part-time."

"Why do you think I lied to him about the job? He

doesn't even want me to do that. Child care eats up most of my salary so to his way of thinking, there's no point. Plus when I'm exercising hard my body weight is so lean I have trouble conceiving."

"Doesn't he understand that you need another outlet besides children?" Darcy had always been proud of her nursing career.

"The truth is, he doesn't see fitness instructor as a real job so he doesn't get why I want to go back to it. I could retrain but why should I when I like what I'm doing?" Alana traced the pattern on the quilt cover. "I know it's selfish, but I simply don't want to have another child when I'm virtually the sole caregiver."

"It's not selfish. Selfish would be having a child and then neglecting it." Selfish would be wanting Alana to have another baby only so Billy would have a playmate. "It sounds like your problems go deeper than work issues to how he sees you as a person."

Alana's eyes filled. "These past few years all I feel like is a mother to his children. We've lost the passion."

Emma was silent. She and Darcy had the passion but not the family life. Was it wrong to want it all? Or merely unrealistic?

Alana glanced at her watch. "I have to go or I'll be late for my class." She squeezed Emma's foot. "That's instead of kissing you and getting your germs. I'll let myself out. Call me later, okay?"

After she'd left, Darcy poked his head in the room. "Billy's asleep. Do you want dinner? It's soup."

"What, no peacocks' tongues and caviar?"

"That's for tomorrow. I can bring it in here, but if you're well enough to get up, it's probably easier to eat at the table."

"I'll get up. Three days in bed is long enough."

She was still weak, though, and grateful for Darcy's arm as he helped her out to the round wooden table in the corner of the kitchen. A sliding glass door let onto the rooftop balcony. Outside, the setting sun had turned the sky pink through the trees.

Darcy started to ladle out a bowl of chicken noodle soup for her when Billy started crying. Automatically, Emma began to rise.

"Stay and eat. I'll get him." Darcy set the steaming bowl before her and left the room. He returned a few minutes later with Billy in the baby carrier.

Darcy moved around the kitchen with Billy, getting himself a bowl of soup, cutting bread. There was something really attractive about a man with a baby. Was it because the baby made the man seem even bigger and stronger? Or was it more emotional, the security of knowing that the father of your child was taking care of both mother and child?

She wasn't under any illusion, though, that just because Darcy had cared for Billy for the past few days that he wanted to be in her son's life permanently. He'd stepped up because that's the kind of guy he was, but it wouldn't last. He was also the kind of guy who slipped away when he wasn't needed. Home and hearth weren't exciting enough for him.

Nor did him taking her in when she was sick mean he wanted to return to them having a relationship. Or that he was ever going to be the family man Emma wanted and needed. Alana didn't realize how good she had it.

"This soup is delicious. Did you make it?" After seeing Darcy with Billy she was ready to believe anything.

"I bought it from the deli. Cooking isn't high on my list of domestic skills. I miss your cooking." Darcy passed her the bread. "When you're feeling better do you think you could teach me to make your chicken curry?"

"I'll email you the recipe." He met that with silence and she mentally kicked herself. That wasn't what he asked. He didn't follow recipes well, learning better by doing. "Or I could show you."

Darcy smiled. "Showing me would be great."

She was surprised to find she already looked forward to being in the kitchen with him. The ties that bound them had long, long threads. She and Darcy were woven together in ways she'd taken for granted when they were married. How long would it take to sever every strand? And how bereft would she feel when that happened?

"You've surprised me, carrying Billy around in the sling," Emma said.

However, he had him facing out, the wrong way around for a baby of Billy's age. His neck wasn't strong enough. She bit her tongue, not wanting her first comment on his parenting to be a criticism.

"It's the only way to get him to stop crying. Isn't that right, mate?" He brushed Billy's head lightly, almost absently, ruffling his fluffy baby hair.

For days she'd been so sick she was barely aware of what was going on. Now that she was awake and feeling a bit better, she burned to ask if Billy had been fed on schedule, if Darcy used zinc ointment when he changed diapers and a million other questions.

It didn't seem right to start grilling him when he was clearly trying hard and when he'd done her a huge, huge favor. Darcy would take even well-meaning comments as criticism. He didn't understand she only wanted to impart helpful advice so that Billy was looked after properly. She had the knowledge and the experience from Holly's babyhood. Didn't it make sense for her to pass that on instead of Darcy having to reinvent the wheel, so to speak? Even so, she bit her tongue.

Darcy seemed to have bonded with Billy, if his affectionate asides to the baby were any indication. She was glad. That's what she'd wanted. But how had Darcy accomplished it so effortlessly when she, the mother, had struggled and failed?

She'd hoped Darcy would one day get to know Billy, but she'd envisaged him picking his son up on a Sunday afternoon and taking him fishing or to his parents' house so he could meet the other side of his family. Staying at his apartment, sharing cozy, intimate meals, while she was grateful, reminded her too sharply of the good times when they were married. And of all she'd lost.

"I appreciate you taking us in," she said as Darcy set a bowl on the table for himself and sat to eat. "It's a lot of extra work and you're not used to looking after— *What are you doing?*"

"Eating my soup?" Darcy carried a spoonful of hot soup from his bowl, directly over Billy's head to his mouth. "What's the matter?"

"You almost scalded the baby!" And then there were the bad times. So much for biting her tongue.

"I didn't spill a drop." He scooped up another spoonful.

Emma put her hand over her eyes. "I can't look." She was barely out of the sickbed and he was already driving her crazy. "Do you do this on purpose?"

"Do what?" There was the faintest edge to his voice.

"And while we're on the subject, he's too little to be carried that way. His neck can't support his head."

"He's fine. Look." Darcy moved his torso slowly from right to left. Billy's head swayed a little but didn't flop. He was holding it up all by himself.

"Well, I'll be damned." Emma put her spoon down. "When did that happen?"

"Two days ago. I was downstairs, tending bar. I had him facing me but he kept swiveling his head at noises, wanting to look around. I was worried he would hurt himself so I turned him around in the carrier. Once he could see what was going on he was much happier."

"You had him in the pub with you?" She pictured Darcy stooping below the bar for stuff, reaching high for mugs, carrying trays laden with glasses. A million possibilities for a baby to bang his head, have something fall in his eyes… She shuddered.

Holly's death had made her paranoid, but she didn't apologize for that. Her job in life was to keep this child safe. The more trouble she had connecting with him, the more determined she became.

"He loves the pub," Darcy said, totally not hearing the concern in her voice. "He must have been very close with his neck strength. I think being forced to hold it up himself has actually helped."

So now he was an expert, after caring for a baby for only a couple of days. "Still, it's not an appropriate atmosphere for a baby."

"He loves music, too. Watch what he can do." Darcy got up and moved away from the table.

Humming the tune of the Macarena and moving his hips and feet, he held Billy's hands and gently guided him in the movements of the dance. Emma clapped a hand over her mouth, sure that this would be too much for her tiny baby. But Billy went from looking bemused to smiling and kicking his dangling feet. He was clearly having fun, and Darcy was careful not to move his head too much. Darcy's smooth voice, perfect rhythm and sexy hips made him a pleasure to watch. Emma laughed, entranced and delighted. Darcy was a natural with Billy.

Darcy wound up the dance with a light bounce on his toes. "Hey, Macarena!"

Billy erupted in a tiny giggle and squirmed as if wanting more.

"Oh, my God, that was too much." Laughing, Emma pressed a hand to her chest. "You should be on *Funniest Home Videos*."

Darcy sat again, one of Billy's feet resting in each palm. "We could do that, upload a clip to YouTube. It'd be a hit."

"You are not putting our baby on YouTube." She put down her spoon and pushed her bowl away. "That was lovely, thank you. I hate to spoil the party, but Billy and I should get going if you wouldn't mind driving us home."

"No can do. Sienna said you needed to rest for at least a week. This is your first day out of bed. You might feel better but you're still weak. You don't want to have a relapse."

"I'm a nurse," she said in her most capable voice. "I know when I'm well enough to move."

"As a nurse, you should have known better than to let yourself get so sick. You should have sought help," he countered in the same reasonable tone.

"I…" He might have a small point there.

"And all your books and papers were spread out on your dining table. It looked as though you were working on something big."

"I do still have a term paper to write."

Darcy reached across the table and laid his hand over hers. The warmth in his fingers matched the warmth in his gaze. "All the more reason for you to stay here. You're not well enough yet to cope on your own."

If ever words should make her hackles stand up, those were the ones. Her whole life was predicated on her ability to cope. But the seeping warmth from his fingers was doing something subversive to her desire to stand on her own two feet. Being looked after was seductive. And that was dangerous.

When she was sick and unable to do more than lie in bed she hadn't thought of Darcy as a man. Now that she was starting to feel better, she was aware of him physically, of his shoulders and his mouth and his dark eyes that always seemed to be smiling at some inside joke.

And she was sleeping in their old bed, a place of a million memories of tenderness and passion. One night, in a moment of weakness and the loneliness that had never gone away, would she be tempted to invite him to share it with her? Just once, for old time's sake. Yeah, they'd seen how well that worked out on the cruise.

She tugged her hand out from under his and cool air wafted over her skin. "Thank you, Darcy, but I don't think that's a good idea."

"Why not?"

The question, put point-blank, was impossible to answer. *Because I'm still attracted to you and I don't want to be. I can't risk falling for you again. You don't want to be my husband, and despite the fun you have with Billy, you don't really want to be a father to our child.*

"My books and laptop are at my apartment."

"No, they're not. I brought them when I moved you in."

She sat back, stymied. "I'm taking up your bedroom. You can't be comfortable on the couch."

"It's no big deal. Maybe you're forgetting how long and wide the couch is." One corner of his mouth quirked up. "How firm the cushions. Great support."

Her cheeks heated at the oblique reminder of the many times they'd made love on that piece of furniture.

"And," Darcy continued, "I'm still hoping you can help me out with the color scheme for the pub."

"You don't need me to be on-site for that."

Billy started to fuss. Darcy unzipped the carrier and pulled him out. "Okay, buddy. Want to go see your mum?"

Emma had no choice but to take the baby. She felt herself tense up when the small solid body landed in her lap. Immediately she held him up at arm's length. "Hello, little man. Have you been a good boy for your daddy?"

She glanced up to see Darcy watching her, an odd quizzical expression on his face. Had he noticed her coolness toward Billy? Could he tell she was only going through the motions, that the warmth in her voice when she spoke to her son was fake? Her mothering ability was on display—and wanting. She hoped Darcy put it down to the lingering effects of her pneumonia. After the way she'd pestered him to have another baby he would be shocked to know that now she wondered if she'd done the right thing in having Billy. And how rotten did that make her feel?

She sat Billy on her knee and faced him toward the table where he could bat at a toy Darcy had left lying there. "Tell me more about your plans for the pub."

"My father gave me architect's drawings of how this place was supposed to be built originally. It has a kitchen and a garden room. Kind of like a beer garden but enclosed in glass so it's usable all year round."

"Sounds amazing. Why have we never heard of or seen these plans before?"

"Dad shelved them. Thought it was too much trouble

I guess. But now that the wine bar is making inroads on my business—"

"Is it that bad?"

"Nothing I can't bounce back from. But this is a good excuse to give the place a facelift. New carpets, furniture, paint, the works."

"That's a great idea. The pub is so dark and gloomy."

"You mean warm and cozy."

"Whatever. Bright colors and better lighting would be a big improvement."

"So you'll stay and help me choose a color scheme and fabrics and paint?"

"I'd be happy to help."

And happy to stay a little longer, if she was honest. She was much better, but the thought of facing her messy apartment, of caring for Billy all by herself again was daunting. Oh, she knew this was only temporary until she felt strong enough to deal with life and her feelings—or lack of them—for Billy. But for now Darcy's offer was a lifeline.

Not because she didn't love her baby enough, but because she loved him too much to be his only careprovider. He deserved so much more than she was capable of giving him right now.

"I can't pay you," he said candidly.

"I would never expect it. In fact, if you say anything like that again I'll have to get insulted."

"We're not married anymore. You don't owe me anything."

"We're friends. You said so yourself."

Their eyes met. A spark of warmth jumped across the table, so strong she had to look down. She fiddled with the top snap on Billy's sleeper. This was exactly the kind of thing she was afraid of—those small, unexpected moments when she and Darcy connected. What happened on the cruise was no accident. There was still so much attraction there. And caring. And yes, way down deep, possibly the remnants of love.

Yet even with all that going for them, they hadn't been able to sustain a marriage. It would be easy to fall for him again. But no way did she want to dive into that deep well of pain.

Billy continued to fuss.

"Maybe he's hungry," Darcy said. "I fed him formula while you were sick, but I expect you want to nurse him again."

"Yes, yes of course." She wanted to succeed at nursing Billy, she really did. It was the part of mothering Holly that she'd found most rewarding in the early days. If she was ever going to connect with her son, breast-feeding would give her the best chance.

"I might go lie down and nurse him. I feel tired again. I guess I'm weaker than I thought."

Darcy helped her into the bedroom to get settled then sat on the bed, still holding Billy. "Your milk should come in stronger now that you're recovering. You need to keep at it. The sucking action stimulates the lachrymal glands, which produce milk in accordance with demand."

It sounded so much like a quote she had to bite back a smile. "Where did you hear that?"

"I read it in a book. I brought over your baby manuals, too. I didn't know how long you were going to be out of action."

Darcy reading up on baby care. Would wonders never cease?

He transferred Billy to her. "I was going to chat about

the color scheme while you feed him but if you'd rather I left, I understand."

"You can stay." Immediately she regretted saying that. In the old days, the sight of Holly nursing used to turn Darcy on. Once the baby was in bed, she and Darcy would make love. But that was then and this was now, and nothing was the same. She lifted her top and un-clipped the flap on her maternity bra, pulling it down to expose her full breast.

Darcy's eyes darkened. As if needing to get away, he rose and walked over to the dresser, putting away some clean socks he'd left there earlier.

Emma sucked in a breath and prepared herself for the pain of Billy latching on. He'd nursed so much in the first months, trying to get enough milk, that even with a few days' respite her nipples were still cracked and raw-looking. She couldn't help the hissed intake of breath as he latched on.

Darcy glanced around. "What's wrong?"

"Nothing." She sighed. There was no pretending. "It hurts like hell."

"Is there anything I can do? Get you some ointment?"

"No, it's fine," she said grimly.

He winced, no doubt reflecting the expression on her face. "Breastfeeding isn't the only way to bond with your baby."

She went still. "Why would you say that? Did Si-enna mention something to you?" It was one thing to talk to her doctor about the problem, quite another for Darcy to know.

"Sienna only talked about your pneumonia. I said that because it's true. There's a whole chapter on bond-ing in one of your books."

"I meant, why do you think I haven't bonded with

Billy?" She set her jaw against the pain as he suckled noisily. "I'm crazy about him."

"You're not fooling me. At first I thought your strange behavior was because you're sick, but after seeing the way you held him in the kitchen…" He sat on the bed again. "What's wrong, Em? Talk to me."

"Oh, Darcy." She bit her lip, trying to control her emotions, but with being so worn down physically, they were too close to the surface. Despite her efforts, a tear spilled down her cheek. She told him everything—all the problems with low milk supply, the colic, the sleepless nights, the stress.…

"I don't l-love him. Sometimes I almost hate him and wish he'd never been born. I'm a bad mother. I've tried to change but the harder I try, the worse everything gets. I don't know what to do."

"I don't think you're a bad mother." Darcy stroked his jaw, frowning. "But I don't know how to fix this. Reading a few baby books hasn't made me an expert."

"Oh, Darcy," she said wearily. "It's not something you can fix. It just is. Don't worry. I'm going to take care of him. You won't be encumbered with me and Billy forever. Once I'm well and your decorating scheme is sorted out, I'll be on my way." She wiped her eyes with the edge of the coverlet. "Sorry. Have you got a tissue?"

He handed her the box from the dresser, his expression troubled. Darcy liked things to be light and happy. He wasn't good with darker emotions. She wished now she hadn't burdened him, or made herself vulnerable. He was being really nice about taking care of her and Billy, but he didn't want to be flung into that well of pain again, either. She would see it in the wariness in his eyes.

She stuck her baby finger in the corner of Billy's

mouth to break the seal then transferred him to the other breast. "You seem to have bonded with him. What happened? What made you change your mind about Billy?"

"I haven't changed my mind about anything, but someone has to change him and feed him while you're out of commission. I saw the way you were with him... not present emotionally. I realized that someone had to be. It's only a stopgap until you come back online."

"Thanks. I appreciate it." It was only a tiny step forward, but the implications were huge. Darcy had acknowledged that they both shared responsibility for their son's well-being. It took a burden off Emma and strengthened the fragile connection between her and Darcy, and between Darcy and his son.

"He's asleep," Emma whispered. Billy's mouth had come away from her nipple. Somehow she hadn't noticed the pain so much with Darcy there.

"I'll put him in his cot." As Darcy bent over to carefully gather him up, his hair brushed her cheek and she inhaled his scent. His face was close to her bare breast and the glistening nipple. Awareness thrummed through her. He hesitated then put his mouth around her nipple and gave one gentle suck.

Oh, oh, oh. It was a cheeky thing to do. But tender and erotic at the same time. The sensation was electric, shooting down mysterious pathways straight to her core. She wanted to push her fingers into his hair and drag him back down for a kiss.

But there was a little something between them. And he was starting to stir. Darcy straightened with Billy in his arms, his gaze somehow both sheepish and ardent as he rocked the baby back to sleep. "Sorry. Impulse."

Feeling her cheeks heat, she pulled her top down. "We should talk about colors."

"I'll put him to bed and get the swatches from my office." Darcy took Billy into the next room. A moment later she heard him going down the internal staircase that led to his office. He returned quickly, his arms laden with samples. He spread them out over the coverlet and sprawled across the end of the bed.

Emma played with fabric and paint samples, matching colors and textures. "Deep coral walls would brighten up the place and go well with the wooden bar and trim."

"Coral?" Darcy groaned. "That's so girlie."

"Pale pink would be girly. Coral is warm and inviting, modern but not cold. And a lot lighter than the wood paneling."

"Don't forget there's going to be a garden room. That will brighten the place."

"About that…don't you think you should accomplish this in smaller chunks? Do a little bit at a time, keep the work and the costs under control."

"That's your way. You want every tiny step perfected before you move on to the next tiny step. It makes more sense to me to do the whole thing at once. Get it all out of the way so I can start fresh."

"Yes, but will you actually do it? Doing it your way it's easier to put things off because the bites are too big to chew. You can do a lot with simple cosmetic changes."

"Structural first. It's logical." The way he said *logical* was deliberately provocative, as if logic was the male province. Which was a joke because they both knew who was the logical one, and it wasn't him.

She batted his arm with a fabric swatch. "Do you want my help with this project, or not?"

After that, an element of flirtation crept into their bantering exchanges. Darcy's laughing gaze slipped now and then to her breasts. Or even more provocative, held her gaze. She began to feel a little breathless. This was dangerous. What she'd always found hard to resist with Darcy was the fun he put into life.

Even something like decorating a pub could be exciting with him involved. She should be doing her term paper not lounging in bed, talking and joking, admiring his dancing dark eyes and the lazy way he sprawled, broad shoulders at an angle, one leg bent at the knee. The other leg hung half off the end of the bed, foot jiggling in that way he had of always being in motion.

Well, the paper could wait a little longer.

As DARCY SAW IT, anyone could be a bartender dispensing drinks, but it took a special personality to be a publican. His father had had the knack of talking to anyone, rich or poor, educated or not, as though they were his most important customer. Darcy had it, too. Now Billy, the third generation Lewis male, watched avidly from a front-row seat strapped to Darcy's chest. Of course, with Emma's smarts, Billy might not be interested in the pub. He might become a doctor or a veterinarian or even an interior decorator.

According to Emma he had colic and cried every night for hours. Darcy believed her but for some reason, since he'd been staying at the pub, Billy didn't cry—as long as he was being carried face-out in the baby carrier.

The kid was a babe magnet. Three young women, all glammed up for a girls' night out, cooed over him and flirted with Darcy every time he moved to their end of the bar. They'd said when they came in they only planned to stay for one drink before heading to Frankston's club scene, but he'd just mixed them a second round of cocktails. Forget renovations, maybe male waiters accessorized with cute babies were all he needed to improve business.

"Hey, Darcy, can I borrow your kid?" Ron, the real estate agent from down the block, leaned on the bar in his rolled-up shirtsleeves.

"Sure, he's due for a diaper change." Darcy laughed at Ron's grimace and removed an empty highball glass. "Same again?" He poured Ron another bourbon and moved along to Tony and his girlfriend, Cerise, a bouncy brunette with sparkling eyes who gazed adoringly at Tony. Tony couldn't keep his hands off her. Ah, young love. Wouldn't it be great to be that innocently happy again?

"Another round?" he asked the couple.

"One more, please." Cerise pushed her empty cocktail glass across the bar, turning to Tony. "Then we have to go to the rehearsal dinner."

"Her sister's getting married," Tony explained to Darcy. "Giving her ideas." Cerise dug him in the ribs with her elbow and he grabbed her hand to hold it. "I'll try a Red Hill pilsner this time. These new beers you got are ace."

"I aim to please." Darcy cracked a bottle, poured it into a glass and set it on a fresh cardboard coaster. It wasn't a bad thing that he was having to lift his game now that the wine bar had opened.

He picked up a towel and started to dry glasses, ignoring the trio of girls and their batting eyelashes. Even sick, Emma had it all over them. He recalled his daring taste of her exposed nipple. Too bold? Hmm, maybe not, if the gleam in her eye was anything to go by.

Bold or not, taking Emma's breast into his mouth had been stupid and reckless, like a child playing with matches. They'd had their day and called it quits for good reasons, reasons that hadn't gone away.

A sudden cheer rose from the crowd of guys watching the football quarter finals. Their team must have got a goal. He concentrated on polishing the glass. Football didn't interest him anymore.

"…surprised you let that dude in here with those," Tony said.

"Sorry, what was that?"

Tony nodded over his shoulder at a pudgy youth moving through the bar handing out flyers to every person at each table. "He was at the fish-and-chip shop earlier. He's working for the wine bar."

Darcy put down the glass, lifted the divider and rounded the end of the bar in a few strides, remembering to hold Billy's head steady. "Here, what are you doing? What are those?"

The kid looked up guiltily. He handed Darcy a flyer. *Buy one drink, get one free. Saturday, 8:00–9:00 p.m.*

In other words, right now. A red haze blurred Darcy's vision. This was a step too far. Give out discounts, fine, but how dare Wayne come into his pub and directly target his customers?

He took the youth by the upper arm and marched him to the door. "Don't come in here with this shit again, you hear me? And you can tell your boss— Never mind. I'll tell him myself.

"Kirsty, watch the bar." He went through his office and pounded up the stairs to the apartment, calling, "Emma, are you awake? Where are you? I need you to take Billy."

"In the kitchen." She glanced up from her laptop and the books spread over the table. "What's wrong?"

"Wayne, at the wine bar." Jaw set, he reached around

to unclick the straps of the baby carrier. His agitated fingers couldn't find the right spot. "Bloody cheek of that guy, sending a kid into my pub with his two-for-one coupons. I saw people leave right after the boy came in but didn't think anything of it." He tried to look over his shoulder and spun in circles trying to see the latch on the carrier. "What's wrong with this thing?"

"Let me get it. You're too worked up." Emma rose and released the straps. "You should cool off before you confront him. Nothing good ever comes from anger."

Darcy pulled Billy free and passed him to Emma. "I disagree. It'll be good giving that bastard a piece of my mind."

CHAPTER ELEVEN

DARCY STEPPED OUT of the pub onto the sidewalk, and the cool night air bathed his heated cheeks. Emma was probably right. Yelling at Wayne like some hothead wasn't smart or mature. Then again, he wasn't trying to win friends and influence people, just save his pub.

He flung open the door to the wine bar and looked around. Yep, there was the couple who'd left his pub not twenty minutes ago, now toasting each other with their half-price drinks.

Wayne was pouring wine into elegant glasses, the ever-present toothpick rolling between his teeth. A waitress came through a door from the back bearing a tray loaded with small plates of hot snacks giving off delicious savory aromas. His stomach rumbled, reminding him that the chicken soup he'd had with Emma was hours ago and he hadn't eaten since.

Wayne passed the wine to the waiter and looked up. A big smile wreathed his face. "Darcy. Glad you stopped by. What can I get you?"

Darcy flung the stack of discount flyers across the bar. "For a start, you can keep these out of my pub."

The toothpick rolled to the other side of Wayne's grin. "Hey, buddy, can't you take a joke?"

"I can take a joke. What I won't stand for is you poaching my customers right out from under my nose. Don't you have any kind of business ethics?"

"Ethics?" Wayne snorted. "Mate, get your head out of the sand. It's a big bad world out there. All's fair."

Darcy heard a snicker and turned to see a pair of women listening in on the conversation. The red fog descended and he spun back to Wayne. "All bets are off...*mate*."

Wayne's mouth turned down, letting the toothpick droop. "Are you threatening me?"

"You can take it however you want." Darcy was past caring how his words were interpreted. His father hadn't worked his butt off to build a pub only for some upstart from the city to sweep in and steal his customers. "My establishment has been in this town for sixty years. It will be here sixty more, long after your wine bar has turned into a juice bar. I *will* outlast you."

Not waiting to hear another word from Wayne he strode across the street to the pub. Behind the bar, he stacked glasses and cleaned up, his movements angry and agitated.

"So, will you be meeting the wine bar dude at sunrise in the parking lot?" Tony asked.

"Ha, that's right," Darcy said. "Dueling cocktail shakers at twenty paces. Care to be my second?" Having it out with Wayne made him feel a tiny bit better, but the aggravation was eating away at him. He couldn't wait until renovations were complete and the pub once again reigned supreme.

"Or how about a little graffiti, or a well-placed rock through that big plate-glass window..."

"Mate, you know better than that—" He caught sight of Tony's smirk. "You had me going there for a moment."

Revenge against the wine bar would be sweet, but it would also be hollow. Rather than tear the other business down it made more sense to build his business up. To put something of himself into the pub so that he could point to that and say, *it's mine*. And someday he could hand it to Billy and say, *Here, son, this is yours. Cherish it*.

The thought caught him by surprise. When had he started thinking about Billy in terms of the future?

His phone rang. "Hello?"

"Darcy," his mother said. "I'm sorry to call when you're working."

"That's okay. I've been meaning to come over but I've had my hands full with Emma and Billy. How's Dad doing?"

"He's being readmitted to the hospital." A tremor came into his mother's voice. "The surgical wound is infected."

Darcy swore under his breath. "Isn't he on antibiotics?"

"Yes, but the medication isn't working. Some sort of superbug has taken hold."

He glanced at his watch. It was almost eleven. "When is he going into the hospital?"

"Tomorrow afternoon. They're waiting for an open bed."

His father was elderly and in the grip of a virulent strain of bacteria. People died from that. "I'll come over right away."

"No, don't. He's asleep."

"I'll see you tomorrow then, around lunchtime." He remembered that his mother and father still hadn't met his son. "I'll bring Emma and Billy."

SHE WAS MAKING LOVE to Darcy. They were lying on a blanket in a meadow, the remains of their picnic scattered. His musky scent mingled with the fragrance of

*grasses and wildflowers. Her hands roamed over his
bare back and buttocks, warmed by the sun. Her body
tightened and their rhythm moved faster as tension grew.
The sweet sensation was about to reach a peak—*

A siren wailed in the distance.

The dream began to fade. Caught between sleep and
waking, Emma moaned. The soft tissues between her
legs throbbed and she pressed her hands there, desperately trying to stay in the dream long enough to climax.
But the sensory image of Darcy had already vanished.

The siren sounded louder. The ambulance was coming closer.

She slipped into her recurring nightmare about Holly.
Only this time it was Billy who was running toward the
driveway and the reversing truck.

"Billy," she screamed. And woke up.

Where was she? The bed was familiar, the quality of
the darkness wasn't. Terror still gripped her, all the more
disorienting because her body was sexually aroused.
Where was Billy?

The bedroom door opened and Darcy came in.

"Shh, Emma, it's okay. Everything's okay." His arms
went around her in the dark, warm and strong. "Billy's
asleep in his cot in the other room. He's fine."

She clung to Darcy as if she never wanted to let go.
"Bad dream," she mumbled.

She sagged against Darcy's chest, breathing in his
scent, recapturing strands of her first dream and weav-
ing them about her as armor against the second dream.
Her hands ran over his shoulders. This was real. He was
real. Solid. Strong. Here for her.

The siren stopped abruptly.

"I heard you call out. You said Billy's name." Darcy
lay down next to her and held her in his arms, stroking

her hair back from her face. His upper body was bare but he wore boxers and his muscular legs stretched out pale in the dim light.

"Don't want to think about it." She shuddered and turned to face him, pressing her body full-length against his through the covers. Desire resurged, a spark that instantly fanned into a flame. She raised her mouth and found his, kissing him urgently.

"Emma?" Darcy murmured against her lips. His hands gripped her, holding her back. "Are you awake? Do you know what you're doing?"

"I'm awake enough. I want—"

"What?" he said huskily. "What do you want?"

She hesitated. What *did* she want? Sex? Love? She was all mixed-up and frustrated. "I just *want*."

"I know that feeling." With his mouth on hers, he lifted his hips and pushed back the covers to get closer. He was already hard and seemingly full of the same urgency as she was.

Emma wasted no time on foreplay. She was aroused and needy and desperate to push away the last shreds of the nightmare. Reaching down, she slipped off her panties and climbed on top of Darcy. Her eyes closed at the heavy hot pulse of his erection against her belly.

"Wait." Darcy reached into the bedside table for a condom.

"Quickly," she urged. Even before he'd covered himself completely she was sliding down his shaft with a long satisfied moan. "Oh, you feel so good."

He groaned and clasped her hips to pull her in close. His mouth found her nipple and he strained up to suckle, molding her other breast with his hand.

They found their rhythm right away, rocking hard together. Emma planted her hands on the headboard and pushed her hips into Darcy's, her need an engine that drove and drove and drove—

It was all over in minutes. Short, sharp and intense.

She sagged over him, panting and damp with perspiration. And ground her hips into his again to capture the aftershocks. "Did you come?"

He gave a low dry chuckle. "Yes. Nice of you to ask."

"I wasn't just using you. Honest."

"I wouldn't mind if you were."

She pulled free and lay beside him, draping an arm over his chest and twining her leg with his. In spite of all the reasons making love to him was wrong, it somehow felt right. "Before the nightmare I was dreaming about making love to you. Then it all went wrong."

"What happened?" He blew softly on her chest, cooling her heated skin and causing her wet nipples to pucker. Her milk was leaking a little and he bent to lick it up, laving her like a cat.

She shivered with sensual delight, unwilling to leave this warm place with Darcy to go back into the nightmare. But he was waiting for an explanation. "In the middle of that dream I heard a siren, maybe out on the highway, and suddenly we were no longer in a sunlit meadow. Instead it was the Saturday of the football final. It was getting cloudy and I was ready to go in. I called to Holly. Only it wasn't Holly. It was Billy." She shivered, remembering Kyle leering at her. She should have gone inside and gotten Darcy. If only...

Darcy pulled her into a warm embrace. He felt so good, so strong and loving. The very real sensation of his body against hers—the prickliness of the hair on his shins, the heat of his skin, the musk of their lovemaking—held her in the here and now, safe from loneliness and sorrow, safe from her memories.

"What happened to the ambulance? The siren?" she added when he looked puzzled.

"It wasn't an ambulance. It was a fire truck. It stopped in the village, right on our street, it sounded like. I was getting up to investigate when you cried out."

Suddenly wide-awake, she sat up. "This building isn't on fire, is it?"

"No. The alarm would have gone off if it was. It must be a nearby shop."

Emma gave him a slap on the shoulder. "You made love to me knowing fire trucks were outside? I don't believe you."

"It could have been a false alarm. Besides..." He kissed her on the lips. "You were pretty insistent. I'll go check it out now. Are you all right?"

She twined a finger through his hair, making it curl in front. "I'm feeling pretty damn good."

"You've been sick. I wasn't too rough, was I?"

"A smoking orgasm was exactly what the doctor ordered." Her voice turned husky. "A girl could get used to this." Oh, God. Had she revealed too much? "I mean the sex."

"Sure, what else?" He searched her face.

The loving, the caring, being held and comforted when she woke from a nightmare into the waking nightmare that was life without her daughter. She needed to remember this was only an interlude. Before long she would go back to her own apartment and be on her own again. It wasn't as if Darcy had asked her to move in for good. "Nothing else."

Darcy eased away a little. "I didn't get a chance to tell you before. My dad's being admitted to the hospital. He's got a golden staph infection."

"Oh, Darcy." She felt so self-absorbed, worrying

about her dreams when he was experiencing something more scary and very real. "I'm sorry."

"I want us to go over to the house tomorrow morning, with Billy. I want Dad and Mum to see him."

"Of course. Whenever you say."

"I'm going to go check what's happening out front," he said gruffly. But before he rolled away from her, he leaned in to kiss her once more, slowly and very tenderly. Then he got up and went out.

Emma lay back on the pillow simultaneously confused and elated, worried and hopeful. Tears leaked from her eyes, and she didn't know if they were happy tears or sad. Damn hormones.

The news about his father was worrying. Was that why Darcy had been eager to have sex, because his father's mortality was breathing down his neck?

Whatever the reason, she didn't regret making love. How could she when it brought them closer together? Even if they had no future as a family, a better relationship between them could only be a good thing for Billy.

A smile tilted her lips. Happy tears, they must be.

DARCY PULLED ON the jeans and shirt he'd left lying over the back of a chair. The digital clock next to the couch read 3:00 a.m. He could hear voices shouting, doors slamming, hoses being reeled out.

And the unmistakable crackling of flames.

He ran down the stairs and onto the street. The Indian restaurant two doors down from the wine bar was on fire. *Too bad it wasn't*— He stopped himself before the thought could form in his mind.

Firefighters had three hoses out, one trained on the restaurant, the other two wetting down neighboring shops.

A police car pulled up. Constable Delinsky and Senior Constable Jackson set up a police cordon, shooing a handful of curious townsfolk behind the rope.

Darcy watched for a while to make sure it wasn't going to spread. The firefighters had caught it in time, but the restaurant would likely be gutted. Shame.

An unmarked car pulled up, and Riley got out wearing plain clothes. After being briefed by his officers, he came over to where Darcy was standing in front of the pub.

"Hey, Darcy." Riley glanced at the apartment. "Did you see anything from where you were?"

Only Emma, on top of him, her naked body filling his field of vision. "No, I was…asleep. Then I, uh, heard the sirens."

He felt no need to tell Riley any more than that. If he wanted to make love to his ex-wife, that was no one's business but theirs. Sex had been short and sweet. And hot. Hot as the flames licking through the caved-in windows of the restaurant, heating his face even from across the street. His groin tightened thinking about Emma riding him, her beautiful breasts swaying above him. He wished he'd had longer to stay in bed with her. He would have liked to make love again, slower, taking his time to pleasure her, to banish all her bad dreams so that when she closed her eyes all she saw was him.

He'd crossed a line tonight. He could no longer pretend that what happened on the cruise was a one-off. He and Emma had been intimate under possibly the least seductive circumstances and it had been awesome.

Maybe he wasn't as over her as he'd thought.

He needed to get his head screwed on straight. Nothing had changed. They were still divorced and, while he was happy to take her and Billy in temporarily, they formed no part of his future. She didn't want it and neither did he. Although clearly it wasn't a big enough deterrent to keep their hands off each other.

Darcy pushed those thoughts away and turned to Riley. "Kitchen fire, probably, eh?"

"It's hard to say at this stage. It's up to the fire chief if he wants an investigation."

"Do you think it could be arson?"

"Possibly. Or it could be purely accidental." He glanced up at the clear, starry sky. "But I think we can rule out a lightning strike or a bushfire out of control."

A couple of firefighters wearing breathing apparatus emerged from the doorway through billowing smoke. "Looks like they didn't find anyone inside," Riley said. "That's a blessing, anyway." He clapped a hand on Darcy's shoulder. "Catch you later."

The fire was under control now, the flames doused, the air acrid with smoke. Yellow tape blocked off the area. The bystanders were starting to walk away. One of the trucks started its engine and slowly drove off.

Instead of going straight upstairs, he walked through the pub with a flashlight making sure that all was well in case it was arson and some nutty firebug had decided to target more than one local business. Nothing appeared to be out of place or out of the ordinary.

He put away the flashlight and went upstairs, tiptoeing past Billy's room to open Emma's bedroom door. She was asleep. He hesitated, torn between wanting to crawl into bed and spoon her the way they used to and knowing that waking up with her would only complicate matters. It would be easier to write off their midnight passion as an aberration if he wasn't gazing into those big blue eyes gazing at him from the pillow next to his first thing in the morning.

Then he heard a cry. Damn. He froze like a statue, hoping the baby would go back to sleep. The next cry was louder and piercing and seemed to penetrate his brain.

"Okay, okay, I'm coming," he muttered.

He went into Billy's bedroom and picked the baby out of the bassinet. Billy rubbed his eyes with his knuckles. He was a small bundle of solid warmth. Darcy was getting familiar with the routine instead of panicking and wondering what to do. He *knew* what to do. "Hey, buddy, what's up?"

Billy's response was to cry louder.

Darcy didn't recall Holly being so demanding. But maybe when she woke in the night he'd simply rolled over and gone back to sleep, leaving Emma to get up. Back then he'd rationalized that because he worked till 2:00 a.m. most nights he needed his sleep. Emma had never complained, never nudged him out of bed. She'd always *wanted* to get Holly.

Hadn't she? It occurred to him that he'd never asked.

Should he take Billy to Emma for her to nurse? No, she was still recovering and needed her sleep. He would feed Billy himself. If he was tired tomorrow, so be it.

Jiggling Billy in his arms in an attempt to keep him quiet, he shut Emma's door and padded out to the kitchen. He didn't know any lullabies so he crooned a Spanish love song while he made up a bottle of formula. At least this part he had down pat. Through trial and error he'd determined the exact number of seconds in the microwave to heat the bottle to perfection.

When he was ready he sank into an armchair in the living room. It was dark except for the glow of the streetlight outside. There were still voices on the street and the sound of vehicle doors slamming. The whirring noise must be the fire hose recoiling onto the truck.

Darcy shut them all out and focused on the baby in his arms. Little beggar sucked greedily. Darcy dabbed at a drool of milk leaking from the corner of Billy's mouth. When Emma was fully recovered she would leave and take Billy with her. That idea should have been welcome—taking care of the baby had been tough. Instead, he felt oddly at a loss at the thought of not having Billy around.

His mind drifted. What if he and Emma were to get back together? The scenario unfurled before him—a second wedding, maybe even an exotic honeymoon in Argentina, where they could dance the tango. Then back home to settle down, in a house, of course. Billy would need a yard to play in when he got older.

Here, the images started to darken. At first everything would be wonderful and they would be happy. Gradually old habits would return. Emma would take over Billy's care again, shutting Darcy out. He would retreat to the bar. She would get pissed at him over being away so much. He would spend even more time with his mates and his pub. And the whole thing would spiral out of control, worse than before Holly died because they were carrying *that* baggage around and for God's sake, they should have known better.

Making love to Emma had been a fabulous mistake. They were being driven by hormones instead of using their heads and working out their problems. If that was even possible. The one with the most to lose if he and Emma came together only to break apart again was Billy.

Darcy stroked his baby's cheek. "Mate, I'm not going to do anything that could end up hurting you."

CHAPTER TWELVE

EMMA WOKE AND glanced at the clock on her bedside table. Ten o'clock. *Billy.* Why hadn't Darcy woken her up to feed him? She sniffed the air and could smell a faint odor of smoke from last night's fire.

She savored these few seconds with no baby crying, no alarm clock warning her to get to work. Her breasts felt full. Her milk was finally coming in strong. The antibiotics had worked their magic and she was feeling almost normal.

She and Darcy had made love. Was that the icing on the cake—or the one wrong thing she should have been smart enough to say no to?

In the middle of the night she hadn't been thinking enough to be either smart or stupid. She'd gone from the dream state to losing herself in mindless pleasure. She'd hoped Darcy would come back to bed after he'd looked at the fire but she'd woken up alone. Had he only come to her for a quick screw? Had he had second thoughts about what they'd done?

They'd shared some good moments through the day—the Macarena, the decorating discussion. But a bit of laughter and banter and hot sex couldn't make up for eighteen months of estrangement.

They needed to talk in depth, but how could that happen if the goodwill wasn't there? Every attempt at talking before their divorce had deteriorated into arguments that left her feeling emotionally bruised. Not because Darcy was trying to hurt her, but because she hated seeing the man she loved, the home and family she'd worked for, slipping away from her.

Holly and Darcy had been part of her. When they were gone, she was no longer whole. Billy was supposed to fill that gap. It was too much pressure on one little boy. Her expectations had been totally unrealistic. Could that be why she was having trouble bonding with him? Poor little guy, being expected to solve her problems when all he wanted was to be loved for himself.

Things had changed, though. When she'd had the nightmare on the cruise, Darcy hadn't wanted to know. Last night he'd put his arms around her and made her feel safe, for once not retreating to that dark place he went to. Had caring for Billy without her hovering over him made that big a difference to his attitude? But if things were so great, why hadn't he come back to bed?

She got up and put on a robe then brushed her hair and swished her mouth out with water from the glass beside the bed. She felt a little shy about seeing Darcy this morning but if they kissed she'd rather not bowl him over with jungle mouth.

She stopped dead, her hand on the doorknob. Where did these expectations come from? Last night was likely just another one-off. She'd been aroused from her dream; Darcy had been…well, he'd been a guy, ready to go anytime.

Did she even want things to progress? She'd learned how to survive on her own, achieved contentment if not happiness. Falling for Darcy again would stir up too many feelings she would rather bury. No, last night had been a mistake. She'd been vulnerable and needy.

She wasn't going to compound that by doing anything so stupid as kissing him good morning.

Billy wasn't in his bassinet. Darcy wasn't in the kitchen. Where were they? From the window she could see the blackened shell of the restaurant up the street. Yellow tape cordoned off the area, leaving a narrow path along the sidewalk for people to pass by. A police car was parked out front, along with a red fire van.

Had Darcy gone down to the pub already? Her breasts were aching now, they were so full. She turned away from the window and noticed the can of baby formula powder on the counter and an empty bottle. He must have fed Billy in the night. Okay. That was nice. She guessed. The extra sleep helped her get better, although she needed to nurse regularly to keep her milk coming in. Darcy knew that. She'd found her baby books lying around, books *she* hadn't read in months.

A faint snore was coming from the living room. She quietly pushed open the door. Darcy was stretched out on the couch. Billy lay in the crook of his arm with his head on his daddy's chest. The two dark heads, the chins with the dimple, even the whorls in their ears looked alike. Her heart melted. How sweet was that?

Darcy opened his eyes and stirred. "What time is it?"

"After ten. Thanks for feeding him in the night and letting me sleep. He'll be awake soon, and starving."

Darcy carefully sat up, adjusting Billy in his arms. "I gave him a second bottle at six."

Emma frowned. "Why would you do that? You know I need to stimulate my milk production."

"I thought I was doing you a favor."

Doing her a favor? Or taking over?

She shook her head. That was crazy. But her warm

fuzzy feelings evaporated. With Holly she'd been the center of the family, the glue that bound the three of them together. Now she felt almost…superfluous. It was understandable that he hadn't consulted her while she was ill but now that she was better, well, she was still Billy's mother.

"What time did you want to see your parents?"

"Could you be ready to go in an hour?" He paused. "About last night. It was awesome but I shouldn't have taken advantage."

He was apologizing for making love to her? He must think it had been a mistake, too.

"As I recall I was a willing participant," she said, stiffly. "However, I think we should stick to what we said on the cruise. Sleeping together doesn't mean we're getting involved or have any emotional commitment."

"I agree," Darcy said. "It's no good for Billy if we're alternately fighting and loving. And I don't want either of us to be hurt again. I'm sure you don't, either. The reasons we got divorced haven't gone away."

Sadly, that was true. "So, no more sex."

"Right. No more sex." Darcy hesitated. "I'll go have a shower." He handed Billy to her and she could smell their lovemaking on his body and feel the warmth of his skin as his arm brushed hers.

No more sex. No more closeness. It was for the best, the smart thing to do, the brave thing. They both agreed. So why did it hurt so much?

Suddenly she wished she was in her own apartment where there were no temptations and where she could retreat from the emotions Darcy invariably stirred up. A few more days and she should be well enough to leave.

Emma nursed Billy while she waited for her turn in

the shower. Her nipples were still sore but not as bad as before. She had to admit, the rest from breast-feeding had aided their healing.

With Billy settled on her breast she took the opportunity to call her sister. "Hey, how are you doing?"

"Great," Alana said. "I got the sixth class Brett promised."

"And Dave?"

"We're not speaking."

"It might be time to pull that ticket to Tahiti out of the hat. I'll look after Tessa."

"Thanks, but I doubt he'll want to go anywhere with me." She paused. "How's things with you?"

"Oh, mostly good. I'm recovering, that's the main thing." Now wasn't the time to go into her complicated ups and downs with Darcy. "I wanted to ask you a favor. Could you help me clean up my apartment? I want to move back as soon as possible."

"Sure, but are you well enough for that?"

"I will be by Friday."

"Okay, I'll meet you there at our usual time."

Emma heard the shower shut off. "I've got to go. We're going over to Darcy's parents' house this morning."

"Right back into the fold, I see."

"No, it's not like that. Catch you later."

She'd missed the Lewises but it was awkward enough being around Darcy in the aftermath of their night together without running the gauntlet of Marge's eagle eye watching to see how they were getting along. With any luck, though, all the attention would be focused on Billy.

And she would hang on to what Darcy had said the other day—they were friends. The lust could be confusing, but the single constant strength between them had always been friendship. That was one thing she didn't ever want to lose.

DARCY WATCHED EMMA strap Billy into the car seat. The baby was blowing bubbles and batting at the dangling plastic keys, but she didn't seem to notice. She never played with Billy, even now that she was feeling better. It made him sad that she was so detached from her son. She'd been such a loving mum to Holly, but she seemed to get no pleasure from Billy.

Their conversation this morning had been surreal. And probably not very honest. They both loved the sex, and it was going to be interesting to see how successful they were at abstaining. He wasn't quite sure what had gone wrong between making love during the night and this morning. She'd been annoyed with him, but why? Surely not because he'd given Billy an extra bottle.

"Are we good?" he asked.

She straightened. "Of course. Why wouldn't we be?"

Lots of reasons, but he decided to stick with the simplest. "This morning something was bothering you. I'd like to know what it was."

She picked up the diaper bag in one hand and the car seat in the other. "We're going to be late. We don't have time for an argument."

"An argument? So it's that bad?" Darcy took Billy's car seat from her. He wasn't good at talking about his feelings, and he couldn't always intuit hers. In the old days he would have brushed off a minor disagreement, but everything had changed. He was no longer sure of her. Plus they were going to his parents' place and his dad was sick. Under the circumstances he'd rather they weren't at odds while around his family. "Just tell me what's wrong in twenty-five words or less."

She sighed. "I'm trying to get my milk back. I really wanted to nurse Billy."

"I thought I was doing you a favor," he said, repeating his earlier rationale. "And I want to participate in Billy's care. If you breast-feed him exclusively, that lets me out."

"Not if I pump some milk for the bottle. But I need to know in advance. We should have discussed it. I felt like you giving him formula was undermining me."

"The way you used to undermine my efforts to care for Holly?"

She jerked back. "What?"

Hell. He hadn't meant to say that. Holly was in the past, and he never wanted to go there again. But the words had slipped out, and with a surprising amount of anger. Darcy struggled to get his emotions under control. If he wanted to spend time with Billy in the future, he needed to keep Emma onside. Which meant avoiding speaking about Holly's death, the topic that stored all their pain and which they couldn't seem to come together on, no matter how they tried.

"I didn't mean to undermine you," he said. "I was letting you sleep." *And bonding with my son.* "You're still recovering."

"No, I mean what was that about me undermining you with Holly? You think it's *my* fault you never spent time with her?" She circled him, eyes wide and disbelieving. "You think *I* came between you and caring for your child? *I* stopped you from changing diapers and getting her lunch?"

"You always got to her first."

"You didn't see when she needed something. You weren't tuned in to her like I was."

"You could have *asked* me."

"One of the few times I did, you dropped her on her head."

"Thanks for throwing that in my face. As if I would ever forget that incident. Have you never made a mistake with the babies?"

Instead of answering that, she threw her hands in the air. "Anyway, you were always at the damned pub."

"I was trying to make a living, to pay for your extravagances."

"What, like food and clothing?"

"Expensive furniture." He flung out a hand at the Italian leather couch and handmade side tables, the walls full of framed paintings. "Original artwork."

"I had to fill my life with *something* of value."

He shook his head. Why was he getting so hot under the collar about not being asked to change a diaper? Especially when he'd screwed up so badly that one time. Maybe he should have tried harder with Holly, but he'd been intimidated by Emma's expertise.

And why was Emma so angry about a simple bottle feeding? It was almost as though she was picking a fight because she was afraid of what she might feel for him after last night.

"Let's not argue about this," he said. "Holly's gone. We can't bring her back."

"That's right. Whenever the subject turns to Holly you retreat. If only—" With a choking sound, Emma turned away from him.

Darcy didn't have to ask what she meant by *if only*. He knew all too well. *If only* he hadn't chosen football over a picnic with her and Holly. *If only* he'd stopped Kyle from taking his keys and getting in his vehicle.

Well, he was sick of it. If only Emma had watched Holly more closely.

"We need to get going or we'll miss my dad." He picked up the car seat and started down the stairs.

"I'll be out of your hair soon," Emma said, coming after him. "On Friday, Alana and I are going to clean my apartment so I can move in over the weekend."

He stopped short. "You want to be back in your own space that badly?"

"I think it's best, don't you?"

It was no consolation that Emma looked as unhappy as he felt. Despite their bickering he was going to miss her when she was gone. He would also miss Billy.

And it was no surprise really, that they were picking fights with each other, trying to manufacture distance in lieu of coming closer. If she was anything like him, making love last night had been so heartbreakingly wonderful it was terrifying. How was it they could share something so magical and yet not be able to resolve their problems?

"Who's a precious baby? Did you see that?" Marge glanced at Roy and their children and grandchildren gathered around her in the living room. "He smiled at me."

One of Darcy's nieces, nine-year-old Dani, tickled Billy's chin with a stuffed horse. Billy chortled and kicked his legs.

Emma sat on a hard-backed chair at the edge of the circle. Darcy's two brothers and their kids were there as well as his sister with her kids. Roy leaned back in his recliner with a blanket over him, wanly delighted with the new addition to the Lewis family.

Darcy's nine nieces and nephews ranged in age from two to fifteen. The little ones played with toys on the floor, the older two monitored their phones and the middle girl cousins, Dani and ten-year-old Lisa, hovered over Billy, clamoring to hold him next. The noise level was typical of the Lewis family gatherings with everyone talking at once.

Emma hadn't expected everyone to be there, but clearly the occasion was a big deal, evidenced by the buffet lunch laid out on the dining table. She used to love that the Lewises were a close-knit family but now she felt under the microscope.

Darcy was the man of the hour as the new father. Seeing him now, she never would have guessed he was the same guy who used to disappear to the pub twelve hours out of every day. Was he right? Had she pushed him away from caring for their daughter because he'd let her fall on her head? Maybe she'd overreacted—Holly hadn't been hurt after all—but it easily could have been worse. Still, how else did parents learn except by doing? He'd managed okay with Billy.

Marge was in grandmother heaven. Emma felt horribly guilty that she hadn't found a few spare moments before now to let her see Billy. After the tragedy of Holly everyone deserved to share in the joy of a new baby.

Courtney, Dan's wife, offered her the bowl of chips. "I hear you and Darcy are back together."

"No." Emma waved away the chips. Where had this come from? Surely not Darcy.

"We've all been hoping this would happen," Courtney went on, apparently thinking Emma had been saying no to the snack. "Dan and I were sure you wouldn't be able to stay apart for long. You two are the perfect couple."

"Darcy and I aren't back together." Emma spoke louder than she'd intended, coinciding with a lull in conversation. Her statement carried across the room loud and clear.

All the adults and even the kids looked over.

"But…" Confusion showed on Courtney's fine, pointed features. She tugged on one of the multiple rings in her ears. "Dan said you'd moved into the apartment above the pub."

"Temporarily. I've been sick with pneumonia. Darcy was helping me out with Billy."

"So you're not going to stay there?" Marge asked. "I thought from what Darcy said, things were working out."

Darcy met Emma's gaze and shook his head. "I meant Billy. Things were working out with me looking after the baby."

"No," Marge said. "You told me you and Emma were getting along really well."

"We are. Or, we do sometimes. It's not the same as getting back together." He reached for a handful of nuts from the bowl on the coffee table. "Now that Emma's feeling better, she wants to move back to her own place soon."

"You should try a little longer, for Billy's sake," Marge murmured.

"We weren't trying to get together," Emma explained. "It was a matter of convenience."

That was met by quiet disapproval from the whole clan. Emma felt her exasperation grow. "We're divorced. There were good reasons for that. I wanted more children and Darcy didn't."

"Now you've got your child. Darcy adores him. What's the problem?" Marge looked around the room for confirmation of her logic. Heads nodded.

"Darcy is *coping* with Billy but the baby isn't the only issue." Emma was outnumbered by a very wide margin. "Tell them, Darcy."

From across the room he looked her straight in the eye. "Maybe we shouldn't rule anything out."

What did he mean by that? And how the heck was she supposed to respond? Emma had a baby to look after. She couldn't rely on *maybe*. She needed absolutes.

She shot a sharp look at Darcy then rose and picked up the diaper bag. "Billy needs a change. Darcy can you give me a hand in the bedroom?"

Mike, Darcy's second oldest brother, laughed. "Darcy, help? We all know he couldn't change a diaper if he tried."

Darcy threw a peanut at him. "I've learned a thing or two in the past couple of weeks."

"I'll help," Dani offered.

"Not this time, sweetie." Emma plucked Billy out of Marge's arms. "Coming, Darcy?"

Dan chuckled as they filed past. "They might not be married, but he sure is whipped like a husband."

Emma stuck her chin in the air and pretended not to hear. She walked down the long hall to the last bedroom, the one Darcy and Mike had shared as kids. Two single beds were made up for grandkids who stayed over. Someday Billy might sleep in here.

She laid the baby on the bed and sat, motioning Darcy to sit on Billy's other side. "Are you saying you want us to try again? Thanks for blindsiding me in front of your family. When did you decide this?"

"I haven't decided anything. I just don't want to rule it out."

"Well, now they think it's all my doing that we're not together. They blame me."

"They love you, Em. They want to see us together, that's all. Especially now that we've got Billy."

"What do *you* want?"

He plucked a thread on the brown patterned quilt. "I like you so much. And it's obvious I'm hot for you. But there's this big wall that goes up between us at times." He glanced up. "You know what I mean? The anger, the resentment...it scares me. I don't know if we can get past that."

Holly, again. Her shoulders slumped. "I know what you mean, but it's not fair that your family's disapproval is directed at me, as though I'm the only one who's holding us back."

"I copped flack when I refused to have contact with Billy after he was born."

"We can't live our lives by what your family wants. When they pressure me, you need to back me up."

"It was your decision to raise Billy on your own."

"Really, did I have a choice? You didn't even come to see me in the hospital. Or you did, but you let my family and friends scare you off. An extroverted guy like you afraid of a few people?" She nodded toward the other room. "Look what I have to put up with."

"You're right. I'm sorry. I'll take my share of responsibility for the situation."

"Thank you. That means a lot to me." But it was two steps forward and one back. Neither of them could commit to trying again.

Billy started fussing. Emma found a rattle in the diaper bag and shook it gently to distract him. Billy's hands flailed, trying to grab it. He was a cute baby, she acknowledged dispassionately.

"Let him have it," Darcy said.

"He's too little. He can't grip yet."

"Try him. He wants to take it."

It seemed like a waste of time. On the other hand, Darcy had been right about placing Billy face out in the sling. Emma positioned the rattle next to Billy's hand. His fingers closed around the handle. His jerky hand movements made it rattle. A wide toothless grin spread across his face. He looked at her and laughed, as if inviting her to share his excitement.

His delight was so pure, so innocent, she couldn't help but smile. She found herself grinning at him unreservedly. "He held it."

Darcy was beaming, too. "He's a child prodigy."

"He's got an awesome smile." How had she never noticed that before? She scooped him up off the bed and peered into his face. He gazed back at her, open, vulnerable, trusting. Something let go inside her. "Hello, Billy."

Billy waved his hand and hit her on the nose with the rattle. Emma laughed and hugged him. Heat pricked the backs of her eyes, and she buried her face in his sweet, baby-smelling neck. His fingers threaded through her hair and clung, as if he, too, wanted to hold on to her and the moment.

She glanced at Darcy, who was digging out more toys for Billy to try to grasp. If he hadn't taken her in, nursed her back to health and taken care of Billy, who knows where she and Billy would be now? Darcy, who she would have sworn didn't know one end of a baby from the other, had just now helped her make a connection with Billy when she would have held back.

Darcy handed Billy a stuffed caterpillar the right size for his small hands to grab and squash while she laid him down and changed his diaper. When Billy got tired of the caterpillar Darcy handed him more toys. Some he grabbed and hung on to, others he batted away.

Had they ever played like this, the two of them, with Holly? Sometimes. Not often enough. She'd always been in a hurry to get on to the next task and get it done, to stick to the schedule she'd set out for herself. Illness, and Darcy, had forced her to relax.

If she went back to living alone now, would she lose the gains she'd made with Billy? But she couldn't stay with Darcy solely for the baby's sake. It had to be because they loved each other and wanted to make it work.

"Emma," he began, "maybe we don't need to belabor the fact that we're not together right now. It's enough that we know where we stand. My father's not well and…"

"He'll be okay, Darcy."

"Will he? I've read terrible stories…" He trailed off, unable to speak his fears.

But Emma knew. She didn't hesitate but pulled him into a warm embrace. As a nurse she believed in the power of medicine to heal the body. As a woman she knew the power of a hug to heal the soul. For long minutes she held Darcy close, her face pressed to his chest over his heart. Gradually she felt him relax and the tension flow out of him.

She eased away. "He might get worse before he gets better. But he's strong. You should hope for the best. I'll go with you when you visit him in the hospital."

Darcy's fingers curled around hers and brought them to his lips. "Thank you."

She looked into his eyes and forgot everything else for a moment—even the baby.

Then Billy made a noise, and her attention landed on the one thing that both brought her and Darcy together, and drove a wedge between them. In spite of the gains they'd made in repairing their relationship, they weren't together again. She had to remember that so she wouldn't feel bad when it came time to leave him.

And that time was coming very soon.

CHAPTER THIRTEEN

GARY, THE BUILDING contractor Darcy had asked to give a quotation on renovations, arrived at 10:00 a.m. the next morning. A wiry man wearing light brown overalls, he polished his smudged glasses on the hem of his shirt and leaned across the bar to examine the plans.

"These were drawn up before the apartment was built upstairs." Darcy unrolled the drawings of that addition and they considered the two sets of plans side by side.

"The garden room is going to completely change the character of the pub," Gary pointed out.

"That's the whole idea."

Gary straightened and glanced around the pub, at the battered chairs, the bric-a-brac, the pictures on the wall. "I used to come in here when I was an apprentice, before I moved to Mornington."

"My dad owned it then. Roy Lewis."

"That's right. How's he doing?"

"Okay, I guess. He just had a hip replacement." Darcy didn't want to go into details. Despite Emma's assurances, his concern for his father hadn't abated. "The question is, is the garden room possible?"

Gary grinned, hands on his hips. "Anything's possible if your pockets are deep enough."

"What if I did it in stages?" Darcy asked, thinking of Emma's suggestion. "Do the cosmetic changes, maybe put in the kitchen this year and save the garden room for next year. Does that make sense or not?"

"Not really. You'd be ripping out nearly new carpeting and paintwork. Waste of time and money."

"That's what I thought. So I pretty much have to do it all at once."

"Unless you didn't include the garden room. If it's light you're after, you could throw in bigger windows, a few skylights. It would be a lot cheaper."

"No, if I'm going to do this, I'm going to do it right." The plans had taken hold of his imagination. It wasn't about beating Wayne and his wine bar anymore, it was about fulfilling the original dream of the pub's designer. When Darcy was finished, the building would be a real landmark.

They talked a little more about the specifics of the garden room. Darcy had a couple of changes he wanted to make to the bar, too, to make it more efficient. Gary promised him a detailed quote in a couple of days and rolled up his copy of the plans.

Darcy walked him out to the parking lot. "If you were to get the job, how soon could you start?"

Gary got out his smart phone and scrolled through the calendar. "If I juggle a couple of things, I could get underway before Christmas, get the bulk of it done. You'll be looking at, say, end of February for completion."

That was faster than Darcy had expected. The pub would have limited seating over the lucrative Christmas season but having the garden room open before the end of summer would be worth it. "Sounds good. Thanks for coming by. I'll be in touch by Friday."

That night Darcy took a rare evening off from the pub. It felt strange to be upstairs while customers were downstairs, but Kirsty and Brad were both working and now that he'd begun on the renovations project, he wanted to make more progress.

He had a notepad and a pen and paper and was compiling a list of steps in the process. First he would need permission from the local council to extend the building. He also needed to see Renita Thatcher at the bank to apply for a loan to cover the costs and work out a realistic repayment plan.

Billy was in a bouncy seat on the floor in front of the TV, enthralled with *Dancing with the Stars*. The volume was down low in deference to Emma, who was working on her term paper in the bedroom.

Her breakthrough in her relationship with Billy was obvious even though she hadn't said anything. She was playing with him more and cuddled and sang to him the way she used to with Holly. Darcy felt better knowing she would be able to love and care for her baby the way she longed to when she was on her own again.

Darcy tried to focus on his plans but the show was doing a special on Latin dancing and before long his gaze drifted to the dancers on the screen. The rumba reminded him of dancing with Emma on the cruise. He reached for the TV control and turned the volume up a little. "Pretty cool, hey, Billy? You should see your mum and I on the dance floor."

Emma walked into the room and perched on the arm of the couch. She wore a simple sleeveless dress of some soft material. Her hair was loose and her feet bare. "I heard music. What's this?"

Darcy reached for the control again to turn it down. "I didn't mean to disturb your work."

"It's okay. I could use a break." She watched for a moment and within seconds her foot was tapping to the beat. "What do you say we show Billy our moves?"

"Em, you know what happens when we dance." He wanted to, no question, but regrets always seemed to follow the high of intimacy. Their relationship was way out of balance and had been for a long time.

"I know it doesn't jibe with what I said yesterday." Now her shoulders were moving. "I know we're not going anywhere. But when we dance, I feel good. I forget about the bad stuff." Her eyes pleaded with him to understand.

And he did, because he felt the same. When they were one with the music and with each other, everything else fell away. For a time.

He got to his feet and took her hand. "We're our own worst enemies."

In answer she twirled beneath his arm to finish snug against his front, her face tilted up to his. Her smile kicked his heart rate up a notch. He turned up the volume and tossed the control on the couch.

The floor space was tiny but that only made the holds tighter, the spins more controlled. Darcy was breathing shallowly even though they weren't exerting themselves. Doing the rumba on the spot was kind of like making love standing up—without removing any clothes.

That could be rectified. He slipped down the strap of Emma's dress and pressed a kiss to the hollow between her shoulder and neck. In the privacy of this room he reverted to the way they used to dance in their own home—as if no one was watching. His hands moved over her, roaming boldly from breast to hip to linger at the junction of her thighs while his hips swiveled and pushed against her back.

The song ended and a commercial came on. Before the mood could be broken he grabbed the controller and flipped the amp onto a radio station that played

Latin music. Effortlessly they adjusted their steps to a tango, wrapping their arms around each other's waists and, cheek to cheek, arms outstretched, glided across the floor.

Turning to face him, Emma held his gaze as she undid the buttons on his shirt. No woman did sultry like Emma. He could feel his pulse rate soar as she slid her hand slowly up his bare chest. Then tweaked his nipples. He'd been hard from the opening bars but now his cock was like granite. He reached around and undid her zipper. The dress slithered down with a little help over her gyrating hips and she kicked it away.

Her face was raised to his, and Darcy leaned down to take her mouth in a long slow deep kiss that lasted until the rest of their clothes were abandoned.

"You're beautiful." He trailed kisses down her neck as he cupped her breast. "Sexy."

Mine.

Where had that come from? At one time he'd thought they were soul mates. She wasn't his anymore, no matter how much he wanted her. But she was his for this dance, for this night.

Thoughts fragmented under the demands of his highly aroused body. An element of possessiveness tempered by tenderness crept into his touch. She would be leaving him soon. He wanted her to remember him when they were both alone in their beds, and know that at their best they were sublime.

Her hands were moving over him, too, touching and stroking and kneading. Their bodies rubbed against each other in another kind of dance they knew as well as the rumba or the tango. Her breath was in his ear as she licked up the side of his neck, pressing her breasts against his chest and grinding her hips against his. His erection pushed against her soft belly. He needed to sink into her, now.

He pulled her onto the couch and pushed her onto her back, nudging her legs apart with his knee.

"We can't do this in front of Billy," she whispered.

Darcy glanced over his shoulder. Billy's eyes were fluttering closed, as if he was trying and failing to stay awake.

Darcy rolled off the couch and gently removed him from his seat. "Time for little boys to be in bed."

Emma sat up as he carried the baby past, nestled against his shoulder. "I usually nurse him to sleep. Or give him a bottle."

"He'll be fine." Disturbing Billy as little as possible, Darcy carried him to his room and tucked him into the bassinet. The baby started to fuss. "Easy now, mate." Darcy found a pacifier and inserted it in his mouth. Billy's eyes closed again as he sucked contentedly.

Darcy hurried back via the bedroom, picking up a condom on the way. He hoped Emma hadn't changed her mind in the minute or so he'd been gone. He rounded the doorway and stopped dead, his breath stolen. She was lying naked full-length on the couch, her arms lifted behind her head, one knee bent. Her pose was an unmistakable invitation. His erection, which had started to flag, leaped to attention.

She opened her arms to him and he lowered himself on top, propped on his elbows. She parted her legs and he entered her slowly, their eyes locked. He dropped kisses on her cheeks and temples, trailed them down her neck. They often enjoyed sexy banter while lovemaking, but his heart was too full to speak.

Spanish guitar playing in the background, he made love to her, the thrum of the strings echoing the passionate beating of his heart. He took his time, pleasuring her every way he knew how, his tongue and fingers strumming her till her body vibrated to a crescendo.

His world contracted to Emma. His body began and ended with hers. He began to climax as she began to fade and his strong final thrusts quickly brought her to another peak. Afterward he lay atop her, breathing hard, slick with perspiration.

Slowly he came back to the room, to the quiet voice of the radio announcer speaking in Spanish and the soft creak of the leather couch with their small movements. And downstairs, the faint clink and buzz of the pub. Funny how he'd heard nothing a few minutes ago.

He turned his face into Emma's neck and simply breathed her in, shutting his ears to the outside world. For now it was only him and Em.

"OH, BILLY. How did I let things get this bad?" With the baby on her hip, Emma picked her way through her apartment, horrified at the mess everywhere. "I must have been completely out of it."

"Ga, ga!" Billy waved his arm energetically.

"I know. Cleaning this will be a big job."

The doorbell rang. Emma buzzed Alana up.

Her sister wore old track pants and carried a shopping bag of cleaning supplies. "Holy moly, Em. What happened in here?"

"I wouldn't blame you if you suddenly remembered a class you have to teach."

"Nah, we can tackle this, no problem. I've got three hours. Should be able to get the worst of it cleaned up." Alana tickled Billy under the chin. "Who's a big boy? Do you want to come to Auntie Alana?" She held her arms out.

Billy buried his head in Emma's neck. "He's tired. It's time for his morning nap."

Alana stroked his head. "How old is he, three months?"

"Fourteen weeks," Emma said. "He's over the colic."

"And you look like you're feeling better. In fact, you're damn near glowing."

Heat crept into Emma's cheeks. Averting her gaze from Alana's, she stroked Billy's cheek. "Darcy's taking good care of us, isn't he, Billy?"

A grin spread over Alana's face. "You dog! You've been sleeping with him again, haven't you?"

Emma headed into the living room. "A lady doesn't kiss and tell."

Alana snorted. "Did you dance again? I blame it all on the rumba."

"It's not only the Latin dancing."

"Then it's worse than I thought. This is what comes of me not keeping an eye on my little sister. While we clean you can tell me all about it."

Emma put Billy down for his nap in a bassinet. When she entered the kitchen she started running water into the sink to wash dishes. She made a mental note to call someone to fix the dishwasher.

"So, are you two getting back together?" Alana found a large black garbage bag and started picking up rubbish. "Is that what you wanted to chat about?"

"For the zillionth time, no. I'm getting tired of having to clarify that." Emma told her about visiting Darcy's family as she placed glasses in the hot sudsy water. "The good news is, I've finally started to bond with Billy."

Alana paused, the rubbish bag hanging from her hand. "I didn't realize that was a problem."

"Well, it was. I didn't find it easy to talk about, even with you."

"You wouldn't, because you're supermum and Super Working Woman all rolled into one."

"Am I really that bad?"

"I'm teasing."

"Seriously."

"Seriously? You are. You put the rest of us to shame."

"Hmph. I think you're exaggerating." It still rankled that she hadn't met her own standards, even if no one else expected her to. "The other good news is that Darcy is taking an active role with Billy."

"I saw he was carrying him around."

"Not just that. He's hands-on taking care of him, even the yucky stuff."

"Really?" Alana raised a skeptical eyebrow. "Mr. I'm-too-busy-having-fun-to-change-a-diaper is handling the yucky stuff?"

"Honestly, he's fantastic with Billy. I wouldn't have believed it if I hadn't seen it with my own eyes. He even got up in the night to give Billy a bottle so I could sleep."

"I thought you were breastfeeding."

"I am. So I was ticked off at the same time as I was delighted. But he's genuinely trying to help me, and help Billy. He never did that with Holly." She rinsed a glass and placed it in the drain tray.

"But you're not getting back together with him. Don't get me wrong—that's probably a good thing, but what's the problem? The sex isn't good any longer?"

"The sex is great. Better, if anything." She let a beat go by. "Part of me would like to be with Darcy."

"Oh, Em. Don't get sucked in. He has this magnetic hold on you. You have to stay far enough away that you don't feel the pull."

"What if I like the feel of the pull? He's fun to be around."

"Have you seriously forgotten how angry, upset and crazy he made you when you were married?"

"It was after Holly died. We were grieving."

"And all those problems are resolved?"

"No. I said *part* of me would like to reconcile. I know we're not ready for that, if we ever will be." She lowered a stack of plates into the sink. "What's going on with you and Dave?"

"We're talking—"

"Great!"

"About splitting up." Alana glanced away, but not before Emma saw that her eyes were glistening.

"Oh, no. No, Alana. You can't. You and Dave are solid. He's a real family man." She pulled her dripping hands out of the soapy water and hugged her sister, rocking her back and forth. Alana's raw grief reminded her of her own marriage breakup. She hated that her sister had to go through that.

"Yesterday we had another big fight." Alana blotted her eyes. "He said he hadn't signed up for an only-child family. And he reminded me that before we got married I'd wanted at least three kids."

"Changing her mind is a woman's prerogative," Emma said, stroking her arm. "Although I understand where Dave's coming from. Darcy and I planned to have more children. When he changed his mind, it altered the whole picture. Kids, and how many, is fundamental to a marriage."

"Children are too important to be bargaining chips in a rocky relationship," Alana argued. "I shouldn't have a baby unless I want it one hundred percent. What if I were to have another child and I resented it and the tension broke our marriage apart anyway?"

Emma had to acknowledge the truth of that, even though it made her feel uncomfortable. If Darcy had given in to her pressure to have another baby immediately after Holly died and then not been the family man Emma had wanted, she would have blamed him even more. She hadn't been fair to him, just as Dave wasn't being fair to Alana.

"When a couple's desires and expectations don't match, there's bound to be trouble," Emma said. "Do you still love him? Do you want to stay married?"

Alana nodded.

"You have to be totally honest with him. Find a way to compromise. I know I said this before, but if you're talking about splitting up, it's the only way." It's what she should have done. Her marriage breakdown had been partly her fault. It was hard to admit, but it was true.

Equally hard to admit was her part in Holly's death. She hadn't been completely honest with Darcy, too afraid he wouldn't love her if he knew what she'd done—and hadn't done—that day. Instead she'd been a coward, keeping her secret bottled up inside, unwilling to let her perfect image slip. And she'd lost him anyway.

"Compromise," Alana repeated bitterly. "I know—I'll have half a baby and Dave can look after it."

"You have a right to expect help. If he wants another kid, he shouldn't expect you to make all the sacrifices. Work it out with Dave, somehow. You've got to. He's a good man, Alana. Tessa needs both of you to be a family." The same as Billy needed her and Darcy. She felt like a fraud. "Don't give up on your marriage. You'll regret it forever."

Alana took a tissue from the box on the counter and handed one to Emma. "Do you still love Darcy?"

Emma hesitated, then slowly nodded. "I think so."

"Maybe you'd better listen to your own advice."

DARCY WENT DOWN the street to the deli for an early lunch. Emma making plans to move out had left him restless and uneasy. Having her and Billy stay had given him a glimpse of how life could be. At his parents' house, where he'd been reminded of the simple joy and comfort of family, he hadn't wanted to rule out a reconciliation.

But although he cared deeply about Emma and the sex was great and he liked having her around, neither of them was willing to rush into another relationship and risk disaster. Over the past year he'd gotten himself on an even keel. If they tried again and failed… He didn't think he could go through that level of anguish again.

He placed his order at the counter then, carrying his number on a metal stand, looked for a seat in the crowded café. Wayne Overton was seated by the window dressed in his signature black on black. The sun gleamed on his bald head. Darcy quickly moved his gaze past Wayne then was forced to return. The only empty seat was at Wayne's table.

"Pull up a pew." Wayne pushed out a chair with his foot.

Darcy plunked his number on the table and sat. "This is awkward."

Wayne took a forkful of pasta and used a chunk of bread to mop up the sauce. "If you'd like to apologize, I'm listening."

Darcy snorted. He glanced around again, hoping to see an acquaintance with a spare seat. Nope, nada.

He cracked his knuckles. Shifted his feet. Then made himself relax. While he didn't like Wayne, he could usually find some common ground with most people. Maybe if he used this opportunity to get to know the man, they could lessen the antagonism and come to an agreement not to poach each other's business.

There was one topic guaranteed to strike a chord with most Australian males. "So, Wayne, what football team do you barrack for?"

Wayne's gaze narrowed. "I'm not into football. I'm from New South Wales. I follow rugby league."

Great, a dead end. Darcy fiddled with the sugar sachets. "Do you play any sports yourself?"

"What do you want, Lewis? It's a bit late for the welcome to the neighborhood schtick."

"Just trying to be friendly. What part of New South Wales are you from? I have an aunt in the town of Wisemans Ferry on the Hawkesbury River."

"Yeah?" A glimmer of interest showed in Wayne's eyes. He pushed his plate away and pulled out a toothpick. "My dad runs a houseboat charter in Brooklyn not far from there."

"A few years ago my ex-wife and I rented a houseboat for a week. Loved it. Gorgeous country. I'm surprised you left. Didn't you want to go into the business yourself?"

"Nah, too much work maintaining the boats." Wayne paused, then volunteered, "I managed a vineyard in the Hawkesbury Valley for a while, but then my wife wanted to move here to be near her family."

"Oh, she's local, is she?" A waiter brought over Darcy's mushroom omelet and coffee.

"I'll have another espresso," Wayne said to the server.

"She's from Red Hill. Her maiden name was Hanson. Glenda Hanson."

"Hey, I know Glenda." Darcy picked up a fork and tucked into his meal. "She played on the state basketball team with my sister in high school. Ask her if she knows Janine Lewis. I'm sure she'll remember."

Wayne chewed on his toothpick. "Janine, eh? I'll ask."

"Small world. Six degrees of separation and all that." Darcy risked a business question. "How are those two-for-one coupons working out for you? They certainly seem to bring in the customers."

"Lots of customers, not much revenue."

"Is that so? How long are you going to keep it up?"

"I'm done. If the wine bar can't make it on its own merits now, it never will."

Yes. Darcy simply nodded. "I got a little hot under the collar the other night." And that was as close as he would get to apologizing.

"Have you owned the pub a long time?"

"Ten years. My dad had it before me for thirty years."

"Bit of history there."

"That's right." Darcy hesitated. "I've probably got you and your wine bar to thank for getting me off my butt and going ahead with renovations."

"Really?" Wayne cocked his head to one side. "I may have to reinstate the coupons."

Darcy looked him in the eye. "I'd like to be friendly but I didn't appreciate some of your tactics."

"Just trying to carve out a toehold. You and your pub have this town sewn up."

"Like I said, it's big enough for both of us."

"Did you hear that the fire in the Indian restaurant was arson? The owner was trying to collect the insurance."

"Not too bright."

"And it pisses me off. The fire could easily have spread down the block to my place."

"I thought this was only a tax shelter for you."

"It started out that way. Now I've grown to like the wine bar. And Summerside. I think I'll stick around."

"The local merchants have a kind of neighborhood watch going for businesses. It's run by the police. Has anyone told you about that?"

"No, but I'd like to know more."

"I'll ask my mate Riley Hemming to get someone to sign you up. He's the senior sergeant in charge of the cop shop."

"I'd appreciate that." Wayne glanced at his watch. "I've got to get back." He hesitated, then stuck out his hand. "Glad we had this chat."

"Ditto." Darcy shook. This time Wayne didn't try to rearrange his phalanges. That, Darcy guessed, was progress.

He finished his meal then strolled to the police station. Riley was in a meeting so he asked for Paula instead. Patty, the Irish girl in dispatch, let him through into the bull pen.

The station was deserted at this time of day. The uniformed officers were probably out on patrol. The far wall had been removed where the extension was going in, the area curtained off with sheets of plastic. The sounds of hammering and sawing could be heard beyond the plastic.

Paula strode out of a room farther along the corridor. "Hey, Darcy. What can I do for you?"

He told her about Wayne wanting information about the business neighborhood watch program. "I know it's beneath someone like you with detective rank, but it's an excuse. I don't get a chance to talk when I'm working."

"You should come over for dinner. Oh, except I'm going to be tied up for the next few weeks. Did Riley tell you the trial starts Monday?"

"This is Nick Moresco's trial?" She nodded. He thought he had problems. Paula had gotten pregnant by a drug lord she'd been investigating undercover. When Moresco got out of jail seven years later he'd gone back to his criminal ways—and had come looking for his son, Jamie. "Is the evidence solid on him?"

"Like a rock. We found his prints at a meth kitchen on the peninsula and a recorded phone conversation that linked him directly to dealers. The case is open and shut. He won't be bothering Jamie and I—or anyone—for a long, long time."

"Great. Well, I'd better not take up any more of your time. Say hi to Riley. We'll celebrate once the trial's over."

Paula walked him out. "How's Emma? I heard she moved in with you. Congratulations on the baby, by the way."

"Thanks. Emma's only staying with me temporarily, while she recovers from pneumonia."

"Oh, okay. Riley thought… Never mind."

"What did Riley say?"

"Nothing. I was trying to read between the lines." Paula smiled sheepishly. "I could blame my being a detective, but really it's me being a nosy although well-meaning friend. I always hoped you and Emma would work things out."

"Not going to happen, I'm afraid." Darcy wrapped up the conversation then headed to the pub. Everyone but he and Emma seemed determined to bring them back together. All the cheerleading from the sidelines wouldn't help them mend their broken relationship unless they could resolve old hurts. He and Emma were stuck in a sort of limbo. They couldn't let each other go. Neither could they reunite. Well, he was tired of it. It was about time for him and Emma to bring this to a conclusion, for better or for worse.

CHAPTER FOURTEEN

EMMA STEPPED OFF the elevator onto Ward 5G North, after seeing Barb in Administration. She hoped she wasn't inviting trouble by arranging to start working again. She was feeling better, but still prone to fatigue. This bout with pneumonia was a hard-learned lesson not to ignore signs of illness in the future.

"Look who's walked right out of the frame of my favorite nurse fantasy." Darcy came out of another elevator. He gave her his most cheeky smile as he lightly touched her back in greeting and his hand brushed her hip.

Seeing him unexpectedly brought a mixture of pleasure and confusion. She fell into step at his side, keeping her gaze straight ahead, even as a warm glow spread through her. She should never have slept with him again. And again. And again. It was like waking a sleeping dog. A very horny dog. "This is my workplace and your fantasies are inappropriate."

"Oh, but they're running rampant with all this medical paraphernalia about. I'll never forget what you can do with a speculum. By the way, whatever happened to your special uniform?"

"It's hidden at the back of my closet." Once, for a costume party, she'd altered an old uniform, making it a tight, micromini with thigh-high stockings and garters and showing generous cleavage, a parody of a porn movie nurse. Darcy claimed it was sexier than black lace.

"Now shush." Two doctors in blue scrubs went past, conferring as they walked. Emma put a few extra inches between her and Darcy.

"It's fun seeing you squirm, but okay, I'll leave you alone. I thought you were cleaning your apartment with Alana."

"We finished. I've just been up to see Barb. I'm returning to work in another week and a half, but cutting back my hours. After getting so sick, I've realized I need to be more careful."

"That's smart. Where's Billy?"

"I dropped him off in child care so he could get used to the caregivers and the environment while I visited your dad." She glanced at Darcy. "I put you on the list of people who are allowed to take him home. Just in case. Is that okay? Maybe I should have asked first."

He looked startled. "No, it's a good idea. Thanks. I didn't think of that."

"Why would you?" It's not as though she'd ever asked him to pick up Holly from day care. She'd taken it for granted that he wouldn't want to or wouldn't be able to. In fact, she'd assumed a lot about his willingness, or lack of it, to help. She felt sad that she'd learned that too late for Holly. But he could have pushed harder. He'd given up too easily.

They turned the corner in the wide corridor. Up ahead was the nurses' station. "Have you seen your dad yet?" Emma asked.

"No, but my mother was in to see him earlier today."

"I'll look at the doctor's notes and meet you in his room once I've checked in at the desk."

Emma greeted the other nurse on duty, and asked

to see the logbook for the resident's comments about Darcy's father. As she scanned the terse notes, her frown grew deeper.

"DAD?" DARCY TOUCHED his father's arm and got no response. His color was waxy yellow, his eyes closed and sunken. The only clue that he was still alive was the beeping of the monitors and his raspy shallow breathing.

One tube dripped something into him via a needle in the back of his hand. Another tube emerged from beneath the sheets and emptied into a bag dangling from a hook on the bed. A clip on the tip of his index finger was wired to a machine that monitored his heart rate and oxygen saturation. The jagged green tracings looked erratic to Darcy's untrained eye. He felt panicky at seeing his father in this condition.

Roy's eyelids fluttered open. "Marge?"

"It's me, Dad. Darcy." He gripped his father's hand.

Roy opened his eyes and glanced around, plucking at the sheet fretfully. "Where's Emma and little Billy?"

"They're around. You'll see them soon." He didn't know if she planned to bring Billy up, or even if she should, given his dad's infection.

"Fine son you have there. Spitting image of your grandfather, my dad."

"He's got the Lewis chin, that's for sure."

Roy gripped his hand with surprising strength. "You've got a second chance here, with the baby. Don't let Emma go again."

This is where he needed to back Emma up. It felt surprisingly hard to defend their agreement to continue with their separate lives.

"We've talked. Neither of us want to get together again. Emma's determined to raise Billy on her own, and I'm going to support her decision. We're friends, though, and I'm going to see Billy lots."

Roy shook his head. "Is that enough?"

Not really, but this was no time to be getting into a discussion about it. "I'm going ahead with the renovations at the pub. I'm trying to build up the business again."

Roy gripped his hand harder. "Why don't you try to rebuild your life? If I've learned anything in the past forty years, it's that women would rather have their man around than all the money in the bank."

That was easy for his dad to say. When Roy had owned the pub it was the only joint in town where people could get a drink. There'd been no restaurants serving liquor, only cafés. Emma wouldn't want a guy who couldn't support himself. And Darcy had too much pride not to provide for his family even if he didn't live with them.

Emma entered the room. "The pub is going to look fantastic when Darcy's finished," she said, clearly having overheard their conversation. Even though she wasn't on duty, she bustled about, adjusting Roy's pillows, filling his water glass.

She gave Darcy an encouraging smile, but her eyes were troubled. What had she found out about his father's condition?

"Emma picked out the paint," Darcy said. "Coral walls with antique white trim."

"Have some water." Emma held the water cup with a straw to Roy's mouth. "You need to keep your fluids up. A little more." She gave his father such a glorious smile Darcy almost felt jealous.

A nurse, Laura, came into the room wheeling a trolley loaded with bandages and supplies. "I'm going to change your dressing now," she told Roy.

Emma propped a couple of pillows beneath his back and helped the other nurse turn him on his side. She glanced at Darcy. "You don't have to stay for this. Go get a coffee."

"I want to stay." If she was staying, so was he.

"Suit yourself." She turned to Laura. "I can do this if you like." Perpetually overworked, like all nurses, Laura made a token protest then thanked her and left to continue on her rounds.

Emma donned a pair of gloves and peeled back the dressing to uncover the surgical wound. The site of the stitches was red and swollen and weeped a yellowish pus that emitted a foul odor. Red streaks radiated down Roy's thigh. He gripped the side of the bed, his face set against the pain.

Darcy swallowed hard to stop himself from gagging. "Is it healing?"

"It's going to be fine." Emma worked swiftly, swabbing the area clean with gauze soaked in some bluish solution. She applied an ointment and then put on a fresh dressing. "All done."

"When can I go home?" Roy asked.

"You'll be out of here in no time."

Darcy recognized Emma's soothing nurse voice, the one that was more about patient morale than an accurate diagnosis.

She bundled away the soiled bandages into the trash and washed her hands at the sink next to the bed. Then she turned Roy onto his back and plumped up his pillows again. She positioned his call button next to his hand. "Press that if you need anything. I'm not on duty today but Laura will help you. Darcy, I'll be at the nurses' station when you're done."

He stayed and talked to his father for another twenty minutes, filling him in on the scuttlebutt surrounding the Indian restaurant fire. His dad's attention waned until finally he closed his eyes. "I'll let you rest. See you tomorrow."

He went looking for Emma and found her chatting to Laura. Seeing him, Laura picked up some charts and headed down the corridor. Darcy waited until she was out of earshot. "How bad is he?"

"Your father's infection hasn't responded to methicillin, the first line of defense against golden staph," Emma said. "This morning he was placed on a stronger antibiotic, vancomycin."

"Will it work?"

"The doctor will know more in a day or two."

"You're not reassuring me."

"I'm being honest. Most patients do recover. A small percentage don't." Her gaze was sympathetic. "The elderly, mostly."

"He's only eighty-one." As soon as he said it, he realized how old that sounded.

"He's strong. He'll pull through." She squeezed his hand. "This isn't the best time to tell you this but…when I return to work next week, I'll be cutting back to two shifts a week." She watched him expectantly.

What was she wanting him to say? "Good. It's good that you won't be working so much."

She was waiting for something more from him, but he didn't know what. Her smile seemed strained. Was she thinking about working, studying and living on her own? Did she like that idea as little as he did? The spotless corridor with the bright lighting seemed a surreal setting for a conversation about their future. He didn't want to talk about her and Billy moving out. He didn't even want to think about it.

"Does my mother know about my dad's condition?"

"The doctor would have told her this morning. It might be a good idea to talk things over with her. Be prepared for the worst but hope for the best."

"That sounds like a good motto for a lot of things."

She hesitated. "I overheard you talking to your father earlier. If you're serious about being part of Billy's life, that…that would be great."

The penny dropped. "Child support. You cut back your shifts and now you need extra cash. I'll start payments tomorrow."

Her cheeks reddened. "I hate to ask. You've been so generous. And if now's not a good time for you, with the renovations and all—"

"It's fine. I really want to do this." He searched her face. "It makes me feel I'm contributing." *Almost like a real father.*

She cleared her throat. "I need to pick up Billy. I'll keep in touch with the nurses about your dad tonight." She left him standing in the corridor, orderlies and visitors brushing past him.

He'd been living in a bubble the past few weeks, with Emma and Billy at his apartment as if they belonged there. Now reality was bursting in. Once she started shifts at the hospital and resumed classes while living in her own place, he would see Billy once a week if he was lucky.

He'd failed Holly. And he'd failed Emma. Whatever happened, he would not fail his son. With his father's life hanging in the balance he realized how important his dad was to him. Oh, they'd disagreed over the years—on how the pub should be run, the rules of darts, whether he should have tried harder to stick it out with Emma— but through it all, Roy had always been there to talk to. Darcy couldn't imagine not having him around.

Now *he* wanted to be there for Billy.

Something had changed in him. He hadn't expected it, hadn't wanted it, but love had conquered fear. He couldn't go back. Even if he only saw Billy on weekends he would be a father to his son.

Instead of going to the elevators he returned to his father's room and sat beside the bed. His father was asleep but he spoke anyway. "Dad," he said quietly, "you have to fight this infection. You've got a new grandson. He needs you." He swallowed. "I need you."

EMMA'S SUITCASES WERE open on the bed, half-packed, a reminder that she was moving out tomorrow. But first she had a lot to do today.

"We'll stop by the university to drop off my term paper," Emma told Billy as she pushed his pudgy feet into booties. "Then we'll go to Auntie Alana's house. If we've got time, we might even get in a little shopping." Summer was coming and she hadn't bought clothes that weren't maternity wear in nearly a year. "After all that we'll come back here to finish packing. Sound good?"

Billy made a noise and shook his rattle for emphasis. He was wearing his best outfit, a new blue T-shirt and OshKosh overalls. His hair had come in wavy and dark like Darcy's but his eyes were like Emma's, a shifting blue-green.

"You don't say? I *so* agree." She strapped him into his car seat.

"You're leaving already?" Darcy stood in the doorway, his gaze taking in the suitcases, her stacks of books in boxes and the piled-up baby paraphernalia by the door.

"No, I'm just going out for a few hours." She hadn't seen him since yesterday afternoon at the hospital. He'd stayed with his father and then gone straight to work. By the time he'd come upstairs she'd gone to bed.

"I plan to go tomorrow." She took a deep breath. "I want to thank you for everything. You've been wonderful to me, and to Billy. I don't know what I would have done without you. I'll be forever grateful."

"Emma, stop. You don't need to say that stuff as though I'm no more than an acquaintance. It's me, Darcy." He came into the room and sat on the bed. "We need to talk about Billy."

Emma glanced at her watch but she sat, too, and tried to relax. A few minutes wouldn't make a difference to her schedule, and Darcy deserved her time. "You did a good job with him. He's going to miss you."

"The little guy has grown on me." Darcy's gaze filled with love as he handed his son a fallen toy. He glanced at her. "I'm not going back to being that guy who doesn't want children. I'm going to be a real father to him."

"A real father," she repeated, slightly stunned but not really surprised. She should have seen this coming. Carefully, she added, "What do you mean by that, exactly? You've already agreed to pay child support."

"I want to see him regularly. I want to be part of his life on an ongoing basis. I want him to grow up calling me Daddy. I want to be part of his future."

At one time all she'd wanted was for Darcy to acknowledge his son. Time had made her greedy. Now she wanted more. She'd hoped any talk of the future would include making plans for them to see each other. Hoped he'd meant what he'd said about not ruling out a reconciliation. She waited for him to say something else, about her and him. About them being a family. He didn't.

"You walked out on me because I wanted a baby. Then I got pregnant accidentally. And you still didn't want to know Billy. Fine. I was prepared to raise him myself. Now you've had him around for all of five minutes and you decide you're going to be a father?"

"Do you seriously have a problem with that? I thought that's what you wanted."

"Darcy, you have a history of always looking for something new and different. Billy's exciting to you now, but what happens when you get bored with him and change your mind again?"

"I'm not going to get bored, or change my mind." He got to his feet, agitated. "Sheesh."

"How do I know that? What if, when Billy is say, two or three years old, you meet a woman and then you're in a relationship and maybe you've got a new baby." She was speaking really quickly, getting it all out in one breath. "And suddenly you stop coming around—"

"I wouldn't do that."

"How do I know? Why should I believe you?" She looked at him and shook her head. "You've been amazing, taking care of me and Billy the past ten days. I'm glad you've enjoyed getting to know Billy. But don't feel you have to keep it up. I know kids and family and stuff isn't your thing."

"I love Billy," he said.

His simple conviction made her want to crumple. If he loved their son but didn't love her, she was destined to a future of seeing him and aching for him.

"Love isn't enough. You have to be present, too."

"I will be present with Billy. I can't prove that in advance. You'll have to take me on faith."

"Darcy, you're a dreamer. You do nothing for years with the pub then suddenly you come up with grandiose notions for a major renovation when a simple paint job and new carpet would do the trick. Maybe some two-for-one coupons of your own. But no, you want to rip down walls, build a glass house, throw in a garden...." She flung her hands about. "Nothing will ever happen. You know that."

"That's not true. I've given Gary the go-ahead." At least he would, tomorrow. "I've been preoccupied with my father, and taking care of you and Billy."

The fight went out of her as she simply gazed at him, all churned up inside. "What about us? Have we got a future? Because I still want the same thing I've always wanted. You, me, our baby—together as a family."

"You said you wanted to raise Billy on your own. I presumed that was because you didn't want to be with me."

"I wanted to but...we're broken."

He reached for her hands and held them in both of his. "Yes, we're broken. But we have amazing sex and I believe we have a true friendship. A lot of couples don't even have that."

Emma clutched his hands, fighting tears.

"Let's try again," he said. "For Billy's sake. We both want what's best for him. Let's live together and be a family. I didn't want a child so soon but it happened and now I'm ready to accept it."

For Billy's sake. Emma tugged her hands away. "I want to be loved, not taken on out of a sense of responsibility, or duty, or some familial urge to carry on the Lewis name."

And he didn't know the worst about her. If he did, he wouldn't be asking her for a second chance.

She grabbed her handbag and keys and picked up the baby car seat. "I have things to do. I'll be back later to finish packing."

"Fine, run away. It's what you always accuse me of doing. Just know this, I will be a father to my son," Darcy said, following her out. "Even if my name isn't on the birth certificate, he's mine. I can't make you believe in me. It's enough that I believe."

Emma hurried downstairs and out of the pub's back door to where her car was parked. She *was* running away. She'd finally gotten what she wanted from Darcy, or at least enough to build on, and she couldn't handle it. What was wrong with her?

DARCY HEARD THE door close and went to the window. With a heavy heart he watched Emma put Billy in the rear seat and drive off. They'd barely begun to sort through their problems and she was leaving. When it came right down to it, she didn't want to talk about what was really keeping them apart any more than he did. Holly's death was just too painful.

He went downstairs and walked through the pub, struck by how shabby the rooms looked in the morning light. Scratches crisscrossed the wooden tables, the chairs looked beat-up and the carpet worn. There were scuff marks on the pale walls and around the base of the bar from countless shoes. Definitely time to update the old girl.

He started removing the framed sepia scenes of Summerside circa 1950s. Although interesting, they added to the general run-down air. His patrons came to drink beer and socialize, not admire the decor, but now he wondered if they simply turned a blind eye to the seen-better-days surroundings. No wonder they'd taken to the wine bar in droves. He'd maintained the old-fashioned look out of a misplaced nostalgia. Sure, the football pennants hanging on the wall opposite the bar had been won by local teams, some that his father had played on, but did anyone even look at them anymore? Probably not.

He'd half hoped Emma would be there to help him take down the photo board and deal with the pictures of Holly. Now he was glad to be by himself. He wasn't sure he could hold it together with all the emotions crowding his heart—his dad's illness, Emma and Billy leaving, his confusion about his feelings for Emma—and he didn't want anyone, not even Emma, seeing him blubber.

He found a big cardboard box and started putting in items. It almost felt as if he was packing up a family home. He didn't know what to do with the individual beer mugs. There were about thirty of them up on the shelves, some hadn't been used in years.

A knock at the door dragged him out of his thoughts. Tony was outside, peering in through the window, a large manila envelope in his hand.

Darcy went to unlock the door. "What's up?"

"Can I ask a favor?"

"Sure, come in."

Tony glanced around. "Why are you taking everything down? You're not selling, are you?"

"Just doing some renovating." Darcy had told most of his regulars his plans, but Tony hadn't been in all week. Maybe longer. "Where have you been lately?"

Tony slid onto a bar stool. "Cerise and I have been looking at rental properties." He slid a sheaf of papers out of the envelope. "Would you be willing to give us a reference?"

Darcy poured coffee and passed a cup to Tony. "No

worries. Are you and Cerise moving in together? How old are you—twenty-three?"

"Twenty-two. Cerise is twenty. And we're getting married. We want you and Emma to come to the wedding."

"I can't speak for Emma but I wouldn't miss it." Darcy was surprised to feel a bit of a lump in his throat. He'd known Tony since he was eighteen, barely old enough to drink. The first time the young brickie had come into the pub he'd been celebrating getting an apprenticeship. Now he was almost done his training and getting married. "You're both awfully young. Surely you're not old enough to marry."

Tony grinned. "We don't want to be ancient like you when we start our family."

Darcy pretended to take a swipe at him. "Who are you calling old?" He guessed to Tony and Cerise, forty *was* ancient.

"What's it like, being a dad?" Tony asked. "Cerise wants to have kids right away."

Darcy felt his face soften. "It's pretty cool when the little dude looks up at you and grins like you're the best thing in his world."

"Awesome."

Darcy hated thinking about how perilously close he'd come to not being a father to his son. Like Tony, he'd thought he had found the right woman in Emma. Unlike Tony, he knew that sometimes life threw curveballs that even soul mates couldn't field.

He was about to lose Emma for the second time. The question was, what was he going to do about it?

CHAPTER FIFTEEN

EMMA WHIZZED THROUGH her stops around town and even managed to find a cute dress on sale. By the time she pulled up in front of her sister's house she was more than ready for a cup of tea. It wasn't Alana she'd come to see, though. She hoped Dave would be in the mood to invite her in.

"Hey, Emma." He opened the door still wearing his business shirt and tie. "How's your little man?" He tickled Billy under the chin, making the baby squirm with delight. "Alana isn't here right now."

"I know. I wanted to talk to you. Can I come in?"

"I'm catching up on some office work but…sure, come in." He led the way into the kitchen, where his laptop and papers were spread over the table. "Help yourself to the tea in the pot. Alana will be home soon."

"I know. That's why I have to be quick." Emma started to set Billy's car seat on the floor.

"I'll hold him." Dave undid the straps and picked him up while Emma got herself a cup of tea.

She took a seat opposite Dave who bounced Billy on his knee. "I hate to interfere in a marriage—"

"Then you'd better stop right there." Dave gave her a hard look. "This is between Alana and me."

"Do you love her?" Emma asked, ignoring him. "Do you want your marriage to last? Do you want to have more children?"

He'd remained stony-faced until her final question. Then his mouth crumpled briefly before he pulled himself together. Tucking Billy in the crook of his arm, he said, "I suppose she's told you all about it."

"Not everything, I'm sure, but enough to know that you two are on a path to divorce if you're not careful."

"What do you suggest I do?" Dave said. "We both agreed before we even married how many kids we wanted. Now she's unilaterally moved the goalposts."

"I'm not going to lecture you on talking it out, or finding a compromise by both working part-time or any of the myriad solutions you could come up with. I'm not going to mention that if you two split you will see even less of Tessa than you do now. You're both smart people. You know all that."

"What then?"

"Support her. Wait it out. She may change her mind. She may not. Just don't give up on her."

Dave rolled his eyes. "We've been at odds over this for more than a year. Tessa's nearly in kindergarten. If we don't have another baby now, it'll be like she's an only. I swore when I was a kid rattling around in our big house all by myself that when I grew up I would never have an only child."

"I know how you feel, not about being an only child, but about wanting another child so badly I thought I would die if I didn't get one. I pushed and pushed Darcy until I pushed him right out the door." Emma leaned forward, wanting so badly for Dave to understand. "That's what you're doing to Alana. Once Darcy left I discovered there was something worse than not having a baby."

"What?" Dave asked.

"Not having my husband and the love of my life at my side. He wasn't with me in bed. He wasn't with me at the breakfast table. He wasn't with me on my birthday or on the anniversary of our daughter's passing. You want lonely? That's lonely."

Dave pulled at a thread on the toe of Billy's sleeper, silenced.

"We don't always get everything we want in life." Emma heard her voice tremble and cleared her throat. "But sometimes we find someone who's so important that he or she trumps everything and everyone else. Don't make the same mistake I did." She rapped the table lightly to make sure she had his attention. "I'm not saying this for Alana's sake. I'm saying it for yours."

Dave glanced up. His gaze flickered, as if something inside had clicked for him.

The front door opened and laughter bubbled through the house, Alana's and Tessa's. Small footsteps thudded on the carpeted floor. A moment later Tessa burst into the room. "Daddy." She threw her arms around his neck in a quick hug. "Auntie Emma and Billy. Hooray." Then like a sprite, she ran out of the room again.

Alana came into the room carrying grocery bags. "Em, I didn't know you were stopping by. You should have texted me. I would have gotten here sooner."

Emma flicked a glance at Dave. Then turned to her sister with a smile. "I was passing and dropped in on the off chance you'd be around. Dave gave me a cup of tea and persuaded me to wait."

"Stay for dinner. We're not doing anything." Alana's quick, sad glance at Dave implied she would welcome the distraction. "I'll put these groceries away then whip up some pasta."

"No, thank you. I've got to get back to Darcy's. It's our last night. I'm moving home tomorrow."

"Oh." Alana put down the grocery bag, her gaze searching Emma's face. "Are you okay?"

"I'm fine." She rose, and as she took Billy from Dave she rested a hand briefly on his shoulder. "It was nice chatting to you."

He glanced up, his mild gray eyes unfathomable. "Yeah, it was good. I'm glad you stopped by."

Alana walked her to the front door and gave her a hug. "Call me if you want to talk. Tonight, tomorrow, whenever."

"Wait!" Tessa skipped down the hall in the frilly pink dress Emma had given her along with the tiara and her fairy wings. "Auntie Emma! You're not going already."

"Sorry, sweetie. I have to." Laughing, Emma added, "You look like the Sugar Plum fairy."

"She adores that dress," Alana said indulgently.

Emma crouched to pull her niece into a hug. Her throat filled as small arms wrapped around her neck. Holly was gone but she still had a precious little girl in her life. "You've grown since I was here for your birthday. Maybe it's time your Auntie Emma took you on a shopping expedition." She glanced over at Alana. "Could I?"

"Be my guest." Alana smiled. "She would love to look at frills and froufrou with you."

"Hooray!" Tessa shouted. "I want a pink tutu."

Emma clapped her hands. "With a feather boa!"

"Oh, good Lord." Alana gave an exaggerated groan. "Tessa, go wash your hands for dinner."

"Dinner's not ready yet." Tessa twirled, lifting her skirts.

"Just give me and Auntie Emma a minute. Go!" Tessa ran off and Alana turned to Emma. "You know how I said you shouldn't reunite with Darcy? I take it back."

"He asked me to try again, to live together. For Billy's sake." Before Alana's face could brighten, she added, "I told him no."

"Why? If he makes you happy, grab hold and hang on with all you've got. Darcy's proven he's a good father. He loves you."

"He hasn't said so." Maybe if he'd said the words she might have had the courage to confess her secret shame in the hope he would forgive her. But if he was only with her for sex and for Billy's sake, it wasn't enough.

"Sometimes guys don't say it in words. Actions mean more than flowery phrases. And you, girl, need to be more receptive and less cautious. Relax and see what happens."

"That's probably good advice." Under ordinary circumstances, but Alana didn't know the whole story of Holly's death, either. "Now I'm going to give you some advice. Hang on to Dave. He loves you. He said so to me this afternoon."

Alana's face brightened. "Did he really?"

"Yes." Emma hugged her again. "Now I must go."

She made one more stop on her way back to the pub—Ward 5G North. She was anxious to see how Roy was doing and if he'd responded to the new antibiotics yet. She'd called the ward several times since she and Darcy had been in to see him yesterday, but the report was always the same—no change. That was to be expected. It took a while for the drugs to kick in. But by this morning, he should be responding.

Tracey was on duty at the nurses' station. "How is he?"

"Roy?" Tracey reached for the logbook. "I just came on. Let me see… Here, you look." She shoved the book at Emma and took the car seat. "I want to see my little sweetie pie. Hey, Billy, how's my big boy?"

Emma scanned the entries from the residents' morning round. *Temp—37.2 C.* Still a slight fever but his temperature was down from the other day. *Blood pressure—160/110. Heart rate—105.* Neither were good, but nor were they worse than before. She read on for the doctor's notes. *Infection appears to be responding to treatment. Continue prescribed course of oxacillin until further notice.*

Emma released her breath. Thank God. She shut the logbook and pulled out her phone, glancing over at Tracey who held Billy and was letting him play with the watch pinned to her chest.

Emma punched in Darcy's number. "I'm at the hospital," she said when he answered. "I've got good news about your dad."

She quickly filled him in on the details. "I'm going in to see him now. I've got Billy with me. I thought that might cheer him up."

"Be careful Billy doesn't get too close. We don't want him picking up an infection."

"The golden staph bacteria is everywhere. We've all got it on our skin. It's only when someone's immune system is impaired, like your father's, that it can take hold. But don't worry. I won't let Billy touch anything. I'm the original clean freak, remember?"

"When do you think Dad will be discharged?"

"I couldn't say. He's not out of the woods yet. Sometimes these infections take time to clear up. But he's definitely on the mend." She paused. "I'll be back after that. To finish packing."

Darcy greeted that with silence. "Tony and Cerise are getting married."

"That's great."

"They want us to come to their wedding."

"Oh. Well, we'll need two invitations. Did you tell him that?"

"No." He was quiet for a long moment. "I'm starting to clear out the pub, getting rid of sixty years of accumulated bits and pieces."

"So you're really going ahead with renovations."

"I told you I was."

Emma thought of all the many and varied mementos, knickknacks and photos. "That'll be hard. I'll help you."

"You don't have to."

"I don't mind." Darcy would be going through a tough emotional time. She wanted to be there.

"Really, it's something I'd rather do myself. If you have to pack, you could leave Billy with me."

"Okay. Fine." She felt stupid for pressing the matter. Stupid for feeling disappointed. She was the one leaving. The one who'd shut him down when he wanted to talk. The truth was, she was scared, mixed-up and confused. She didn't want to remarry just for Billy's sake. She wanted Darcy to love her. He'd spoken of reconnection, friendship and sex. Where was the love she wanted so badly, the love she needed and, yes, deserved, in spite of everything?

When she moved out he would want to see Billy, not her. Stupid of her to think they were going to hang out together like a family. Stupid to believe he'd changed how he felt about her because they'd made love. Stupid, stupid, stupid, for falling in love with him again and leaving herself vulnerable. Hadn't she had enough heartache?

"Actually, that would be good." She managed to say it coolly. "I'll see you in a bit."

"Em? Thanks for calling about Dad."

"No worries."

She clicked off and retrieved Billy from Tracey. "Come on, mate. We'll see your grandpa quickly and head home—"

She caught herself but not before the thought had formed. When had she started thinking of the apartment over the pub as home? Not because it was so homey but because Darcy was there. The sooner she was disentangled from him and out from under his roof, the better off she'd be.

DARCY WAS ON a stepladder, untacking pennants and listening for Emma's return when he heard the rear door to the pub open.

"We're back." She put Billy's car seat on a table and pushed her hair behind her ears. Her shoulders in a sleeveless dress were lightly sunburned, making the faint freckles stand out. Her bare legs ended in thin strappy sandals.

Darcy climbed down the ladder and dropped the stack of dusty, faded pennants into a box. He felt a bit awkward with Emma. Already she seemed to be withdrawing from him. Was it appropriate to kiss her on the cheek like a friend? But she wasn't *just* a friend. Her cheek would never be sufficient.

"Thanks again for checking on my dad."

"He's looking so much better. He's going to be fine." She gave him one of her hugs, moderate on the Emma scale but still full of warmth and caring. It was just like her to set aside their differences to offer her support.

He hugged her back then released her reluctantly. Their gazes met, and her eyes were filled with compassion and guilt and wariness. Darcy leaned over the car seat. His love for his son was less complicated than the confused mixture of emotions he felt for Emma. "Hey, monkey face."

"Nice way to talk to a baby." But she couldn't hide a smile.

Billy blew a raspberry. Darcy gasped melodramatically and wiped a drop of moisture off his cheek. "Who taught you that? Who taught you to spit at your daddy?"

Billy waved his arms and laughed. In his tight fist he held the plastic ring of keys.

"He's really got a good grip now," Darcy said.

"He's changing every day." Emma stroked her baby's cheek. "Aren't you, bub?"

"Then I need to see him every day."

She glanced at him then away, her blue-green eyes as unfathomable as the deepest ocean. "It's hard to imagine the pub any different than it is now."

What was that look? That evasive answer? Was she going to have a problem with giving him access to Billy? He supposed every day wasn't practical but damn it, this was his child. "I'm looking forward to seeing the pub as it was originally intended. It will make the place feel more like mine."

Plus, Emma's barb about his procrastination had hit home, and he was determined to prove her wrong.

"I said some things…" she began.

"Never mind. You were right. I am a dreamer, but I'm determined to do this."

"I really hope it works out." She picked up the car seat. "I'll go nurse Billy and put him down for his nap. Then I'll come and help you."

"What about your packing?"

"Packing can wait. This is part of my history, too." She headed for the stairs.

Now for the job he'd been dreading the most. Darcy started to take down the photos on the big corkboard opposite the bar. Many were yellowing and curled at the edges, some completely obscured by newer layers. There were pictures of Darcy and his brothers and sister as kids—fishing off the pier, playing at the beach and eating ice cream in the park. He'd never quite understood his father putting family photos in the pub until he'd had Holly, and he spent so much time there that he wanted a pictorial reminder of her while he worked. It was equivalent to an office worker having framed photos of his wife and kids on his desk.

There were quite a few snapshots of him and Emma, of them with Holly, of Emma and Alana on a sailing dinghy, their hair blowing back from laughing flushed faces. The bay waters in the background reminded him of the cruise. It hadn't turned out anything like he'd hoped. Instead of finding a new woman who would take his mind off Emma, he'd entwined his life inextricably with hers forever through Billy. A year ago he would have kicked himself for being so dumb. Now he thanked God for his good luck. When he thought of how close he'd come to not having this child…

"You're not throwing these out, are you?" Emma pulled the framed photos of 1950s and 1960s Summerside out of the box.

"I was going to take them to the secondhand shop."

"If they were reframed and hung on the newly painted walls they would look fantastic. The pub has a lot of character. I don't think you should mess with it too much. Just streamline it a bit, make it less cluttered, with new furniture in an old-fashioned style."

"Yeah, that's exactly what I was thinking." It was, although he hadn't known it until she'd articulated it.

"You should paint upstairs while you're at it," Emma went on. "Even renovate the kitchen, make it bigger. With a decent cooking space you might even learn to cook."

"You were going to teach me how to make your chicken curry. Guess it's too late now."

"I'll invite you over next time I make it."

"Okay." He tossed a broken frame into the discard box. "Actually I was thinking of buying another house. Someplace with a yard."

"Another house?" she repeated, looking a bit shocked.

"Did you think I was going to live above the pub forever? It was only a stopgap." He had the craziest urge to ask her again to marry him. But he tamped that down. Why subject himself to another rejection?

"I—I didn't think about it at all. It's nothing to me."

"You're a terrible liar."

She straightened. "What do you mean?"

He walked over to her and tweaked a lock of her hair. Somehow they'd gone from being intimate to standoffish, and he didn't know how to get back to closeness. So he resorted to teasing.

"You're jealous," he said, and her eyes widened. "You'd love to have a garden again. To grow your plants and to let Billy play outside in the grass."

"You're wrong. I'm over gardening. An apartment is so much less work." She turned away and started pulling down the horse brasses a friend of his father's had brought back from England once upon a time. "If you had a yard, a fenced backyard, somewhere safe, it would be good for Billy…when he visits you."

She was over gardening. Just like he was over football because of the association with that awful spring day nearly three years ago. Their biggest interests—besides

Latin dancing—had been destroyed, along with Holly. It was wrong. He was tired of living in limbo.

He crossed the faded crimson carpet to the corkboard to pick out his favorite photo of Holly, one of him holding her as a baby. With a fingertip he traced the outline of his daughter's tiny face. So small. He closed his eyes and was enveloped by the memory of her soft, soft skin and her sweet baby smell. He could hear her giggle, and the way she called, "Daddy!" when he came through the door at night.

Too many times he'd given her horsey rides and piggybacks then handed her off to Emma for the bath or the feeding. Emma should have let him do more. He should have insisted. Until Billy, he hadn't realized how much bonding came from mundane acts of physical caring.

Billy was the one who mattered now. Yet to pretend Holly had never existed in the hopes that he could forget the grief and pain clearly wasn't working and it dishonored her memory.

He carried the baby photo of Holly over to Emma. "Don't you think Holly and Billy look a lot alike, even though she had your coloring?"

Emma stiffened. She glanced at the photo, looked at him, and then slowly reached out to take it. Her fingers trembled as she held it.

Darcy slid his arm around her shoulders and drew her in close. "Just a little, about the eyes?" He heard her breathe. Then she sniffed. He tightened his hold.

"Sh-she was so beautiful."

"She was an angel."

"Oh, Darcy." Emma turned her face into his chest with a sob. "I miss her so much."

"I do, too." His other arm wrapped Emma and drew

her in to hold her tightly. His tears spilled into her hair as she wept in his arms.

Grieving together was so simple, so basic and necessary to the healing process, yet they'd never done it. It was his fault. Guilt and recriminations had gotten in the way. And he'd never been brave enough to face the pain.

"I wish I'd been able to talk about her," he murmured into Emma's hair. "I'm sorry."

She drew in a ragged breath. "I know it hurts."

He went on holding her for a long time after both their tears had dried. His chest ached with the sadness, with Emma's pain, with the loss of his daughter. But he felt more at peace, as if he'd moved out of that limbo state and could look forward and back instead of peering blindly through the fog.

"Come over here and sit down." He pulled Emma to a table and brought over the stack of photos of Holly. "Let's look at these together. It might be less painful."

Emma nodded tearfully. She took the top photo. "I remember this day. It was really hot and her ice cream melted before she could eat it."

"She was so funny, trying to lick it off her elbow."

"The neighbor's dog got most of the ice cream, as I recall." She gave him a ghost of a smile. Then picked up another photo. "She was so cute in this little dress I made for her. The pattern could expand to two sizes up. I was going to make her another and another as she grew." She went quiet.

Darcy put his hand over hers. "We had her for eighteen months. We need to be grateful for that and not think about what might have been."

"It's so hard," she whispered.

"I know. It's hard for me, too, especially thinking I

should have spent more time with her, done more with her, the way I've started doing with Billy."

Emma's face suddenly crumpled. "It's my fault."

"Mine, too. I was intimidated by your knowledge. It was easy to let you take over."

"No, I mean, it was my fault she died." Emma looked at him, her face wet. "All this time I've blamed you for not going on the picnic because I couldn't bear to admit that I should have stopped him."

"I don't know what you're talking about," Darcy said. "You're not making sense."

"Kyle. I knew he was drunk. I saw him stagger when he came out of the house. And when he spoke he slurred his words. I tried to get his keys off him but—"

"Go on."

"He was hitting on me—"

"What?"

"He was always hitting on me. Usually I ignored him, but that day he was leering down my blouse, touching me, making suggestive remarks about how he could come over at night while you were at the pub."

Darcy swore. "I can't believe this! Why didn't you tell me? If I'd known, I would have decked him. He wouldn't have been able to walk, let alone drive. Why didn't you come inside and get me?"

"I should have. He wouldn't hand over the keys, and he was too big for me to take them off him. I should have gone straight into the house and got you. But I knew that as soon as I went in he would have driven off so what was the point? I just wanted him out of my yard and away from the house."

"Oh, Emma." Darcy got a sick feeling in his stomach. "It wasn't your fault. The guy is a prize jerk. And I'm at fault, too. I should have been a more responsible host and kept a closer eye on how much people were drinking."

"It's not very realistic, though, is it? People should be responsible for their own behavior. Footy parties are notorious for drinking games and overindulgence...."

She was letting him off too lightly. "Emma—"

"Wait, I'm not finished. I want to say this, get it all out." She wrapped her arms around herself. "I was so angry and upset, so focused on Kyle that I wasn't paying attention to Holly. I went back to gardening. I wanted to get my pansies in. I always plant pansies on footy grand final weekend. And tomatoes on Melbourne Cup Day, the first weekend in November. Holly wanted me to throw the ball to her. I told her to wait. She threw it anyway. It bounced off a tree trunk and rolled onto the driveway. Holly ran after it as Kyle backed up."

She started to cry again. "I let Kyle get in his vehicle and drive knowing how drunk he was—"

"It's not your fault." Darcy pulled her back into his arms. "You just said you tried to get the keys, but he wouldn't give them to you."

"I should have been watching Holly. If I'd played with her instead of being so bloody-minded about sticking to my gardening schedule..." She gulped a sob. "If you were out there, you would have been playing with her and the accident never would have happened."

"But I wasn't outside with her, was I?" Darcy said bitterly. "I was inside, drinking with my mates. That's what I feel so bad about, what I could never talk about. I was drunk, too. Too drunk to realize Kyle shouldn't have been driving. And because of that, our daughter is dead." He stroked Emma's trembling back. "I'm sorry, so sorry."

"I'm sorry, too." She hugged him fiercely then eased

away and gazed at him with a tearstained face. "We've both been beating ourselves up for not being responsible enough, playing the *if only* game. We've got to stop or we'll never be able to move forward. It was an accident. A horrible, pointless, tragic accident. But an accident, nevertheless."

"You're right." He pushed her hair off her face, his palm sliding against the tears he wanted to kiss away. Something held him back. He was looking to her for answers, but in her eyes he saw his own doubt, uncertainty and fear reflected. They'd hurt each other so badly. "We've finally got everything out in the open. The question is, where do we go from here?"

Emma bit her lip and looked at him sadly. "Maybe now we can move on with our lives. Separately."

CHAPTER SIXTEEN

EMMA AWOKE TO the sound of the birds at dawn. Darcy's arm was draped across her ribs, and his hand cupped her breast in sleep. She lay still, savoring the hush of early morning in the apartment, the quiet rhythm of Darcy's breathing.

She turned in his arms and watched him sleeping. With one delicate finger she pushed back a lock of dark hair. How on earth was she going to leave him? Last night their lovemaking had been silent and tender and sweet, as if they were saying goodbye with their bodies.

Every cell in her screamed to stay, to take his offer to try again. Probably they could make it work as a platonic, friends-with-benefits relationship with the added bonus of sharing a love of their son. But having known passion with him during marriage, she wasn't content to build another union on such a lukewarm foundation, with all the attendant uncertainty surrounding their feelings for each other. In some ways, negative emotions had bound them together as much as they'd torn them apart. If they ever were to start fresh, they needed to start on a positive note.

It was time to start afresh. To see what kind of woman she was without the crippling burden of grief and guilt she'd carried with her for so long.

Quietly she slipped out of bed, pulled on a dressing gown and went into Billy's room. He was lying on his back, eyes wide-open, gazing up at the mobile of colorful parrots.

"Hey, Billy," she said softly.

He smiled and wriggled his body, looking as delighted to see her as she was to see him. Emma picked him up and cuddled him, loving his warm wriggly body and his soft baby scent. "Come on. It's time we went home."

Two hours later she was packed and ready to go. She went to tell Darcy, who'd just woken up.

"It's early." Darcy dragged on a pair of shorts and a T-shirt. "Stay and have breakfast."

"Thanks, but no." Her suitcases were piled in the hallway. The cot was broken down and Billy's high chair and other paraphernalia lined up next to it. Now that she was ready she wanted to get going before she lost her resolve and agreed to stay longer. Or forever.

But ever since her confession, while Darcy had been sympathetic and comforting, he hadn't asked her to stay. She'd blamed him for Holly's death all this time as a way of covering her own guilt. Why would he want to be with her now that he knew the truth about her?

"I'll be in touch about setting up regular times for me to see Billy," Darcy said.

There it was, confirmation, if she needed it, that he'd changed his mind about trying again. Last night's lovemaking was for old time's sake, a punctuation mark at the end of a long and sometimes tortuous story.

"I'll email you my work and university schedule. We'll sort something out." At least her son would have a father, even if he didn't have the traditional two-parent family. She would have to be content with that.

Darcy surveyed the luggage and furniture. "Gary's

coming this morning. I'll bring your stuff around in the truck later."

"I'd appreciate that." Oh, God, this was hard. They were so stiff and formal with each other. "Good luck with the renovations. If there's anything else I can do to help, just ask."

"You've got your plate full, too. But thanks for choosing the paint and fabrics." His gaze fell on Billy in her arms and pain and love washed across his face. "Can I hold him one more time before you go?"

"Of course." It almost broke her heart to see Billy snuggle into Darcy's shoulder and the tender, gentle way Darcy stroked his son's head and whispered secrets in his ear. She stood close, wishing she could enclose the three of them in a group hug. But that seemed going too far.

All the way down the stairs and out through the back of the pub she chatted about the lovely weather and Darcy's father in the hospital and her parents in Broome and Alana's job and…and…

By the time they reached her vehicle she'd run out of words to hold her there. She unlocked the door and Darcy put Billy in his car seat. He made sure the straps were snug and the catch securely fastened. "See you soon, mate."

When he straightened, his eyes were glistening. "Keep in touch."

"I will."

He held out his arms to her, so obviously trying to avoid being emotional that he did it almost jokingly. With a nervous laugh she went into his embrace. She aimed for his cheek. He aimed for her mouth. They bumped faces, laughed and tried again. A quick kiss on the mouth, a burning meeting of the eyes. Then Darcy quickly turned and walked into the pub.

Emma blinked a few times and got into her car and drove away. It really was that easy. Not.

THE APARTMENT WAS too quiet with Emma and Billy gone. Darcy roamed the rooms, crowded with furniture, and felt the emptiness seep into his bones.

This was nuts. They'd been with him for less than two weeks. Now he had his life and his space back, he could get on with renovating the pub. At least if he kept busy, he wouldn't notice their absence as much.

He heard the buzzer that let him know someone was outside the back door and wanted in. His heart picked up. It was an hour too early to be Gary. Maybe Emma had changed her mind and come back. Darcy pounded down the stairs. Or she'd forgotten something, although the rooms had been bare when he'd looked through them.

He yanked open the door, puffing a little. Alana stood there. "Oh, it's you. Hey."

"Hey, yourself. Boy, you really raced down the stairs. Were you expecting a strip-o-gram or something?"

"Huh? What are you talking about? I thought Emma might have forgotten something."

"Ah," she said knowingly. "Missing her already, are you?"

Darcy gave her a look but didn't respond.

"Does that mean she's already left?" Alana asked. "I came to help her move. I should have called first."

"You missed her by ten minutes." He waited for her to make her excuses and leave. "If you hurry, you can probably help her carry her suitcases up."

She turned to go then paused. "Can I ask you something?"

"Sure. Do you want to come in for coffee?"

"No, thanks—this will be quick. I just wondered if you really do like being a father again. Because you were so certain before that you didn't. Now Emma says you're some kind of superdad. Are you being genuine or just making the best of a bad deal?"

"Did she tell you to ask me this?" Darcy said, mystified. He didn't think he could have been clearer to Emma that he truly wanted to be a father to Billy.

"No, I'm asking for myself. I'm curious."

"Because…?"

"Dave and I are talking about, well, about a lot of stuff, but mainly about having another child. I'm considering it, but I'm not sure. What if I do agree and have a baby and then regret it?"

"I couldn't speak for you. And you won't know for certain how you'll feel until it happens. All I can say is that when I looked into Billy's face I fell in love with him instantly."

Alana chewed on her bottom lip. "Instantly, really?"

"I would never have predicted that would happen. Mind you, it must be different for everyone. There's no right or wrong."

"Do you really think so? I've been feeling guilty about not wanting a baby."

"Don't. You can't help what you feel. What you need to figure out is how much of your not wanting a baby is due to being pressured by Dave."

"Exactly!" Excited, she stabbed a finger at him. "He doesn't get that. I don't think even Emma does."

"If she hadn't pushed so hard, I might have come around to the idea and we would never have gotten divorced." Seeing Alana change gears to rev up in Emma's defense, he held up a hand. "I said might. I was to blame for other things."

"But you're right," Alana said, subsiding again. "I could ask Dave for a moratorium on baby talk for six months so I can sort out how I really feel."

"That sounds like a good idea. You've got nothing to lose and everything to gain. In the meantime, keep talking to Dave. Who knows, maybe whatever it is you're afraid of is just in your head."

"What makes you think I'm afraid of something?"

"Everyone's vulnerable on some level."

She glanced at her feet, and scuffed the pavement with the toe of her running shoe. "I'm afraid of only being a mum. I'm afraid if I stay home all the time I'll get stupid and boring. Dave's ex-wife was an engineer. She's running her own company now."

"And we saw how well their marriage worked out. I'd guess Dave doesn't care about his wife's profession so much as what kind of person she is."

"He and his ex both worked all the time and hardly saw each other. The kids were in day care ten hours a day. Dave hated that."

Darcy nodded sympathetically. "He's probably afraid your family will go the same way if you start working too much."

"It's all about finding balance, isn't it?" Alana said. "But he's got to find that balance, too."

"The main thing is having the same goals, the same commitment to the relationship."

"Wow, you are so understanding." Alana gave him a mock punch to the arm. "Are you sure you're not a girl?"

Darcy laughed. "As a bartender, I'm an agony aunt to half of Summerside." His smile turned wry. "Now if only I could sort out my own life."

HOLLY WAS SITTING in the stroller, her bright red-gold curls peeking out beneath her sun hat. Emma pushed her around the zoo. They stopped to watch the monkeys swinging between the bare-limbed trees in their enclosure. Holly giggled and pointed at their antics. Emma was happy. They always had a good time at the zoo. Darcy had taken a rare day off and come with them. She glanced around, wondering where he'd got to. Then she saw him, coming toward them holding a bobbing red balloon.

He kissed Emma on the cheek. "Look what I got for the baby."

"She's hardly a baby anymore," Emma said, laughing. She kneeled down and turned the stroller around.

Holly wasn't in the seat. A baby boy smiled up at her. He didn't look like Billy, but somehow she knew it was.

"You can't just replace Holly," Darcy said. Then he handed Billy the balloon as though nothing was out of the ordinary. "But we can go look at the lions."

Emma woke up. She kept her eyes shut, hanging on to the image of Holly. She could still see her so clearly as if she were alive, laughing and real. This was the first dream she'd had of Holly that wasn't a nightmare. It wasn't even sad. It was…happy. There was even a certain peace.

She opened her eyes and reached for the photo of Holly she'd rescued from the corkboard and put in a frame for her bedside. It still hurt to look at her, but now the pain was tempered by memories of the joy and love her baby had given her. Thanks to Darcy.

Outside her window, birds piped in the dawn and her room slowly grew lighter. She would have to get up soon. Billy usually woke around six. Although her nursing classes were over for the year, exams would begin in a few weeks and she had to study. For the moment she lay there thinking and enjoying the quiet before she had to get on with her day.

Confession was supposed to be good for the soul. She had felt better telling Darcy her awful secret. He'd been wonderful, making her feel that it wasn't her fault. She knew it wasn't, not really, but she'd lived with the guilt for so long she hadn't been able to get it out of her mind until he'd absolved her.

Darcy was buying a house for Billy, for when his son came to visit. That was a big investment, especially when he was already stretched with the renovations on the pub. She couldn't tell herself any longer that he wasn't a good father. He'd proven himself beyond all doubt. Unfortunately, now that he wanted to be a father, he didn't want to be married to her.

Or did he? He'd made love to her as if he adored her. When they danced, he looked into her eyes as if she was the only woman on earth. He showed he cared in so many practical ways. She couldn't ask for more. So why hadn't he said he loved her and that he wanted to get back together for *their* sake?

Maybe he was happy with their present arrangement. They were friends again, a huge advance from where their relationship was a year ago. He could see Billy as often as he wanted. He had his hands full with the pub. The sex, well, she couldn't see that continuing unless they made some sort of commitment. The times they'd made love had been fantastic, but she wouldn't be happy doing it again without knowing they had a future.

The clock radio came on. Six o'clock. Time to get up. The newsreader droned in the background as she moved between the bathroom and her room, washing, getting dressed. Across the hall Billy was babbling to himself in his crib. Was it coincidence that he'd gotten over his colic and his general grumpiness when Darcy had come into their lives? Maybe it was because she was less stressed. Maybe it was simply his natural development. Now when he woke in the morning he didn't immediately cry to be picked up. His morning soliloquies were a great delight. No intelligible words, of course, just pure sound but she would swear that to him, he was making total sense.

For the next hour she was occupied in her routine of feeding Billy, having breakfast, tidying up. While she hadn't been paying attention, the seasons had moved along, and spring was in full bloom. She left the door open to the small balcony off the living room so Billy could sit in his playpen with his toys in the fresh air and sunshine.

It was so inviting she stepped outside. In the backyard of the house next door, an old man was working in his vegetable patch. Suddenly she missed her tomatoes. At this time of year she should have the seedlings planted and the stakes in the ground ready to tie up the trusses.

The balcony caught the sun for most of the day. She couldn't buy a house with a yard and a garden, but a few potted plants would provide some much-needed greenery. Although it was too late in the year to start plants from seed, the garden center would be bursting with seedlings.

"Come on, Billy, we're going shopping."

Then she thought about trying to carry large pots plus bags of soil plus seedlings and push Billy in the stroller. Darcy had mentioned yesterday that he had the contractor coming again today, so she didn't want to burden him with babysitting duties. She could wait for the weekend.... Or she could ask Marge.

As she was dialing the number she had a better idea. "Marge, it's Emma. When I saw Roy yesterday he was doing much better. Do you have any more news?"

"He's coming home the day after tomorrow." The relief in Marge's voice was palpable.

"Oh, then I guess you're busy getting ready for him."

"Not really. I've been doing nothing but house-work and baking to keep busy while he's been sick." She paused then added hopefully, "Did you need me to look after Billy?"

"I do need your help. I want to go to the garden center, but I can't manage on my own. Would you be able to come? There's a café there. We could have lunch."

"I would love that. I'll buy Roy some potted freesias for his homecoming. I can be ready anytime. When do you want to go?"

At the garden center, Marge pushed Billy in the stroller while Emma maneuvered the trolley through the outdoor aisles. Three big bags of potting mix lay beneath large black plastic pots. Now she was select-ing tomato seedlings—cherry, roma, beefsteak, black Russian...oh, and some of these heritage varieties. Was that too many for her tiny balcony? She'd thought she was over gardening, but cruising through these aisles gave her planting fever.

"Darcy was over last night," Marge said.

Emma's ears pricked up. "Oh?"

"Do you think he'd like lemon basil?"

"Darcy?"

"Roy. Darcy and I went to visit him."

She loved Marge to bits, but the older woman's con-versation tended to be fragmented. "I think he'd love it."

"He talked about you."

"Roy?"

"Darcy."

"Did he say anything in particular?" Like he was thinking of asking her to get back together. Would he talk about that with his mother? They were close but...

"He said you two are going to work out an arrangement about Billy." Marge touched her arm and smiled. "I'm so happy about that. I was thrilled when you rang this morning. I don't see why we can't still see each other even if you and Darcy aren't married."

"You're Billy's grandparents. I will always want you in our lives." Emma gave her a hug. "We're friends, no matter what happens between Darcy and I."

So, Darcy hadn't mentioned anything about wanting a future with her. What if he didn't think she wanted him? She'd told him she was fine on her own, that she wanted to raise Billy herself. She hadn't said any different, so why would he think she'd changed her mind?

Where do we go from here? he'd asked. She knew where she'd *like* to go—straight to the church and get married again. Then home with him and Billy, to start afresh. She wished she'd told him that instead of leaving. Yes, they shared heartbreaking memories, but also many, many joyous ones. She'd learned the hard way to cherish the good and endure the bad.

A year ago she'd been prepared to meet someone else, someone who shared her dream of a home and family. She'd come full circle to Darcy. There was no one she'd rather travel through life with. He was a link to her past, a joy and comfort in the present, and part of her hopes and dreams for the future. She loved him. How could she ever have thought she could replace him? It was like Latin dancing. She didn't want any other partner but him.

Emma looked at her trolley, full of dirt, pots, fertilizer and seedlings. She had everything she needed to make something grow. All she had to do was plant, water and hope for the best. Trust and pray that he cared enough to give her a second chance.

DARCY LOADED THE last of the boxes of stuff he and Emma had taken off the walls of the pub into the back of his truck. When his dad was feeling up to it, he might enjoy looking through everything and deciding what he would like to keep as a memento.

The tables and chairs were stacked near the back, ready for the workmen to take to a local furniture refinisher. He liked the old bentwood chairs, and the round wooden tables with the turned legs had character. Sanded down, with a fresh coat of varnish, they would look better than modern furniture. He would buy a couple of the tall tables and chairs, though, for along the window onto the street.

The mugs he'd decided to keep on their shelf above the bar. Not many people still used them, but as long as his father and his friends were around, he would maintain the tradition.

Walking through the empty pub with the bare walls gave him a funny feeling inside, part nostalgic, part regretful, part looking forward to what came next.

On the bar sat the box of family photos he'd taken off the corkboard to be distributed to the appropriate people. He and Emma could divide between them the photos of Holly. A photo of the three of them was on top. How would they divide that? He could tear the paper down the middle but to actually separate himself from Emma? In the two years they'd been apart he'd found out he couldn't do it. It had felt like ripping off a limb, or tearing out his heart. She was part of him. She always would be. Having her and Billy living here for even a short while was the happiest he'd been in a very long time.

When she'd said she wanted them to go their own separate ways, he'd been gutted. Sure, he'd been the one to leave the first time around, but he'd changed since then. And yes, she'd been great about letting him into Billy's life, but she'd made it clear they weren't a family.

Riley came through the door wearing his navy pants and white shirt uniform. He walked in, gazing around. "You're really doing it."

"Yep," Darcy said. "It reminds me of the time we jumped off the end of the Frankston pier when we were twelve. We didn't know how deep the water was or if we would drown or swim."

"John broke his fool leg as I recall. Those were the glory days, all right. How long will you be closed for?"

"A couple of weeks, until the worst of the construction is over." Darcy moved behind the bar. "Coffeepot's still on. Interested?"

"Always." Riley leaned on the polished mahogany. "If you're short of something to do while the pub is down, you can come and work with Summerside's finest as detective."

"I think I'd do rather well at that. A publican gets to be pretty observant." Darcy set two mugs of coffee on the bar. "We notice things."

Riley's eyebrows rose. "Give me an example."

"You, my friend, have just come from the barber, where your hair has been freshly cut."

Riley passed a hand over his dark glossy hair. "It's that mousse crap they put on that gave it away, isn't it? I hate that stuff."

"No, it's the thin border of paler skin around your

hairline. And the sprinkling of dark hair trimmings on your shirt."

Riley grinned and brushed off his shoulders. "Very impressive. Can you tell me what I'm thinking right now?"

"I said I had powers of observation, not the ability to read minds." He wished he could read Emma's mind. She'd been brooding over something the other day. He would like to know what it was. She'd seemed to like staying with him at his apartment. Was it possible she regretted leaving? The place was too small, too cluttered with furniture, for the three of them for very long.

"Seriously, what are you going to do with yourself? Are you going on a holiday?" He eyed Darcy over the rim of his cup. "Perhaps with a certain mother and child?"

"I want more than a weekend with Emma. I want the rest of my life with her," Darcy said, spilling his guts. "I've never stopped loving her, not even when I thought I had. How am I going to convince her to risk another chance on me? I screwed up so badly the first time."

"Just you? Marriage is usually a team effort."

"Okay, we were both at fault. But that's because we were hurting."

"Have you got that sorted now?"

Darcy thought of the afternoon when they'd taken down the photos. He was afraid of the strength of his feelings sometimes. Love, grief, regret…they seemed too big for his chest to contain.

He and Emma had done more than mourn their daughter's loss, although that had been cathartic. They'd both opened up for the first time since Holly died, gotten some things off their chests they should have been able to talk about at the time, but hadn't. Guilt was a terrible burden. "I reckon we have got it sorted. Maybe not completely but we've made a good start."

"Then what are you waiting for? Go jump off that pier."

CHAPTER SEVENTEEN

EMMA PICKED UP the landline to dial Darcy's number. There was no dial tone. Odd. "Hello?"

"Emma?"

"Darcy? I just picked up the phone to call you."

"I dialed, but it didn't ring."

"Great minds think alike." She smiled, glad to hear his voice. "What were you calling about?"

"You go first."

"No, you." She paced the kitchen. Why was she so nervous? It wasn't as though she was going to propose over the phone. She was only calling to ask him out on a date.

"How's Billy?"

It was always his first question. She loved him for it. "He's in his high chair, spreading pabulum all over the tray." She moved the receiver close to Billy. "Daddy's on the phone."

Billy slammed his hand into the puddle of mush and splashed it onto his face. "Goo!"

"Did you hear that?" Emma said. "I think he understood what I was saying."

"Clearly. And he thinks my name is Mr. Magoo."

"Did you call to ask after Billy?"

"Not entirely." Darcy cleared his throat. "I was wondering if you and Billy would like to go on a picnic."

A picnic.

Why a picnic? Picnics were a symbol of everything that had been wrong with their marriage. If only he'd gone on a picnic with her and Holly—

No, she couldn't stay stuck in that mind groove, blaming him for what happened. That afternoon at the pub when they'd cried in each other's arms should have cured her of that. Guess it was harder than she thought to change well-worn thought patterns. But she would, because if she ever wanted to be with him again, they needed to start on a clean slate.

And maybe a picnic was symbolic for him, too, of a desire and determination to make up for the past, and to show her that he was willing to change.

"Em, are you still there?"

"A picnic would be lovely. What should I bring?"

"I've got it covered. I'll pick you up in an hour."

She clicked off the phone and picked up Billy, twirling with him in her arms. He giggled. "We're going on a picnic. We're going on a picnic."

Humming a salsa beat, she danced to the nursery to change his diaper and dress him in a clean T-shirt and track pants. Then she carried him to her bedroom to get herself ready. Stroke of luck that Darcy had wanted to see her today, the day she'd chosen to make her bid for his future. Was it a coincidence or was it a sign the universe was conspiring to bring them together?

Still holding Billy she stood before her closet. "What should I wear, skirt or shorts?" Billy had no opinion on the matter, being more interested in chewing on a lock of her hair. "Don't do that, sweetie. I should have asked Darcy where we're going. Will it involve sitting on grass in a park or rocks by the sea? With you coming we'll have to go someplace baby-friendly. A skirt probably wouldn't be out of place."

It was only a picnic. But after months in maternity clothes she figured she deserved to get a little girlie. It had been a while since she'd had a big occasion to dress up for—even if Darcy didn't know it was a big occasion.

Oh, God, what if he rejected her proposal? There they'd be, halfway through their sandwiches and lemonade, and everything would turn awkward. Would they finish eating in silence or pack up and skedaddle? She shook her head. Idiot. Of course she would wait until after they ate to say anything.

"Your mother is a tad nervous," she told Billy. "Nothing to be alarmed about."

She laid her clothes on the bed then sat in the rocking chair by the window to nurse Billy. While he fed, she practiced the speech she'd written last night in which she convinced Darcy they should try again. At two pages, typewritten, it was hard to remember word for word so she'd also written out notes on index cards.

"I'll go over them on the way to the picnic grounds," she told Billy. "I know, he's going to think I'm crazy, and it'll be tricky not to let him see what's on the cards. I'll pretend I'm studying for an exam."

The doorbell rang. "There he is." She tucked the index cards in her purse and went to let Darcy in.

He smelled so yummy and citrusy with musky low notes that she gave him a peck on the cheek just to get a better sniff. "Mmm, you've been bathing in awesome sauce."

His low laugh, a little self-conscious, rumbled in her ear. She handed Billy into his arms. "Sorry I'm not ready. I still have to get dressed."

"You look great."

She was wearing her oldest pair of shorts and a faded T-shirt. "Have you had your eyes checked lately? I hear that forty is the magic age when people start needing glasses."

He rolled his defective eyes and she hurried to her bedroom. *Nice. Be snarky about his age. That'll get him hot for you.* And she'd been doing so well for a moment with the kiss on the cheek and the compliments.

She put on the light summery skirt, a camisole and a sheer blouse in an aqua print that brought out the blue in her eyes. Added a touch of fragrance and some fine gold jewelry he'd given her one Christmas. Brushed her hair again. *Breathe.*

When she entered the living room Darcy was on the floor, playing with Billy. He stood and gazed at her so long she got nervous.

She touched a dangly earring set with teal-blue tourmaline. "I'm overdressed, aren't I?"

He swallowed. "You look perfect. Absolutely beautiful."

"Thank you." *Breathe, damn it.* He looked pretty gorgeous himself in an indigo-blue cotton shirt and black knee-length shorts. "Shall we go?"

Emma slipped on flat sandals. Darcy carried Billy in his car seat. And for once the elevator cooperated by showing up quickly.

In the foyer of the apartment building, Emma started for the door to the parking garage. "We should take my car since I've got Billy's seat." She hadn't thought about having to drive when she'd written her index cards.

"I bought a car seat of the same model yesterday and installed it in my truck so we can transport him in either vehicle." Darcy pushed open the entry door for her to go through.

"Aren't you full of surprises?" she said, moving past him.

"You haven't seen anything yet." He secured Billy in the truck cab. Then he turned to her with a bandanna in his hand. "And you're not going to see anything else until we get where we're going."

"What? No way. I *need* to see." She stepped back, hands out to ward him off as he advanced on her. "You can't— Hey!"

He spun her by the shoulders and quickly tied the folded cloth over her eyes. "Resistance is futile."

"This *is* kind of kinky." She touched the cloth. But how was she going to study her index cards? "Or is this your answer to my alleged backseat driving?"

He opened the door and helped her inside and with her seat belt. She felt her handbag being placed in her lap. "I want you to sit back and relax. Enjoy the ride. It'll take about half an hour to get where we're going."

How far could they travel in that length of time? Depending on direction it could be down the peninsula to Rosebud or toward Melbourne as far as Mordiallic. Or maybe he was taking her up to the Dandenong Mountains?

Darcy started the engine and pulled away from the curb. Emma tried to figure out where they were going by the speed and the direction they turned. She knew they got onto the freeway for a short time, but after they got off there were so many twists and turns she was completely boggled as to where they were. Darcy, of course, wouldn't give her a single clue. She'd forgotten how maddeningly stubborn and immune to her probing he could be. There was no noise from the backseat. Billy must have fallen asleep.

Finally Darcy stopped the truck. "We're here."

"At last. Now I can take off this bandanna."

"Not yet." He pulled her hands away from the cloth

and placed them in her lap. "Be patient. Sit there while I unload then I'll come back for you." He paused. "Promise you won't peek?"

"I promise," she lied. As soon as he was out of the vehicle she was peeking.

"I mean it, Em. I'm trying to create an effect. It'll be spoiled if you look too soon."

He *had* gone to a lot of trouble. And she had to admit, the suspense was exciting. This was part of what she loved about Darcy. She never knew what to expect, but whatever he planned was always entertaining.

"Okay, I won't look."

While he unloaded the truck—and it took at least ten minutes so he must have brought a lot of gear—she tried to mentally go over everything she wanted to say to him. How she'd always loved him. How much she needed him. The many ways he enhanced her life. The ways she hoped she could make him happy. In every category she'd prepared examples, of course.

Her door opened and he removed her seat belt. "You can come out now. But don't take off the blindfold."

His hand at her elbow, he guided her first over pavement then onto grass. "Watch your step. It's a little bumpy. Easy…over to your right. Take off your sandals."

She put a hand on his shoulder and slipped off her shoes. She could hear birds close by and in the distance, a lawn mower. She raised her face and smelled a sweet fragrance, jasmine or daphne, on the breeze. "Where are we?"

"You'll see in a moment. Step onto the blanket. Sit down. Carefully…right down to the ground. There are pillows."

She lowered herself to her knees, felt around and located a large cushion. He helped her lean against it.

"Ready? I'll take the bandanna off now."

After so long blindfolded, the sunlight made her eyes hurt. She scrunched them shut, then slowly opened them a crack. They were seated on a big blanket strewn with soft cushions in a meadow. A picnic basket sat to one side and a cooler. Billy was in his car seat, still asleep.

Emma gazed around. "Where are we?"

"Can you guess? You get points for each correct statement."

On second thought, not a meadow and not a park, either. It wasn't that big. A hedge bordered one side and a fence bordered the other side. A quiet residential street formed a third boundary. And down the sloping grass in front of them was a tangle of bush and then tall pine trees and eucalypts. It was an empty lot.

"Is there a creek down there?"

"Two points." Darcy pulled a bottle of champagne out of the cooler and two flutes out of the picnic basket. "Five points if you can tell me the name of the creek and the town."

"It looks like Summerside. But how could that be Oh, you drove around in circles and doubled back. Very clever." She'd hoped for someplace more picturesque and romantic to propose to him, but this was very pretty. "Are we on private land? Are we allowed to be here?"

He poured the sparkling wine and handed her a glass. "I have permission from the owner. And yes, this is Summerside. Two and a half points."

"You said five."

"You have to name the creek."

Four creeks ran through Summerside, two with multiple branches. She only knew of one that had such tall trees along its banks. "Earimil Creek?"

"Is that your answer or are you guessing?"

He was teasing her. Emma sipped her champagne, in no hurry to end the game. They had all afternoon, a bottle of bubbly and a basket full of food—which from here looked to contain all her favorite delicacies. He had gone to a lot of trouble for this picnic. Soon she would be asking him a question—one that could change their lives.

"It's my answer."

"Five points to the lady in the sexy blouse."

"I don't want points. I want a kiss."

"Raising the stakes, are we?" Dark eyes gleaming, he leaned across two feet of blanket and kissed her. Only their lips touched. His mouth was firm and bold and tasted deliciously of contrasts—warm and slightly salty from the sun and the olives, cool and sweet from the champagne.

He left her breathless and wanting more. More kisses, more laughter, more tenderness. More time together. More *certainty* in their relationship. "What's your next question?"

He spread perfectly ripe brie on a cracker and offered it to her. "Don't you want to ask me anything?"

"Why are we here?"

"Ah, one of life's age-old questions. I presume you're speaking metaphysically—"

She threw a pillow at him. "You know what I mean. Why here and not in a park?"

His teasing smile faded, and his expression grew intent and serious. He might have been about to reply or he might have been going to put her off, but she would never know because Billy woke up and started crying.

"Good timing, old man." Darcy unclipped him from his harness and pulled him out. "Does he need to be fed?"

"No, I fed and changed him before we left. He should

be good for another hour at least. I think he's starting to teethe." She reached for her oversize handbag. "I have a teething ring in here somewhere."

Darcy laid Billy on the blanket. "Is that better, mate? Were you folded up too long in that car seat?" He turned to Emma. "Isn't he a bit young to be teething? I thought I read that teeth don't come in until they're about six months old."

"That's the average age but some start earlier." She dragged out her wallet, hairbrush, keys, index cards. "You either have a phenomenal memory or you've bought your own baby books."

"I went online to some baby sites." Billy stopped crying and rolled over, reaching for the things Emma had taken out of her purse. "Hey, buddy, those are your mum's cards." Darcy tried to take them off him.

"I'll get them." Emma lunged for the cards. Too late. Billy clung to the cards and the elastic band that held them loosely together slipped off. They tumbled to the blanket. Billy picked one up and put the corner in his mouth. "Give that to me, sweetie."

While she tugged the card out of his tight little fist Darcy gathered the rest together. "Don't look at those," Emma ordered desperately. "They're just study cards for an exam."

"What class is this for? 'I know all your favorite meals and can cook them the way you like them.'"

Her cheeks flamed. "Stop, please, just stop."

He glanced at Emma. "'I love the way you sleep with your lips slightly parted? It makes me want to kiss you.' Who does that? Are you seeing someone else?"

"No, you idiot. *You* sleep with your mouth open." She was the idiot. Hearing her words aloud made them sound ridiculous. Snatching the cards out of his hand she shoved them back in her purse and gave the teething ring to Billy. She felt like such a fool.

"Emma." Darcy's voice was impossibly gentle. His hand touched her bare knee. "You are the most organized person I've ever known, but this is bizarre, even for you. Why did you write those cards?"

"Because I love you," she said fiercely. Her eyes shimmered, but she forced herself to look at him. "I wanted to tell you all the many different ways I love you. I wanted to give you reasons to love me. I wanted to ask you to marry me—again. I didn't want to forget a single thing I intended to say because if you said no then, I would always kick myself that I'd gone about it wrong, or hadn't been persuasive enough, or hadn't said the right thing." She dropped her gaze, unable to bear the astonishment in his. "It was a dumb idea."

"It's incredibly sweet. And the answer is yes."

"I beg your pardon?" She needed to hear it again, have it confirmed.

"Yes, I will marry you." Darcy scooted across the blanket and wrapped her in his arms. He laughed, exulted, and pressed kisses over her face. "I love you, too. I never stopped."

She grabbed his face and kissed him properly, long and slow and deep, until Billy's kicking feet eased them apart. She picked the baby up and cuddled him.

Darcy kept his arm around her, his face close. "Now ask me again why we're here."

"Okay, I'll bite. Why are we here?"

"I want to buy this block of land and build a house on it—for us. I've already put in an offer, subject to approval from you." He tipped up her chin so he could look directly in her eyes. "I came here today to ask you to marry me. You beat me to it."

"I've always wanted to live next to the creek."

"I know. That's why I chose this one."

"But can we afford it? You're renovating the pub."

"We'll manage. The quote Gary gave me is afford-able. And I have a feeling the pub is going to be more popular than ever when the renovations are complete." He searched her face. "So, should we buy this land and build ourselves a dream house?"

"Oh, Darcy. Yes! I love this spot."

"That is the correct answer. Ten points to the woman who won my heart."

"I don't want points. I want…" She leaned up to whisper in his ear.

"We might get arrested if we did that in public."

"We'll wait till we get home." Emma leaned back against his chest and looked out at her future backyard. Rainbow lorikeets flitted among the gum trees. Somewhere a kookaburra laughed. "It feels good to have dreams again."

"And a family." Darcy's arms tightened around her. "Maybe this time— No, there's no *maybe* about it. This time, we will survive whatever comes our way— together. I don't ever want to lose you again."

"Love will see us through," Emma said softly, her fingers splayed across his hand, snug in the arm that wrapped around her and Billy.

Love wasn't simple. The journey was full of ups and downs. But as long as she and Darcy were together they could handle any curveball life threw at them.

* * * * *

COMING NEXT MONTH FROM

H HARLEQUIN®

super romance®

Available April 2, 2013

#1842 TALK OF THE TOWN • *In Shady Grove*
by Beth Andrews

Neil Pettit and Maddie Montesano share a history and a daughter. But that's it. Their relationship has been, well, *tense* for years. That wasn't a problem when Neil lived out of state. But now that he's in town, sparks are flying and everyone's talking about where they'll end up!

#1843 RIGHT FROM THE START by Jeanie London

A divorce mediator, Kenzie James has seen it all when it comes to commitment. And she can tell Will Russell is *not* a good bet. So why does she look forward to their encounters at work? Luckily she knows better than to fall for this single dad...or does she?

#1844 THE FIRST MOVE by Jennifer Lohmann

Seeing Renia Milek again is a clear sign to Miles Brislenn. Back in high school he might not have had the courage to approach her, but this chance meeting...? He's not letting it pass him by. The attraction is clearly mutual, until Renia's past threatens to come between them.

#1845 A BETTER FATHER by Kris Fletcher

Sam Catalano needs to prove he's a good father to his young son. And to do that he needs stability, which is why he's bought the summer camp he used to attend. But buying it puts him in conflict with Libby Kovak—his old flame and the rightful owner.

#1846 YOU ARE INVITED... • *A Valley Ridge Wedding*
by Holly Jacobs

The best man? Mattie Keith—maid of honor—thinks Finn Wallace is anything but. She's the legal guardian for his nieces and nephew, but he's suing for custody! They've vowed not to let their conflict spoil their friends' wedding, but when temperatures and attraction rise, promises may be broken....

#1847 THE SUMMER PLACE by Pamela Hearon

When it comes to fun and games, Rick Warren and Summer Delaney are definitely on opposite sides. Summer has a lot at stake in making this camp program work and proving she's right. Too bad the working rivalry is sparking a big attraction!

HSRCNM0313

SPECIAL EXCERPT FROM

H **HARLEQUIN**®

super romance®

Talk of the Town

By **Beth Andrews**

Maddie Montesano shares a history with
Neil Pettit...and a daughter. Their relationship
has been rocky and it could get worse with
Neil back in Shady Grove...
Read on for an exciting excerpt!

Maddie Montesano swung her crowbar at the wall, focused
on finishing this demolition. The back of her neck prickled
with a warning of being watched...and let her know who
stood there.

When it came to Neil Pettit, it was like some sort of homing
device was imbedded inside of her. *There he is! The man of your
adolescent dreams!*

It was annoying and as powerful as it had been when she'd
been young and stupid with love for him.

Well, she'd gotten over Neil a long time ago.

Neil leaned against the doorjamb, his broad shoulders filling the space as he lazily slid his gaze from her head to the toes
of her work boots.

There should be a law that when a woman saw her ex, she looked hot. Sexy hot…not sweaty, I've-been-working-and-am-a-total-mess hot.

"Hey, babe. Looking good." His greeting was the same as in high school when he'd wait by her locker. Oh, how her heart had raced with so many wonderful, conflicting emotions.

"It's the tool belt," she said, not bothering to keep the flatness from her voice.

He grinned at her tone, one of his slow, panty-melting smiles. It was more potent now than it'd been twelve years ago. "It's not the tool belt." He came closer until the toes of his sneakers bumped against her boots. "It's the whole package."

She rolled her eyes. "Please."

Golden stubble covered his cheeks and she noticed the dark circles under his eyes. He looked tired and that hint of vulnerability had her weakening. Not allowed.

"Something I can do for you, Neil?"

His expression changed. "Is Bree here? I'd like to see my daughter."

What are Neil's intentions?
Find out in TALK OF THE TOWN
by Beth Andrews, available April 2013
from Harlequin® Superromance®.
And be sure to look for the other
three books about the Montesano siblings
in Beth's IN SHADY GROVE series
available later in 2013.

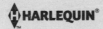